BLOOD BONDS

An Otherworld Novel, Book 21

YASMINE GALENORN

A Nightqueen Enterprises LLC Publication

Published by Yasmine Galenorn

PO Box 2037, Kirkland WA 98083-2037

BLOOD BONDS

An Otherworld Novel

Copyright © 2019 by Yasmine Galenorn

First Electronic Printing: 2019 Nightqueen Enterprises LLC

First Print Edition: 2019 Nightqueen Enterprises

Cover Art & Design: Earthly Charms

Editor: Elizabeth Flynn

Map Design: Yasmine Galenorn

ALL RIGHTS RESERVED No part of this book may be reproduced or distributed in any format, be it print or electronic or audio, without permission. Please prevent piracy by purchasing only authorized versions of this book.

This is a work of fiction. Any resemblance to actual persons, living or dead, businesses, or places is entirely coincidental and not to be construed as representative or an endorsement of any living/ existing group, person, place, or business.

A Nightqueen Enterprises LLC Publication

Published in the United States of America

ACKNOWLEDGMENTS

And so, we reach the end of the road. I had no clue this series would last for twenty-one books, back in 2005 when I first conceived the idea. It's been a long road, and it's one I'm both happy to end, yet not without a bittersweet pang. But I've told the stories I have to tell for the Sisters, and I have other worlds to explore. I won't say I'll never write another story in Otherworld, but for now, it needs to rest.

To those who have remained glued to the adventures of the sisters—thank you for the love you've given this world of mine. And thank you for understanding my need to explore new characters and stories and offer you new worlds of adventure. If you love Otherworld, I urge you to give my Wild Hunt series a try—it's promising to shape up to be another expansive world.

Thanks also go to my husband, Samwise, who has been my biggest supporter as I've shifted my career to the indie side. He was there at the birth of Otherworld, and he's been there by my side through this journey. And thank you to my friends who have cheered me on—especially Jo and Carol and my niece, Jade. Thank you to my assistants Jenn and Andria for all their help. And thank you to my fellow authors in my UF group, who have helped me learn what I needed to learn in order to take my career into my own hands.

A most reverent nod to my spiritual guardians—Mielikki, Tapio, Ukko, Rauni, and the Lady Brighid. They guide my life, and my heart.

And of course, love and scritches to my fuzzy brigade —Caly, Brighid, Morgana, and little boy Apple. I had other furbles at the very beginning of Otherworld, but these four are seeing me through the end of it. I would be lost without my cats.

Bright Blessings, and I hope you enjoy the last Otherworld book. All stories have an ending, and all journeys have a sunset. For more information about all my work, please see my website at Galenorn.com and sign up for my newsletter.

Brightest Blessings,
~The Painted Panther~
~Yasmine Galenorn~

WELCOME TO OTHERWORLD

They're the D'Artigo sisters: savvy half-human, half-Fae agents of the Otherworld Intelligence Agency. Camille is the Queen of Dusk and Twilight. Delilah is a two-faced werecat and the Autumn Lord's only living Death Maiden. And Menolly is a vampire princess and married to a gorgeous werepuma Amazon. It's been four long years since they first found out about Shadow Wing...and now, they're facing the end of the line. It's time for the D'Artigo sisters to extinguish Shadow Wing's evil forever, before he goes mad and tries to unravel the world...

MAP OF OTHERWORLD

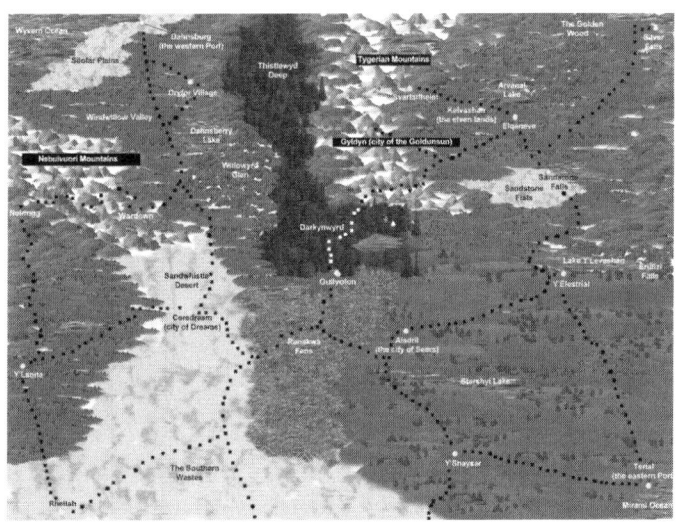

CHAPTER ONE
Menolly

I FLIPPED ON THE LIGHTS AS I ENTERED MY OFFICE, dropping my backpack on a chair by the door. The meeting had been frustrating, and my temper was at a low boil. I decided to hit the gym before I went back to my suite, to work out the irritations of the evening. But first, there was more work.

A glance at the clock told me it was midnight, which meant that I had to answer my email, answer my snail mail, and take care of a dozen other administrative tasks before I could knock off for the evening. I had quickly learned that being a princess of the Vampire Nation wasn't all powder puffs and tiaras. It was an endless roundabout of diplomacy. I had come to hate the bureaucracy, and I wondered how Roman had managed to put up with it as long as he had.

As I headed toward the massive walnut desk, Nerissa entered the room. Since she had been forced to quit her job with the FH-CSI, she had taken up a position as my secretary. It was well below her qualifications, but it gave us more time together, and now she was on my schedule, at least partially. She woke up at noon, and went to bed around four in the morning, so we had a lot more overlap than we used to have. Luckily she didn't need as much sleep as a human would.

"How did the meeting go?" she asked, wrapping her arms around my waist.

I leaned up to give her a long kiss. We'd spent a leisurely hour in bed when I woke up, making love and cuddling. The scent of her fragrance still lingered on my skin. Even though I didn't have to breathe, I could smell her perfume. A quick thought that it would be fun to play hooky and sneak back to bed ran through my mind, but one look at the pile of mail on my desk quashed that thought.

"It was a royal pain in the ass. There are problems over in the European quadrant of the Vampire Nation." I shrugged. "And these are problems that aren't going to be solved through a Skype meeting. Roman has to make a trip over there. He wanted me to go along, but there's no way I can get away at this point. At least he understands that."

"Problems? What sort of problems?" She moved a pile of file folders over to the to-file box and tidied up a stack of letters I was working away at. A number of vampires were so old school that they refused to use email, so we still kept the post office on their toes.

I returned to my chair, leaning back against the soft, supple leather. Nerissa took her place in the chair next to my desk, setting down her tablet. She leaned her elbows on the polished wood, resting her chin on her hands as I swept my braids back to catch them in a ponytail.

"One of the regents over there—Harriman—seems to be going rogue. He's refused to curtail the attacks against the human population like he's supposed to, and in fact, there are reports that he's actually encouraging them. When Roman phoned him a few days ago, he wouldn't take the call and his valet confided to Roman that he's afraid for his life. So Roman had a couple of our agents in the area look into matters, and they think that Harriman's inner predator is out of control."

"Which means trouble," Nerissa said.

I nodded. "Yes, precisely that. And it means that we have to take action as soon as we can. We don't dare let him rile up the vampire populace. The last thing we need is for him to gather an army behind him. We're still trying to convince a lot of the old-school vamps that they're better off following our way, and even though they answer to Blood Wyne, there's a lot of dissent—especially over on the continent."

The old-school vampires of the Vampire Nation had resisted Blood Wyne's decree, which severely curtailed which humans that vamps could drink from, and how much blood they could take at one time. We weren't exactly fighting an uphill battle, but it wasn't easy, and we had been forced to put down a number of the vamps who had outright refused.

"Uh-oh," Nerissa said. "Are you afraid he's going to start a civil war?"

"I'm not sure, but Blood Wyne's afraid of that. And with her experience, if she's worried a civil war might happen, then we all should be on the alert. The Queen has an excellent read on the various regents, and she's scary smart. And a vampire civil war would be hell on anybody else living in the area."

Nerissa sighed. "So you think she'll really take him out?"

"Blood Wyne won't, but Roman will. He has express orders that Harriman isn't to walk out of this." I tossed the pile of letters on the desk and began cleaning my nails with the letter opener. "Blood Wyne is as ruthless as they come. She won't hesitate to destroy anyone or anything who defies her rule. We can just thank the gods that she has a strong sense of community responsibility. I don't know how she's managed to keep her inner predator under control for as long as she has, but I'm just grateful that she has it in check."

"I suppose we better start going through some of your mail." Nerissa looked about as excited as I felt. She was qualified for so much more, but the fact that we were married, not only to each other but also to Roman, Prince of the Vampire Nation, meant that neither of us were allowed out in public without a retinue. Our lives had changed drastically over the past six months, and I had a suspicion that she was as uncomfortable as I was with a number of those changes.

I stared at the stack of envelopes in front of me. "I hate this shit."

"So do I, but apparently it's part of our responsibility and so we have to do it." She gave me a steady look. "I love you, Menolly, you know that. I love you more than I've ever loved anybody. But if I had known what it would mean for our lives when we married Roman, I would have thought twice. I'll follow you anywhere, but you need to know that I'm feeling terribly claustrophobic living here.

And living with a bunch of vampires isn't exactly my idea of *happy happy, joy joy.*"

I pressed my lips together for a moment. Her comments stung, but at least she was honest. That was one thing that we had learned the hard way. Communication was vital if our relationship was to survive. Honesty suited us both, regardless of whether it caused pain.

Setting down the letter opener, I turned to her. "I know. I know you're not thrilled about our life at this point. I feel the same way. It's like we've been locked away in an ivory tower. I don't know what else we could have done, though. Blood Wyne could have killed me if I refused. At least Roman's a good sort." I paused, dreading the answer to my next question. "Do you want out? Blood Wyne will never let me divorce her son, but I doubt if she'd keep you here if you said you wanted to leave." I was praying she would say no, praying that our love would be strong enough for her to stay.

Nerissa quirked her lips. After a moment, she shook her head. "I love you more than I hate the confinement. Maybe things will change. But no, I'm not going to ask for my freedom. I'm not willing to give you up."

Relief flooded through me.

"I'm *so* glad you said that. I can't imagine life without you. Maybe there's some way we can ask Roman to ease up on requiring so many bodyguards and curfews and everything that goes along with this life. I'll tell you one thing. If this is what being royalty is like, I wouldn't recommend it to anybody." I paused, thinking. "It must be worse for Camille—she's the actual queen of her Barrow."

We started in on the mail again, sorting through the charity requests, the invitations, the thank-you notes, and a dozen other categories of correspondence that came our way.

A text message on my phone put a stop to the tedium. I glanced at it, at the same time that Nerissa pulled out her phone. We were both included in the group message, from Delilah.

BE HERE AT THREE AM. CARTER'S ON HIS WAY. HE'S FOUND OUT WHAT THE GEMS ARE.

AND WITH THOSE WORDS, our lives once again shifted.

ROMAN'S VALET was packing for him when I entered his room. Nerissa and I had our suite, and Roman had his own. When we married him, we had insisted on a private living area, and he had agreed. At first, he seemed to feel left out, but now he just seemed relieved. Nerissa and I hated clutter, and preferred a modern look. Roman's room looked like a Victorian antique shop had exploded all over it.

As I entered the room, I found him sitting on the bed, reading something on his tablet. He glanced up, a smile spreading across his face. Holding out his hand, he motioned to me, and I allowed him to draw me down beside him. He wouldn't kiss me in front of his valet, it wasn't considered proper, but he stroked my hand before letting it drop.

"Hello, my love. Did you come to help me pack?" His

eyes glinted with laughter. He knew just how much I hated packing and anything to do with boxes and suitcases.

"Fat chance. You're on your own there, bub. Sink or swim. No, I wanted to talk with you before you left. When are you headed out?"

Blood Wyne owned her own jet. It contained a sun-free cargo space where vampires could travel safely during the day. Several international airlines were starting to offer the same services, but Blood Wyne's jet was piloted by her own captain and was filled with security guards. While a vampire could travel halfway across the world in just a few hours on their own, providing they didn't have to carry luggage, Roman not only had a dozen suitcases, but also an entourage. Which meant flying via plane.

"We leave at two AM. I have to be down at the airport in ninety minutes. I'm so not looking forward to this trip. Staking Harriman isn't going to be easy, and Mother wants him to suffer a little first, as a lesson to other regents over on the continent."

"Translation: you're going to make him regret defying your mother." I shuddered, glancing at Rubicon, the valet. He kept his gaze firmly on his job, which was, right now, packing Roman's clothing. His loyalty had been tested time and again, and he had come through with flying colors, but I still thought it odd that Roman felt comfortable talking so freely in front of him. I was far more suspicious than that.

Roman shrugged. "Mother calls the shots." But the expression in his eyes told me that was exactly what he was thinking. He didn't have a problem with torture, not when it came to things like this. "Are you sure you don't want to come with me?"

I snorted. "I think you know the answer to that. I have no interest in witnessing the…interaction. Besides, I have to stay here. We're getting close to discovering…"

I paused. Roman might trust Rubicon with his secrets, but I wasn't about to. The secrets I carried had far too many ramifications to chance them reaching the public. And while I knew that Rubicon was loyal to Roman, I still doubted his loyalty to me. There had been a lot of outcry over my ascension to Roman's side, and I was never sure just *which* vampires had disapproved of our marriage.

Roman snapped his fingers and Rubicon turned. "Leave us for a moment, if you will. I'll text you when to return. Don't go far." As much as Roman loved his traditions, he had also embraced technology as part of them.

"As you wish, milord." Rubicon exited, firmly shutting the door behind him.

Roman waited for a beat, then turned to me. "So Carter's found out what the gems Shadow Wing carries are?"

I nodded. "Nerissa and I are headed over to the house as soon as I get done talking to you. Finally, after four years, we have an endpoint in sight."

"What do you have to do? And when are you going to do it?" Roman held my gaze, his expression somber.

"We figure out *how* to destroy them. And then our plans are to summon Shadow Wing through a demon gate. When Shamas returned from the grave, he returned a far stronger sorcerer than he entered it. He can create a demon gate powerful enough to bring Shadow Wing through. After all the battles through all the years, we finally have a chance to end the demonic war."

"Should I stay? I can ask my mother to send someone in my place."

Roman was serious, but I shook my head.

I kissed him gently on the lips. "I appreciate the offer, but I can't tell you exactly when we're going to do this. It could be tomorrow, it could be a week from now, or maybe a month. All I know is that it has to be soon. The longer we wait, the more chance there is that Shadow Wing's power will grow. Besides, your mother would have a fit if you turned Harriman over to someone else, and even I would agree—you have to be the one to squash his rebellion. It has to come from the throne. No, you worry about him. We'll take care of Shadow Wing. This is our fight, Roman. Not yours."

Roman pulled me to him, holding me by the shoulders.

"This may be your fight, but it's my fight as well because we're married. You and Nerissa are my wives, and while I know full well that neither of you love me the way you love each other, we *are* a triad. You two have done so much to fit into my world. I want to help you any way I can."

Feeling restless, I broke away, pacing the length of the room.

"Honestly, the way this war has run, I'm not surprised that in the end, it's coming down to us against him. I haven't mentioned my feelings to Delilah or Camille yet, but I have a sneaking suspicion they feel the same way. Sometimes, turning points in history balance on the shoulders of one person. Or a small group."

Roman nodded. "True enough. I've seen that play out

time after time through the centuries. And what strikes me so much is that *usually* the vast populace never knows what's gone on behind the scenes. Or they never find out they were ever in danger. Saving the world can be a private affair, and usually it's best if it's kept in secret."

He stared at the suitcases, then his gaze flickered to me again. "I'll go. You're right. Mother made it clear that dealing with Harriman is *my* duty, but I'm not happy about leaving you. Text me if you need me, although I'm not so sure how cell phone coverage is where I'm headed. Harriman lives in an isolated mountain range, but he rules his region with a bloody fist. That's another thing we've been trying to discourage. When it comes to interacting with the general population, fear isn't the best motivator. Although my mother doesn't hold with that thought when it comes to the Vampire Nation proper. She has most of the vamps cowed in front of her."

I shrugged. "Let's face it, we're top of the food chain predators. We don't have a lot of enemies, except for each other. If Blood Wyne tried to be diplomatic among our *own kind*, she'd never get anywhere. They'd stake her within minutes. She *has* to play the bitch queen when it comes to our own people."

I felt odd, calling the Vampire Nation my "own people," because I still identified with being half-Fae like my sisters. But when I was with Roman, I tried to blend into his world.

"You're right about that. I suppose I'd better get back to packing." He pulled me to him and wrapped his arms around my waist. "Promise me you'll be careful. I won't ask you to keep out of trouble, because we both know that isn't in the cards for either of us. Especially not with what we're facing—with what *you're* facing. I was hoping to be in on the end of the game with the war, but I don't know how long it will take me to corral Harriman. If I'm not here when you face Shadow Wing, remember how much I love you, and remember your strength."

He kissed me then, holding me tight as his lips played over mine. We were both cold as the grave, cold as death, and yet a warmth spread through my body that I seldom felt. It was true that I didn't love Roman like I loved Nerissa, but I was deeply fond of him, and I loved him in my own way.

"You promise *me* that *you'll* be careful. If Harriman *has* given into his inner predator, then chances are he suspects you're coming for him. And who knows what spies he has in the court? Be careful, my liege, and come back whole and safe." I kissed him again, and then crossed toward the door as he texted for Rubicon to return.

"Menolly," Roman said. "Give Nerissa my love. Hold tight to each other, and if you need to, turn to my mother. She picked you to be my wife for a reason."

As the door opened and Rubicon entered, I gave Roman a solemn nod. Then, taking my leave, I returned to the office where Nerissa was waiting. We headed down to my new Jaguar that Roman had bought me as a wedding present. He wasn't thrilled that I still insisted on driving myself, but he put up with it.

As we sped into the night, I couldn't help but wonder what Carter would have to say. And just how long it would be before we were facing Shadow Wing.

CHAPTER TWO
Delilah

SHADE AND I WERE WAITING FOR THE OTHERS WHEN IRIS came through the door. She was wearing a long blue dress and a quilted jacket, and her hair was done up in a massive beehive formed of braids, with a ponytail coming out the top, like Barbara Eden on the old *I Dream of Jeannie* TV shows. She had a pensive look on her face, but given the reason for the meeting, I wasn't surprised. Hanna offered to take her jacket and Iris gave her a grateful smile.

"Would you like some tea?" Hanna asked, draping her jacket over the coat rack.

Iris nodded. "That sounds wonderful. Peppermint, please? And do you have any crackers? Saltines?"

Hanna gave her a long look, then turned to bustle around the kitchen, setting the kettle on the stove and getting out china cups and a plate for crackers.

"Add some cheese to that tray, please," I said. Turning to Iris, I said, "Sit down. Shade's in the living room, watching the news." I glanced at the door. "Where's Bruce?"

Iris shrugged. "Taking care of the twins, where else?" She let out a long breath. "Delilah, I need to talk to you before the others get here. It's important, especially given with what's on the agenda, and I need an ally for later tonight when I have to tell everybody else. Especially Camille."

I frowned, worried. The past few weeks, Iris had been acting strange, seeming moody and quiet. But she had been reticent, and we had been busy with Shade's and my wedding, and trying to figure out what exactly I had seen through the vision of Shadow Wing, so I hadn't got around to asking her what was wrong. We hadn't had a chance to sit down and talk for a while when I thought about it.

She settled in her chair and motioned for Hanna to join us. "If you don't mind taking a break."

"I could use one. Today I overhauled the linen closets and washed every scrap of bedding in the house." Hanna poured the tea and carried the tray over to the table. The two women had become close friends over the past couple of years since Hanna had come to live with us.

I sipped my tea, then bit into a saltine and cheddar, smiling as the taste blossomed on my tongue. "What's going on?"

"I think I know," Hanna said, staring at Iris. "Am I right?"

"You're right." Iris paused, then nodded. "I won't beat around the bush. I'm pregnant again. And it's twins again. Mallen says I'm having two girls this time."

I sputtered around the cracker and cheese, then after

wiping my mouth on a napkin, reached out to take the house sprite's hands in mine, squeezing them. "Oh, Iris! Congratulations! But the twins are barely a year old! How are you going to handle four babies?"

She snorted. "Good question. However, that brings me to what I wanted to tell you about. I need your support before I tell the others, because I'm so hormonal I can't handle a lot of flack tonight. And I'm sure to either burst into tears or rip them a new one if they argue."

I slowly let go of her fingers. Holding her gaze, I cocked my head to the side. "You're going to tell me something I really don't want to hear, aren't you? What is it? What's going on? Are you okay? Are the babies okay?"

She took a long breath and held it for a moment, then slowly exhaled. "I'm fine. The babies—both inside and out—are fine. But… Well, here's the thing. We're nearing the end battle. I've been here since the beginning. But now…with two young children not out of the crib, and two more on the way…" She glanced up at me, tears trickling down her cheeks. "I can't put them in danger, and I can't risk my babies losing their mother. I swore to you I'd be here to help, but I'm afraid I have to break that promise."

My heart dropped, but I understood. The danger was real, and Iris had more to lose than just about any of us. I struggled to keep my own emotions in check. "Of course you have to do what's best for your family. I understand. And the others will too. If you need to back away, we'll support you."

She let out another breath before she straightened her shoulders. "I'm glad, because that brings me to the next matter."

"There's more?" I swallowed a mouthful of peppermint tea, ready to hear the worst.

She nodded. "The Duchess has invited us to come live with her in Ireland for the duration of my pregnancy, so that she can help out. Bruce and I talked it over and we think it would be best. Even though she scared me at first, Bruce's mother has proven an invaluable help with the babies, and Bruce and I need the help."

My stomach clenched. The thought of losing Iris was physically painful. She had become a part of our family, and the realization that she and Bruce were leaving—that they really wouldn't be around anymore—hurt like hell.

"Delilah? Are you angry?" Iris was crying in earnest now.

I hung my head, trying to hold back the tears. "No, please don't think that I'm upset at you. Watching you walk out of our lives hurts, but I don't want you in danger. The truth is, there's no way to guarantee your safety here. There are too many factors at play. It's better if you're safe. Just…don't stay away forever, *please*!" I knew I sounded needy, but there was only so much adulting I could handle at one time.

Iris sniffed and dabbed her eyes, then blew her nose on the tissue that Hanna offered her. "Oh, we won't. When Shadow Wing is taken care of, we'll come back. At least… I'm sure we will. But given I'm going to be ballooning up again, given two babies in the oven, and I've got two to care for already, I imagine we'll be away for at least a couple of years." She looked miserable, but then shrugged. "The Duchess is a goddess-send. I remember how intimidated I was of her at first. Now, she's practically frothing at the mouth for more grandbabies."

I was about to say something when a knock sounded on the front door. Shade answered and then came traipsing into the kitchen, followed by Camille and her husbands. Vanzir followed them. I sniffed back my tears and smiled, watching her wings shimmer. She usually kept them under wraps, but when she was alone with us she let them shine, even though Tabby always wanted to come out to play with them. I kept my inner kitten under control as much as possible, but now and then I couldn't help it, and I'd change shape and take a quick swipe at them.

"Menolly here yet?" Camille asked, glancing around. She frowned as she looked at Iris, who was still red-nosed and teary. "What's wrong?"

"Nothing, really," I said, wanting to spare Iris from having to repeat her news over and over. "We'll talk when Menolly gets here. Meanwhile, are you hungry?"

Camille nodded. "Yeah, we were supposed to have dinner with Aeval, Titania, and the Merlin—who's just back from Ireland—when you called. Vanzir and I told them to go ahead without us, but I'm famished." She poked around in the fridge, bringing out more cheese, along with some cold cuts and bread.

Hanna jumped up. "Let me fix you and the boys a sandwich, Camille."

Camille handed over the food. "Thanks, Hanna." She sat down between Smoky and Morio. Trillian sat near Shade, and Vanzir stretched out at the end of the table.

"So," Camille said. "Carter has found the answer?"

"Well, *an* answer. I just hope it's the one we're looking for. He's on his way." I turned to Shade. "You should go get Roz. He's still down at the studio."

Within fifteen minutes Carter had arrived. That he had made the trip underscored how important this was. He hardly ever emerged from his apartment. The demigod tended to be a recluse. His coppery-colored hair seemed longer than when I had last seen it, trailing down mid-back. His horns were showing, which meant he was comfortable around us. When he *did* go out, he usually cloaked up under a glamour. He propped his cane against the table, and within a minute he was sifting through a pile of papers.

As he sorted out his notes, Menolly and Nerissa arrived.

I slid into a chair and cleared my throat. "I guess we're all here. Shall we start the meeting?"

The big wooden table had been home to so many meetings in the past that a flash of nostalgia hit me as we took our places around it. The house had felt empty since everybody else moved out. This place had been home since we first came over Earthside, but now it belonged to Shade and me and felt so much quieter than we were used to.

Hanna brought a platter of grilled cheese sandwiches to the table, along with a bowl of potato chips, and everybody dug in. As we set to eating, Carter took a sip of his tea and then leaned back, staring at us.

"I'm ready. I'm sorry this took me so long, but the research was complicated. Shall I begin?"

I nodded. "Please."

"First, I found out exactly what the gems are that you saw in your vision. *Two jewels, jet as night with sparkling white centers.* The information wasn't easy to dig up, but I finally came across a mention of them in a series of notes that I took a hundred years back. I knew the jewels sounded familiar."

A shiver ran up my back. The vision I'd had of Shadow Wing had shown me two glowing jewels, one beneath each of his horns. I had known right then that those gems were the key to defeating Shadow Wing.

"So you really know what the gems are?" Camille asked, her eyes lighting up.

He nodded. "I do."

"Then, do we have hope?" asked Nerissa.

Carter nodded. "You do, but this won't be easy."

"Don't keep us in suspense," Smoky said. The dragon looked as somber as the rest of us.

"All right, here it is," Carter said. "What do you know about the Beasttägger?"

Camille frowned, tapping the table with one nail. "Wasn't he the Demon Lord in control of the Subterranean Realms, the one Shadow Wing assassinated?"

"Correct." Carter held up a printout. "This painting of the Beasttägger was made thousands of years ago. I still possess the original, but it's much too fragile to carry out of the vault, so I made a copy of it."

The painting was that of a horned demon. Unlike Shadow Wing, he had no wings, but he was massive and powerful, with flaming hooves.

I shuddered. "He was a freakshow, that was for sure."

"Look closely and tell me what you see." Carter handed the printout to me. I studied it for a moment, frowning, before I gasped.

"There! Right under his eyes, on the lower outer corners." I slapped the print down on the table and pointed. Camille and Menolly studied the image for a moment, then Camille tapped the Beasttägger's head.

"*Gems*." She looked up at me. "Are those the same ones that you saw at the base of Shadow Wing's horns?" Camille handed the printout back to Carter.

I nodded. "They look exactly the same. Even in the printout, it's obvious. How did he get them? What are they? Are they the same ones belonging to Shadow Wing? Or different?"

"One question at a time. It took me awhile to figure out just what they were, but the gems on this painting are the Beasttägger's *soul receptacles*. One contained his own soul. The other, that of the Demon Lord *he* replaced." Carter sat back, a mildly horrified look on his face.

"Soul receptacles—I don't like the sound of that," I said.

"What are they?" Morio asked.

"They're magical gems that can contain souls." Carter leaned forward. "Given Delilah's description, it's my belief that Shadow Wing has been implanted with a soul receptacle containing the Beasttägger's soul. The other contains his own."

"Do all Demon Lords have souls that reside outside their body?" Nerissa asked.

Carter shook his head. "No. That research took me awhile, but I've ascertained that *this* is how the Demon Lords control so much power. They always move up via assassination. And when they assassinate their opponent, they trap the former Demon Lord's soul in one of the gems, and implant it within themselves. This forces their own soul into a similar gem."

"What happens if they don't transfer their own soul over?" Iris asked.

"If they didn't have a second soul receptacle ready, they would end up allowing the former Demon Lord to operate through them, as their own soul would be bounced out into the astral realms, severed from their body."

"Sort of like possession? Or a walk-in?" Morio finished his sandwich and pushed his plate back.

"Right. But when implanted with both gems, the host is able to utilize both the energy of their captive—the former Demon Lord—as well as their own powers. Two soul receptacles will work together, but three won't. So you'll never find anybody using three at once."

"So Shadow Wing essentially has the energy and knowledge of two Demon Lords' souls? No wonder he's so tough." Camille rubbed her head.

"Yes. Think hard, though, about what a victory over him would mean." Carter had a self-satisfied smile on his face.

I ran through the possibilities in my mind. "If we manage to destroy both gems, then we not only destroy Shadow Wing but the Beasttägger as well. And that… would break the chain of command in the Sub-Realms? Which means Trytian's father can take over without being challenged."

"Correct, and it means you would be breaking a chain that stretches tens of thousands of years. This has been how the Demon Lords kept control of the Sub-Realms." Carter looked delighted. He let out a contented sigh. "I love finding out new information like this."

I laughed. "You're such a geek."

"Ah, yes, but a stylish one, I hope," he said smoothly.

"So, what are the gems, exactly? And how do we destroy them?" Camille glanced at me before watching Carter again. So much depended on his answer.

Carter held her gaze. "They're actually a form of magically treated diamond. Which means that not only are they incredibly difficult to destroy, but they're magically impervious to most of the elements. There's only one thing I've learned of that can destroy them, and you know what I'm about to say."

Camille hung her head, waiting, before raising her gaze to him again.

"The combined power of the spirit seals. And *this* is where you and the Keraastar Knights come in." He turned to her, a solemn look on his face. "There are very few soul receptacles in existence. They're actually chips scattered from the Spirit Seal when it was broken. The demons managed to get hold of them before they were forced into the Sub-Realms."

The room fell silent. Camille closed her eyes and reached for her throat, where the Keraastar diamond rested. For so long, we had wondered what part the Keraastar Knights had to play, and why Shadow Wing was so intent on gathering the spirit seals. Now we knew. It was self-preservation. As long as the Keraastar Knights were scattered, Shadow Wing was safe. But now, the circle was complete and he had to know it was only a matter of time before we came for him.

"So then…we really *can't* leave his destruction to Trytian's father and hope it works. We *have* to face him ourselves," Camille said.

Trillian rested a hand on her shoulder. Smoky and

Morio both tensed. The three of them would protect her to their deaths, but this was one battle they couldn't fight for her.

"Do you know how this will play out? Do the prophecies say anything about the end?" I asked Carter, holding his gaze.

He shook his head. "I'm no prognosticator. I'm a researcher. I can't tell you how this will end, or what Camille's supposed to do, but she and the Keraastar Knights are the endgame in this battle. Everyone here can help, but in the end, it's up to them to deliver the final blow."

"We need to summon him to a place where, if he gets free, he can't do much damage. Or at least, where he can be contained," I said after a moment's thought. "We can't just gate him over into the open where he could run amok."

Camille glanced over at Smoky. "What about the Dragon Reaches? I figure that if nothing else, your people can tear him apart, even if you can't destroy the soul receptacles. The dragons pledged to help us."

Smoky pressed his lips together, looking somber. His hair—down to his calves—twitched, belying his nerves. After a moment, he said, "I'll have to talk to my mother and the Wing-Liege. I can't approach the Emperor on my own. I fear that they'll look upon the action against Telazhar as fulfilling their promise to you. What time frame are we talking about?"

"We can't wait too long," Vanzir said. "There are rumblings from the Demon Underground that Shadow Wing is draining his army for power. He's a Soul Eater, so he can eat their essence and their magic."

"He knows that the end is near, and he's gathering his strength," Camille whispered. "Vanzir's right. We have to move fast. We've run out of wiggle room."

"That's about the size of it," Vanzir said.

"Speaking of the demon army," Carter said, pulling out a folded piece of paper. "I received a missive this morning from Joreal addressed to you."

"Joreal?" I cocked my head. The others looked as clueless as I felt.

Carter arched his eyebrows. "Trytian's father."

Blinking, Camille let out a soft sound. "Do you realize that in all this time, Trytian never once told us his father's name?"

Trytian had been the son of the daemon general who was leading a war against Shadow Wing down in the Sub-Realms. The daemons bore no love for the demons, and they viewed Shadow Wing as unstable and reckless. Trytian had fallen in our last battle, and even though he'd been a pain in the ass, we all felt his loss.

"We've always just thought of him as 'Trytian's father.' It never occurred to me to ask for his name," Menolly said.

"So, what's the news?" Smoky asked. He bore no love for Trytian, though he had honored his death.

"Shadow Wing has truly become the Unraveller. He's not only tearing apart everything he touches in the Sub-Realms, but he's absorbing as much magical energy as he can. He's eating the souls of his followers right and left, and those who have stayed in his service have turned into a death cult, bent on shoring up his revenge. The most fanatical are offering themselves to him, freely advancing to their deaths to shore him up. Once you managed to regain all the spirit seals, Shadow Wing realized that he had lost his chance to break out via ripping open the portals. So he's doing what he can to beef up his powers so he can force his way through. And he blames the three of you for his losses."

"If I thought that he was actually locked down there for good, I'd say leave him be and forget about him. But given all of the rogue portals popping up, and with him gathering power, we don't dare rest until we've destroyed him," Camille said. "The prophecy with the Keraastar Knights has played out as foretold, and we're near the end. We need to make sure he's dead and can never rise again."

"So what's next?" I asked.

Camille stared at her hands. "I'll talk to Grandmother Coyote. Maybe she can give me some direction about how I'm to use the Keraastar Knights against him. She helped set this in motion four years ago."

Iris slowly stood. "Before we continue, I need to say something." Her expression was strained.

"What is it?" Menolly asked.

Iris glanced at me and I gave her a nod.

"Go ahead. You have to tell them sometime."

"Right." She let out a sharp breath. "Delilah knows, but the rest of you don't. I've been feeling off for the past month, so I went to see Mallen. I'm pregnant again. And as much as I want to help you in this final battle, I can't walk into it carrying life in my womb."

I reached out to catch her hand. "You've stood by our side through this whole ordeal. You need to take care of you, now."

Camille was out of her chair, hugging her as soon as she finished speaking.

"Iris, you're part of our family. There's no chance we'll ask you to put your life on the line when you have young ones to care for. Nor would we allow it, even if you want to. Right?" She flashed Menolly a sharp look.

Menolly looked crestfallen, but nodded. "Camille's correct. Knowing this, we wouldn't let you fight, even if you wanted to. In fact, as much as it pains me to say so, I think you should leave for the duration of the fight. We still have many enemies, and the woods surrounding this house have never been truly safe."

I walked over to stand behind Iris, placing my hands on her shoulders. "I'm glad you said that, because Iris is going to move to Ireland. At least until the new babies come."

"Babies?" Camille blinked. "You're pregnant with twins again?"

Iris laughed then. "Yes, it seems to be in my blood. I'm so glad you don't feel that I'm abandoning you. I'd never do that—but…" She paused. "Delilah's right. The Duchess has asked Bruce and me to move to Ireland so she can help with Maria and Ukkonen, while I'm brooding the new buns."

Out of the corner of my eye, I saw Roz staring at the table with a gloomy look. He had fallen for Iris years ago, but given he was an incubus, there wasn't a chance in hell that she would have taken him on. He had managed to accept that his love was unrequited, but it was still obvious that he still had feelings for her.

"When do you leave?" he asked.

"In a couple days. I know this is short notice, but

Undutar is pushing me to hurry. For some reason, she feels it's unsafe for me to stay here." Iris was Undutar's priestess, and when a goddess spoke, her priestess jumped. That was just the way things were.

"We'll do anything you need to help." I couldn't imagine what it was going to be like when she left, but everything was changing around us. It was like a whirlwind had settled down in our lives, gusting us this way and that.

"I appreciate it. Truly. Of course, we'll tidy up the house and make sure it's locked up. If you could check on it every now and then, we'd be grateful. I figure we'll return in about eighteen months—once I give birth and we find a nanny willing to come back and help us." Iris slowly took her seat again. Her voice was clouded. "I can't believe I'm leaving. I've been over in Seattle for decades… in the US for centuries. Now, I'm uprooting my life and moving off across the ocean again." She glanced at me. "We talked about going to Finland, but my family and I are so estranged that we decided it's just better to accept the Duchess's gesture and go where we're wanted."

After that, the conversation broke apart.

Camille had to leave, so we agreed to get together the next day and go talk to Grandmother Coyote. Menolly wouldn't be able to come, given the daylight, but not all of us needed to go. Carter promised to continue searching for more information before heading out into the night.

After everyone had left, Shade and I curled up on the sofa in the living room. Hanna entered the living room, carrying a tray containing a bowl of Cheetos and some hot cocoa. She set it on the coffee table.

"If you're good for the evening, I'm off to bed," she

said. "It's been a long day for me, and tomorrow I want to tackle cleaning all the rugs."

"Go ahead." I waved her off. "You've done enough for one day. Go relax and sleep." After she left, I leaned my head against Shade's chest. "I'm sad."

"Why, love? Because Iris is leaving? You know it's safest for her and her family to go." He wrapped his arm around my shoulders, stretching out his legs and resting them on the coffee table. For a dragon shifter, he was remarkably relaxed.

"Yes. No. Oh, I don't know why I'm upset. I've managed to handle all the changes so far, but I'm starting to feel boxed in by chaos. I know that sounds odd, but I'm a cat. I don't like change. It's not easy for me." I inhaled his scent, closing my eyes as it calmed me down. He was cinnamon and spice, pumpkin pie and falling leaves and rain on the window—all things shadowy and autumn.

"I know, love. And things are bound to change even more."

"I suppose." I shrugged. "Menolly said Roman's off to handle some crisis overseas. Some big issue with one of the regents over there, and if they don't nip it in the bud, she said it could turn very nasty, very quickly. At least she didn't have to tag along."

"What? Did Dracula pop his head out of the shadows?"

I laughed, but then sobered. "Not quite, but too close for comfort. Apparently, some old-school vamp over there wants things to return to the days when the Vampire Nation considered humans to be on the same level as cattle."

"Ouch, that sucks, no pun intended. I'm glad she didn't

have to go along, though. I don't think she and Nerissa have adapted too well to Roman's life yet."

"I know, but there's nothing Camille or I can do to help. Maybe they're just war-weary. I suppose we all are. Once Shadow Wing's dead, then we can get on with our lives and find a way to make all the changes work." I grabbed a handful of Cheetos, staring at them. They were my favorite food in the world. "Just three more months till we see Jerry Springer. I can't thank you enough for the tickets."

Shade had managed to find tickets to see Jerry Springer in January, when he was coming to Seattle. Over the years, my obsession with the talk-show host had waxed and waned, but it had never fully died, and I was looking forward to fulfilling one of my bucket-list goals.

Shade slid his hand out from behind my head and stretched. "I will never understand your fascination with that man, but whatever floats your boat, honey."

Laughing, I picked up the remote and turned on the TV. "Want to watch a movie?"

Shade nodded. "Whatever you like."

I flipped through the channels until I found Godzilla attacking Tokyo, and we watched late into the night. We moved on from Godzilla to Mothra and then to giant ants mutated by radiation, and my anxiety faded as I lost myself in worlds where monsters were sure to be defeated, and the good guys always won.

CHAPTER THREE

Camille

SMOKY WAVED ME OVER TO WHERE HE WAS SITTING AT ONE of the desks in the office. "My mother responded." He held up an envelope. An ornate wax seal marked the back, Vishana's symbol.

"Can you guess what her answer is?" I asked, sitting beside him, running my fingers up his arm. It had been over a week since I had managed to catch some bedtime with any of my husbands, and I was feeling the lack. I really didn't appreciate it when royal duties interfered with my sex life.

He stared at my fingers for a moment before a lock of his hair rose up to coil around my wrist, bringing my hand to his lips where he kissed each finger in turn. Only then did he answer me. "Honestly, I don't." Opening the envelope, he slid out the single sheet of paper, folded once, and set the envelope down on the desk. He scanned the note, then sighed and handed it to me.

I read what Vishana had written.

My son, the Wing-Liege and the Emperor regretfully decline to host the final assault on Shadow Wing in our lands. We will send help, if you need, but we cannot allow the Demon Lord into the Dragon Reaches. —Love, Mother

---

"They really said no?" I stared at the note, willing it to change before my eyes. "I know that they helped us with the battle against Telazhar. But I thought for sure they'd go one step further." I crossed my arms, disappointed. But I couldn't really fault them. They had helped us more than we ever expected during the assault on Elqaneve and the other lands in Y'Eírialiastar.

"I have another idea," Smoky said.

"What's that?" I read the note again, just in case we had missed anything. But it was short and not-so-sweet, and not-so-helpful.

Smoky straightened. He was tall, over six-six. I had found out he was still a growing boy, at least as far as dragon shifters went, and he had sprouted up two inches in the past few months.

"What if we build an arena in which to contain him over in Otherworld? We could ask the techno-mages from Elqaneve to help us. Sharah's done a remarkable job in recruiting new members for her team, and we could build a chamber that would be almost impossible for him to break out of."

"One problem with that," I said. "If it's an anti-magic chamber, we can't just gate him into it. We'd have to gate him outside of the chamber and then drive him in. We'd have, what…five minutes in which to engage him before he realizes what's happening and either kills somebody or escapes."

Smoky frowned. "True enough. But what about gating him right outside the walls, then immediately trigger a ring of anti-magic spells to surround him? At worst, it will confuse him, which would give us the extra time to drive him inside."

"That might work," I murmured. "Damn it, I wish your kin would just help us out." I had come to love my dragon in-laws, but they could be stubborn lizards.

"Well, give us some credit. We did help with Telazhar." Smoky shrugged. "Besides, given the fact that the prophecies state it will require the Keraastar Knights to destroy him, surrounding him with a ring of dragons won't make much difference. We might be able to defeat him momentarily, but if you and your Knights are the only ones who can kill him, then having the dragons at hand won't do any good in the long run."

"I'm off," I said, standing up and slipping into my jacket. "Speculating is futile until we know more. Hopefully, Grandmother Coyote can clear up a few things. Delilah said she'd be waiting for me. I'll be back in a few hours."

"Drive safe, my love." Smoky kissed me, long and slow, warming my heart as well as my body. "Do you want me to come with you?"

I shook my head. "No need. I'll be fine. Just try to figure out anything you can to help matters. Think some more about that anti-magic arena idea. Maybe there's something there."

GRANDMOTHER COYOTE WAS one of the Hags of Fate. Four years ago, almost to the day, she had tipped us off to what we were facing with Shadow Wing, but there had been a price. And there would always be a price for her aid. Sometimes, it was steeper than the help was worth. Other times, it was well worth the effort she asked.

Followed by my guards, I headed to the back of the Barrow. At my request, a side road had been put in, giving us easier access to our vehicles instead of having to go all the way to the parking lot at the front of Talamh Lonrach Oll, the Fae Court Sovereign Nation. They waited till I was safely in the car and headed toward the gate before backing away. I always had the feeling they weren't happy about me driving myself, but I wasn't going to knuckle under. Aeval and Titania both knew just who they were taking into the Court of the Three Queens when they chose me, and I wasn't inclined to compromise more than I already had.

The drive from Talamh Lonrach Oll to our old house took me about half an hour, though traffic was light during the early afternoon, and I wasn't all that worried about being late.

The weather was blowing up a storm. The wind gusted past at a steady clip and the clouds were crowding in, threatening rain with their dark thunderheads. I could have sworn it was already dusk even though it was only mid-afternoon.

As I approached the land where Grandmother Coyote's lair was located, I eased off the road onto the embankment and parked behind Delilah's Jeep. She was sitting in the driver's seat, reading something, but when she saw me she jumped out of the car.

I made sure my jacket was snugly buttoned up and slipped into the storm. Inhaling deeply, I stretched my arms wide as I reveled in the silhouettes of the tall firs and cedars, and the smell of wood smoke in the air from down the street.

"Wilbur?" I asked, indicating the whirl of smoke that drifted past.

Delilah nodded as she hurried over to me, hands jammed in her pockets. "Yeah. Wilbur. Say, are we going to include him in this battle? He's been there for us a lot of times, even if he is a pain in the ass."

I shrugged. "I'm not sure, but actually, now that you mention it, he might be able to help Shamas. He's a sorcerer, too. Or rather, a necromancer, but his powers are similar." I shivered as I began to cross to the field leading to Grandmother Coyote's tree.

The Hags of Fate ruled over destiny, but they neither wove it nor created it. They observed, and when it was needed, they intervened. They could predict the most likely future, and together with the Harvestmen and the Elemental Lords, they were the only beings who were immortal. They existed outside of time, yet walked through the world when they chose.

The woods surrounding Grandmother Coyote's place were darker than I remembered. It had been awhile since we had last come here, wandering through the undergrowth in search of her tree.

"It's going to get cold tonight," I murmured, my wings shimmering through my jacket. When the weather was too extreme, it was harder to control their appearance.

"Do your clothes ever get in the way of those things?" Delilah asked. "They look like they've been dusted in glitter."

I shook my head. "I can control how far they manifest in terms of solidity. I prefer to keep them out of sight most of the time, because they're a distraction and kids like to try to play with them. And *cats*," I added, staring at her pointedly. "I can feel them, but they don't exist in this realm the way my jacket or dress does." I paused, then giggled. "Some nights, though, I like to go outside under the moon and dance around. They make me feel graceful, and they also connect me with the Moon Mother more. I know it sounds silly, but I pretend I'm flying."

Delilah snorted, but she gave me a look that told me she understood.

I glanced around the wooded lot. "That way," I said, pointing to a barely discernible trail. I had been here far more often than the others, but it was still tricky. If Grandmother Coyote didn't want to be found, she set a good camouflage. I set off, firmly treading through the knee-high grass that was dying back for the season. The trees were laden with leaves, but they had changed color, and all it would take was one good, strong wind to catch them up and send them spiraling to the ground.

Delilah followed me as we pushed on through the thicket, ducking to miss the massive spider webs that the orb weavers strung from tree to tree. These woods were a haven for the striped spiders. In fact, the entire Pacific Northwest was rife with them during the summer and autumn. They came out to play in the vegetable gardens, feasting on the bugs, and then in autumn, when the mist was rising off the ground, they abounded, weaving their webs and fattening up, then laying their egg sacs in hidden crevices so that next year, a new generation would be born. I found them fascinating, though I didn't like them on me. With their jointed legs, they reminded me of aliens, a hive mind of ruthless predators. And yet, the orb weavers kept to their webs, seldom intruding within the homes and houses around them. Oh, sometimes one would have eyes bigger than its stomach, stringing a web across the sidewalk, but most often, if we left them alone, they left us alone.

A rustling to my right gave me pause. I stopped, turning to scan the bushes. The occasional bloatworgle stumbled through the woods around here. They were dangerous, breathing fire. But none of the minor demons appeared—merely a red fox who scampered across the path to the other side and vanished beneath a huckleberry bush. I silently wished him well, hoping he would find plenty of fat mice to fill his belly. I didn't dare say that aloud, though, given Delilah had made friends with some of the mice around the area, and as strange as it seemed, she watched over them. When we had first come here, a mouse helped her out when she was in her tabby form. She was still helping out the mouse's family to return the favor, even though Misha, the original mouse, had long departed for the Summer Lands.

We broke through the thicket into a clearing. Across the grove was a giant oak, the trunk huge compared to the towering fir trees surrounding it. I motioned for Delilah to follow me over to a fallen nurse log. The decaying trunk was covered with mildew and mushrooms, with moss and ferns growing out of the decaying wood. I sat down on the end, and Delilah joined me.

I held out my hands. Closing my eyes, I whispered, "Grandmother Coyote, we're here. Come out, come out, wherever you are. We need to talk to you."

There was silence all around, with only the rustle of leaves in the wind to keep us company.

One beat. Two. Three beats. And then, another.

Slowly, from behind the massive oak, a cloaked figure stepped into a glimmer of moonlight that broke through the clouds. The moonglow hit Grandmother Coyote square on, illuminating her. Luminous and brilliant in her age and wisdom, she held up one hand, crooked a finger, and motioned for us to follow.

I stood, silently crossing the lea, Delilah by my side. As the moonlight from the waning crescent struck us, it splashed a cold, ethereal glow across our skin. Delilah shivered, but for me, it was like nectar, and I let it wash over me, the essence of my Lady who watched from above.

Still silent, we followed her to the trunk of the oak, which was wide enough to drive the car through and then some. But it was bigger inside than it appeared. A light emanated from the trunk, forming a doorway. I took a deep breath and stepped inside, into the lair of Grandmother Coyote.

⚔

ONCE WITHIN THE TRUNK, we found ourselves on a path, compacted dirt and pebbles. The path led down a corridor, surrounded on either side by clouds of mist. I wasn't sure what lay beyond the mist, and I didn't want to find out.

We walked for a while—I don't really know how long because time seemed suspended within the realm of Grandmother Coyote—and finally came out into a cave. There was a table in the center of the cave, and three chairs surrounding the round slab of oak. Grandmother Coyote motioned for me to sit opposite of her, and Delilah sat to my left.

"So we're back to the beginning, are we?" Grandmother Coyote leaned back in her chair. What she truly thought of us, I had no clue. She was impossible to read, her face impervious, a topographical map of a timeless life. Within the nooks and crannies of her wrinkles existed the whole of time, and her eyes were those of an endless observer.

I nodded. "It felt fitting to come to you for advice. I assume you know why we're here?"

Grandmother Coyote continued to stare at me. "You have the spirit seals. You know Shadow Wing's secret. And now...I cannot volunteer information. You must ask." Her gaze never left my face.

I wondered if there was *anything* she didn't know. As if she were reading my thoughts, a toothy grin spread across her face. When Grandmother Coyote smiled it was more disconcerting than if she frowned. Her teeth were like steel, sharp, and able to gnash through bone.

I took a deep breath and glanced at Delilah for moral support.

"Go ahead," Kitten whispered.

Turning back to Grandmother Coyote, I said, "I assume there's a price for your help?"

"Oh, my girl, there's a price for everything in this world. And the price for my help this time is steep. You hold the reins of fate in your hand, Camille. Are you all willing to pay my price for my help?"

I thought about everything that had happened in my life, both the good and the bad. I had faced loss when Mother had died. I had faced the darkness of my own mind when Hyto had captured me. But joy and love had rewarded me so many times over. I was my father's daughter, and even though he was dead, I would not make him ashamed.

I steeled myself and said, "I will pay the price."

Delilah cleared her throat. "Camille won't pay the price alone. I promise to help her. And Menolly would as well, if she were here. All three of us will see this through." Her voice was steady. Kitten had grown up over the years, her timidity gone, and in its place a strong warrior had emerged. The Death Maiden had won out over the scaredy-cat.

"The deal is set, then." Grandmother Coyote slowly reached beneath the tablecloth and brought out a small velvet bag. She handed it to me.

"Draw three bones, as you did the first time you came to me. Then place them on the table in front of you."

I silently reached in the bag. The bones were finger bones, from every race of creature. I had brought one of them to Grandmother Coyote, the first price she had charged me. Bad Ass Luke, as we had called him, had been the first demon we fought. And he had been the first sign Shadow Wing was on the rise.

I let my fingers play over the bones. Three of them sparked against my skin, and I removed them and placed them on the table. One was long and slender, one short and stubby, and the third looked to be a finger bone from a creature that I didn't recognize.

Grandmother Coyote stared at the bones.

I closed my eyes, leaning back. I could feel shadows wandering through the room. Behind us, around us, standing over our shoulders, the shades of the past were alive and thriving in Grandmother Coyote's lair. I thought about asking about them, but I didn't want to interrupt. The silence hung heavy. I knew that Delilah's eyes had grown wide, but she said nothing, either.

After a time, Grandmother Coyote expelled a lungful of air. For some reason, that surprised me. I wasn't sure that she even *had* to breathe, considering she was one of the Immortals. But her sigh filled the room, swirling around us with a magic of its own. I tensed, almost afraid to break the mood, as if it would shatter the magic into shards, like a mirror breaking.

"Delilah, I see the shadow of a girl. She dances around you in fire and ash, in bone and falling leaves. She's a flickering flame, hard to grasp, harder still to hold onto. She will grow to be a queen, weaving her webs throughout the lands during the autumn days. I tell you this: you must not fear who she is to become. You must claim your own nature, lest she spin you around in circles. You are her *guide*, but you cannot possess her. You can merely direct her."

Delilah blinked, letting out a little gasp. "Is she the only child I will have?"

"Remember this: even though you will give birth to her, this autumn flame is no youth. From the very beginning she will be older than time. She will be her *father's* daughter. However, though she will stay with you but a fleeting moment—at least what will seem like it—you will open your home to others who need mothering. One does not have to give birth to be a parent. Those who will grow up remembering you as their mother will do so out of love, not blood."

Swallowing hard, Delilah murmured a "Thank you," and pressed her lips together. I couldn't tell if she was upset, or relieved.

Grandmother Coyote looked at the second bone. "I see a split path before Menolly. You will tell her that a fork in the road is coming, and her joy and happiness depends on which route she takes. Obligations come and go, and while it is necessary to keep one's word, there are ways she can do so without shuttering herself away in a tower like Rapunzel. She is not to think in terms of either/or. There are ways to make everyone happy in her life. The only restrictions will be those she puts upon herself."

Without missing a beat she turned to me. "And so, while your sisters' fortunes have little to do with the matter at hand, that is what the web weaves for them. For you, I see this: Surround the problem with the solution. Circles are infinitely strong, their shape an infinite loop. A circle of energy can surround and shatter an adversary. But you *must not break the chain*. There must be trust. Hands must hold tight. And no matter what happens, *do not give into the fear*. The chain is only as strong as its weakest link, so reinforce that link and you can win."

"Who is my weakest link?" I asked. "I assume it's one of the Keraastar Knights?"

"Perhaps," Grandmother Coyote said.

I closed my eyes, then realized what she was saying. "*I'm* the weakest link. I'm the one with the most to lose, therefore *I* am the weak link. How do I fix this? How do I steel myself so that my fears over what *might* be don't interfere and break the spell?"

Grandmother Coyote shrugged. "How do you fix anything? How do you strengthen a girder or beam? You reinforce it. Remember, the core is the strongest part. Strengthen the core, and the shell will follow." She leaned back. "Focus that combined energy on Shadow Wing's gems and you can shatter them as surely as a word can shatter silence. Not every battle is fought on a physical level. Sometimes magic is the only strength you have. Sometimes it's the only hope."

And with that, she fell silent.

CHAPTER FOUR
Menolly

I STARED AT THE PHONE. I HAD JUST OPENED CAMILLE'S email. I slowly placed my pen on the desk, and pushed away the thank-you note I had been writing to the Ladies of the Night Society—a vampire club for gentrified members. They had held a meeting in my honor a week ago, and it was expected that I express my gratitude for their kindness. If it had been up to me, I would have sent them an email thanking them, but among the upper-crust vamps, decorum dictated a decidedly old-school approach to things such as thank-you notes and invitations. Probably because a lot of them were old school to begin with.

Camille had been to see Grandmother Coyote and come away with—as usual—cryptic answers. But the message for me had been clear enough. The Hags of Fate thought I could keep my obligations *and* be content and happy. I no longer questioned how the Immortals knew what they knew—there was no use pondering some of the universe's mysteries. What I *did* know was that when the Immortals gave advice, it was best to follow it.

A knock on the door stirred me out of my thoughts.

"Menolly?" Erin Mathews peeked into my office. She was my daughter—the only person I had ever turned into a vampire.

I looked up from my desk and, welcoming the interruption, motioned for her to come in.

Erin was looking good. Her vampire glamour had fully taken hold and gone was the dowdy, middle-aged look she had sported as a human. She was my only child, so to speak. I had sired her when her life was on the line, and she had made the choice to be turned rather than to die.

"Erin, hey, what's up? Gearing up for the tour?"

Erin had been offered the chance to go on tour with Wade Stevens, the founder of Vampires Anonymous, to create chapters of the support group on a nationwide basis. It had been hard for me to say yes, given my worries over the vampire hate groups out there, but I had to cut the cord sometime. Erin needed to grow into what she was meant to become. And this movement could put both Wade and Erin in the spotlight. I had no doubt they were on their way to becoming ambassadors between the living and the undead.

She shrugged. "We're making progress. There's a lot to iron out." She paused, then added, "I wanted to thank you again for letting me go. You could have said no. You could have ordered me to stay in the security department."

I considered my response. Erin was still in the starry-eyed phase of being sired and she looked up to me.

"I almost didn't agree because I was worried about you. But my sisters reminded me that there's a lot of work to be done, and that even if you were to stay here, I can't protect you all the time. I trust you, Erin, and I believe that you'll do great things. But if you need me, I'm just a phone call away." I gazed at her for a moment, then suppressed a smile as she knelt before me.

"It's been a long road, these past four years," she said. "One moment I was owner of the Scarlet Harlot and president of the Faerie Watchers Club, and the next…I was dying. And you saved me." She looked up, a grateful look on her face. "I'll always be grateful to you for that, regardless of what happens. But you're right, you can't protect me every moment, and I'm hoping that I can make a difference in the world."

Her words echoed in my head.

"Sit down for a moment." I motioned for her to take a seat and she rose, crossing to the chair next to my desk as I returned to my own chair. I rested my elbows on the polished walnut.

"There's something I've never told you. But now, I think you should know. Years ago, when I was turned, I swore to myself that I would never turn another soul into a vampire. After what Dredge did to me, I couldn't imagine putting someone else through it." I paused, debating on whether to continue. Erin knew that I had been tortured, but I'd never given her the specifics.

She nodded. "I know you weren't given a choice. You weren't dying, like I was, when he caught you."

"No, I wasn't. And he spent the entire night focused on causing me as much pain as he could without outright killing me. I'll never get rid of the physical scars, though I've healed a lot of the emotional pain. But there are some acts…some wounds you never forget. No matter how much you heal, no matter how much you let go, there are some journeys from which you never fully return. So even though you were dying, it was incredibly hard for me to bring myself to turn you. And I probably wouldn't have, if it hadn't been for Grandmother Coyote."

Erin blinked. "Grandmother Coyote?"

"Yes. The first time I met her, Grandmother Coyote gave me some cryptic advice. She also scared the shit out of me, but that's just the way she is. But at a meeting of the Supe Community Council, Grandmother Coyote came up to me and she told me that I was going to have to do something I had vowed never to do. That when the time came, I needed to go through with it, as much as I didn't want to. I didn't know what she was talking about at that point, but then you were kidnapped by Dredge's freakshow followers, and he put me in a spot where the only way to save you was to turn you."

Erin stared at me. "I never knew why they kidnapped me, not really. You mean, he did it to torture you?"

"Yeah, he did it to force me into what, at the time, seemed like a no-win situation. He had lost control of me after turning me, so he was looking to make my life as much of a hell as possible."

She ducked her head, staring at her feet. "I'm sorry I was a party to that."

"It's not your fault. *You* did nothing. Dredge was a sadist and he knew you were a friend, so he used you to hurt me. But...Grandmother Coyote had foretold that I needed to follow through. She said that a long thread of destiny hinged on my action—or inaction. That destiny is you, Erin. And I'm pretty sure that what you and Wade are about to do is going to change the world for vampires and humans alike. I see you both ushering in a new age of understanding between the living and the undead."

She hesitated for a moment. "I hope you don't regret turning me. I wanted to live, and I'll do my best to make you proud. To make you feel that it was a good thing you turned me. I'll keep control of my inner predator, and I'll follow in your footsteps. I want to make the world a better place."

I smiled softly. "You already have done that, Erin. I don't regret turning you. I only regret that it was necessary. But you're helping pave the way for others."

"I'm doing my best," she said. She added, "We head out on the road in two days. Do you have any advice for me before I leave?"

"Treat yourself with respect, treat others with that same respect. Corral your inner predator. Turn to Wade if you need help. He's got a sensible head on his shoulders, regardless of his mother. Do yourself proud, Erin. Go out there and change the world." I thought about hugging her, but I wasn't a huggy person and neither was she.

Erin stood. She gave me a low bow. "Permission to leave, Your Highness."

I remembered Camille's advice to me when I married Roman. *Assume the title and wear it like you mean it. If you don't, nobody will take you seriously.*

I brushed Erin's hair back from her face. "Go, and may the gods be with you. Keep us informed of your progress. I wish you all the luck in the world."

And with that, Erin turned and walked out of the room and out of my life, for at least the foreseeable future. I wondered how long she'd be gone—the project was supposed to take a couple of years. Feeling both proud and worried, I returned to my duties.

By midnight, I had finished up most of my drudge work—the thank-yous, and the answers to all sorts of requests—and Nerissa and I took a break. She was hungry, and I wanted out of my office. We returned to our suite where she could eat in peace without feeling like a sideshow. Granted, all the human employees and servants in Roman's mansion ate, but they did so out of sight. Most of the vamps weren't used to food around them and I knew that Nerissa felt out of place because she needed to eat.

She opened a can of soup to heat while piling a piece of bread high with sliced turkey and cheddar. I dropped onto the sofa and leaned back. Roman had promised when we moved in that we could have our own private suite of rooms and he had made good on his word. We had a living room–kitchenette, an office–library, a workout room, a storage room, and our bedroom. The bath was huge and he had installed a soaker-tub, as well as a double-sink vanity.

"Erin came to say good-bye today. I doubt if she'll get a chance to see me again before she and Wade head out," I said, staring at the ceiling.

Nerissa cut her sandwich in half. "Want a drink?"

"No, I had a big breakfast." I had drunk two bottles of waffle-flavored blood, thanks to Morio. He had taught one of the witches Roman kept on staff how to spell a bottle of blood so it tasted like anything but what it was.

"How do you feel about her leaving?"

I considered the question. "Worried. Proud. Hopeful. I told her, finally, about Grandmother Coyote's prophecy. And speaking of the Hags of Fate, Camille visited Grandmother Coyote last night. She had a message for me. For us, I assume."

Nerissa shuddered. "Uh-oh. Is that a good thing, or a bad thing?"

I read her Camille's email.

"So then, the Fates think we can make this life work." Nerissa sat down opposite me, her sandwich and a mug of soup in hand. Placing the mug on the coffee table, she curled up on the sofa, resting her left arm on the arm of the sofa and balancing the sandwich in front of her. "I hope so, because I really need a little more freedom, and I can only see the net tightening as the years go by."

"We'll make it work, I promise," I said. I was about to ask her what her view of the optimal situation would be when my phone jangled. I glanced at my texts. "Hmm, it's from Carter."

"What does he want?" Nerissa bit into her sandwich, wiping her chin with a napkin.

I scanned over his words. "He wants us to come over. He says he has further information, but it would be better if I visit him rather than my sisters. I wonder what's up." I knew that if I called to ask, he wouldn't budge. Carter was secretive when he felt it benefited the situation.

"When does he want you over there?"

I texted him back, asking. A moment later, he answered.

"He says tonight, if possible. In the next hour or so. I might as well go now. I finally finished answering all the correspondence on my desk, and since Roman's away, there isn't much going on here." I glanced at her. "You want to come?"

Nerissa shook her head. "No, I'll stay here and get in a

quick workout before I take a bath. Besides, Carter asked for you, not me. Go ahead. I'm good."

She looked so comfortable and settled that I didn't have the heart to cajole her into going out with me. I gave her a quick kiss on the cheek, then lingered for a moment, nuzzling her ear.

"Come back soon," she whispered. "We can lock away the world and pretend that we're the only ones who exist."

I stroked her cheek, then reluctantly pulled away. "I'm holding you to that."

As I threw on a light jacket and headed for the door, she turned on the TV and went back to her dinner.

CARTER LIVED IN A BASEMENT APARTMENT. He could have lived just about anywhere. Hell, he was the son of both the Titan Hyperion and a demon. As a demigod, he could have lived anywhere. He certainly didn't have to hole up in a seedy part of Seattle, in an underground rat hole. To be fair, he kept the apartment nice—in a vintage sort of way—but it was still a basement apartment in a rundown neighborhood. But Carter seemed to like it, and that was all that mattered.

I parked my Mustang in one of the spaces I knew was included in his magical circle of protection. He had hired a high-powered witch to cast protection charms for him and his place, and that included a few parking spots next to the sidewalk.

As I clattered down the stairs, I wondered who would be opening the door this time. Every few months, Carter found himself a new housekeeper/lover. We had broached the outer skirts of the subject a few times, just enough for me to know that Carter was into some hardcore S&M play, and he was definitely the top. He didn't act it on the outside, but then again, he was half-demon and he had the horns to prove it.

He took me by surprise when he opened the door himself. "Menolly, I'm glad you're here. Come in."

I raised my eyebrows as he moved aside to let me in. "What happened to Mera?" His latest concubine had been a member of the Elder Fae, and I figured she would last longer than most.

"I asked her to step out for a few moments," Carter said. He ushered me into the living room, where a tall man was standing. He looked familiar, though I couldn't place him, but he *felt* odd. Not human, though he looked to be so. "I asked you here because I felt you'd be the most adept in meeting Joreal."

For a moment, the name didn't ring a bell, but then I remembered our conversation from the night before. *Trytian's father*, the daemon general who was leading a roust against Shadow Wing. And that was where the familiarity came in. Like his son, Joreal had wavy dark hair, and angular features. He was larger, though, with broad shoulders and brilliant blue eyes. And he had a mean look to him that did wonders at setting off my "Danger danger Will Robinson" alarms. But I smoothly stepped forward, stopping in front of the daemon. I considered holding out my hand, but decided that a nod was as good as a shake.

"How do you do, Lord Joreal? I'm Menolly D'Artigo. Please allow me to express our sorrow at your son's death. Trytian died honorably, and he helped us more than we had any reason to expect." I had learned *some* diplomacy since taking my place as Roman's wife. A little sugar went a long way in sanding out the rough patches.

"My son had a soft spot for humans," Joreal said with a stoic face. "And by human, I include your own kind. He did what was required, and his death wasn't in vain. I can only hope that his sacrifice will be worth it."

He clasped his hands behind him. As he appraised me with his gaze, I held my ground. Daemons were not as unpredictable as demons, but I was still wary. The fact that he was standing in Carter's living room said something for his nature, but I had learned long ago not to offer trust before it was earned.

Carter seemed to sense the standoff as he smoothly passed between us carrying a tray of tea and cookies. The tray contained a bottle of blood as well. I had to hand it to Carter, he was gracious to a fault. He sat down in a chair in between the two of us, and motioned for me to sit on the loveseat and Joreal to have a seat on the sofa. As the daemon took his place, I slowly sat down.

"Carter called me here because he says you have the means with which to destroy Shadow Wing." Joreal was blunt to a point. He didn't waste any time with small talk, though I rather doubted whether any of the daemons found chit-chat to their liking.

"We think we do, yes." I wasn't sure exactly what Carter was up to. We had been secretive for so long, protecting our fight for the spirit seals so no one else would find out. Although since Trytian had known about them, it made sense that his father did as well.

"Then we must coordinate. I do not want my armies to get in your way if you truly can destroy him. As you know, we are waging a major offense against him down in the Subterranean Realms. The Unraveller has gone rogue. He's an unpredictable factor determined to throw the Sub-Realms into chaos." He paused, holding my gaze. His eyes were like ice, although I knew mine were just as frosty. "Carter thought it best that we meet to discuss a possible alliance."

I readied a question to which I already knew the answer, but I wanted to hear it from Joreal himself. "Once Shadow Wing is gone from the Sub-Realms, who plans to take over?"

Joreal wasted no time. "I will take over. It's time to take control away from the demons. They're far too chaotic. I have plans, once Shadow Wing is destroyed, to seal off the Sub-Realms for good."

Now *that* I hadn't known. We knew, thanks to Trytian, that Joreal was looking to wrench away control, but that he planned to wall off the Sub-Realms from the other worlds was new information. I wondered what his reasoning was, although I wasn't about to fault it.

But I had to ask. "Out of curiosity, why are you sealing them off?"

"I don't believe that either demons or daemons should interact with the other realms. We're not all out for absolute control and destruction, contrary to what you may think. Some of us are reasonable. But I'm also a purist. I think too much intermingling between those who inhabit the Sub-Realms and the non-demonic is a bad idea. My son didn't agree with me, but since he was involved in the fight against Shadow Wing's ill-advised attempt to gather the spirit seals, I supported his endeavors and his communications over here."

I had the feeling that humanity as a whole, as well as the entire Supe community, had just been insulted. On the other hand, the fact that Joreal didn't believe in mingling with humanity made me feel a little better. And the fact that he was willing to confine his own kind to the Sub-Realms was another positive mark.

"I see," I said. "I think it would benefit my sisters and me if we were to sit down with you and discuss our strategy. Perhaps you can help. We face one major obstacle."

"And what is that?" Joreal asked.

"What to do between the time we gate Shadow Wing over here, and the time my sister and the Keraastar Knights can affect an attack. We're not at all sure that we can contain him at that point." I sat back, chugging down the drink Carter passed to me.

"Well, we'll just have to figure out a way to help you, because down in the Sub-Realms, even my comrades and I know that the only way to defeat Shadow Wing is through the Keraastar Knights. The great Fae Lords set up that prophecy, foolishly."

"Why foolishly?"

Joreal snorted. "Because by enacting such a destiny, they insured that my own armies can never fully throttle him. It's as though they gave Shadow Wing a form of immortality when they created the Spirit Seal. In their attempts to lock us away in the Sub-Realms, they effectively offered him the chance to go undefeated."

I had never thought of it that way, but Joreal was right. Thanks to the prophecy and the Spirit Seal, the great Fae Lords had very nearly created an impervious enemy. When they divided the worlds during the Great Divide, they had, in essence, sealed their own fates.

"Why don't you let me call my sisters and set up a meeting? If they can't make it tonight, can you come back tomorrow night?"

Joreal arched his eyebrows, reminding me for all the world of Trytian. The smirk on his face reinforced the familiarity.

"I was hoping that you could make it tonight. I don't fancy staying up here for another day. But if not, I will make myself available."

I thanked him, and excused myself to step into Carter's kitchen to call my sisters.

CHAPTER FIVE
Delilah

"Will it live?" My eyes were glued to Tim's fingers as they flew over the keys. I needed my laptop to be ready by the time we met with Joreal, and it had chosen to conk out on me an hour ago, blue-screening for all it was worth. "I really need it later tonight."

I still couldn't believe that the daemon general had actually come over Earthside to meet us, although I had a feeling Carter had a great deal to do with the matter. When Menolly had called the night before, Shade and I had been out on a date and I had set my phone to ignore. By the time we got home, it was too late to set up the meeting. And Camille was unavailable as well, so we had agreed to meet tonight.

I was uncomfortable having Joreal come to our house, even though Trytian had been here numerous times, so we were meeting at Carter's, even though the space was limited. Camille wanted to bring the Keraastar Knights with her, so that we could all have input. Menolly had offered to hold the meeting in a conference room in her mansion, but the head of security had put up a fuss once he knew she was bringing a daemon home with her. Rather than just throw around her authority, she had decided to let this one go.

Tim glanced over at me, his fingers pausing midair. He shook his head, a somber look on his face. "I'm thinking you need to buy a new laptop. I can get this one working, but I can't guarantee how long it will last, or even whether it will save the data appropriately. What the hell did you do to it?"

I stared at the ceiling. "I might have been in my tabby form a couple days ago, and I might have gotten a tad rambunctious and knocked it off the table." Embarrassed, I confessed, "I didn't even remember doing it until Shade reminded me this morning, after I tried to turn the laptop on and it wouldn't boot up. And I suppose it didn't help that I also spilled a bottle of soda on it. I did that last week. I dried it out and it seemed to work, but maybe the insides got gummed up from that, too?"

As he sat back in his chair, Tim let out a long sigh. "I thought by now I had taught you how to treat your electronics. I can give you a loaner for tonight, if you like. Even if you bought a new one today, we'd just have to set up all your programs again and that would take at least a two days, given how much software you have on here. If you want, I'll buy one for you, and get it ready."

I groaned, but handed over my credit card. "Go ahead and do that. And if you have a computer I could borrow, I'd appreciate it. Maybe make it one that isn't your favorite?" I didn't anticipate another rousing fight with the computer in my tabby form, but I couldn't guarantee anything. I could control my panther herself for the most part, but Tabby had remained an irrepressible force within me.

"Wait here." Tim rose and went into the back room of his shop. Ever since he had opened his computer consulting business, he had been slammed with customers, and both he and Jason were doing well in an economy that was struggling. He returned with a computer that looked like a clone of my own. As he sat down and opened it up to set up a temporary account, Jason peeked in from the back. A tall black man, he had a smoothly shaven head and muscles that had muscles of their own.

"Hey love, I'm headed out for the garage." When he saw me, Jason waved. "Hey Delilah, how are you doing? How are your sisters? I haven't seen Nerissa for a while. She decide to stop her training sessions at the gym?" In his spare time, Jason taught martial arts.

"We're fine, although it's odd with Camille living out at the Barrow, and Menolly and Nerissa living over at Roman's. I'm pretty sure that Nerissa's been kept busy at the mansion. But we're all doing okay. How are you?"

"Business is good, life is good, I can't complain. Did Tim tell you our news?" Jason moved forward, to stand beside his husband.

Tim shook his head. "I was going to as soon as I finished with the computer, but I might as well do it now since you're here." He turned back to me, looking as excited as a kid in a candy shop. "Jason and I are adopting!"

My heart warmed. Jason and Tim would make incredible parents, and any child would be lucky to have them. "Congratulations! I'm so excited for you. When?"

"We're adopting twins. They're two years old—a brother and a sister—and they lost their parents in an auto accident early this year. One of them is a special-needs child, the boy, and the state has had a hard time adopting them out because of that. There are in foster care right now, but they can't stay there much longer. The state's trying to adopt them out together, and while they've had a lot of requests for the little girl, so far nobody's wanted to take the boy on as well."

Jason produced a picture from his wallet. The children were adorable—and they were obviously twins, dark skinned with shiny black hair. But the little boy was missing his lower left leg.

"Was there an accident? Or a birth defect?"

"The children were in the car accident with their parents. Althea came through unscathed, but Douglas lost his leg. They don't have any other family—no one who's in a position to take them on. They're actually children who belonged to one of my customers. Unfortunately, he let his car maintenance slide for too long, and his brakes gave out while he and his wife were busting ass on the freeway, trying to get home so they could get the kids to bed at a reasonable time," Jason said. "So at least they aren't going to total strangers."

I nodded. "Well, they're absolutely lovely. I hope you let me babysit. I love babies."

Jason beamed, and Tim was looking misty eyed.

"I'd better get going," Jason said, "but we're going to have a party when we bring them home next month. I hope you can make it."

As Jason headed out the door, Tim's gaze followed him.

"So you're going to be a papa again?" I asked. Tim already had a daughter from a previous marriage, but his ex-wife still bore a grudge against him and didn't let him see her very often. Tim wanted to be a good father to his daughter, and he did the best he could under the circumstances.

He nodded. "Jason and I knew we wanted children, but we just weren't sure about the method we were going to use. Whether we were going to adopt or go with a surrogate. And then, the news about the twins came through the grapevine, and we knew exactly what we had to do."

"Well, you and Jason are going to make wonderful parents. Now, if you show me how to use this, I'll get a move on and get the rest of my day going. Take my credit card number and just charge whatever computer you think I need to it."

As Tim dove into showing me how to use the loaner, I couldn't help but wonder if by this time next year I'd have a child. On Samhain, in less than a month, Shade and I were fated to go through the last ritual that would pave the way for me to carry the Autumn Lord's child. Remembering Grandmother Coyote's message, I had also started thinking about adopting. I had always wanted a litter of my own werekitties, but Shade couldn't give them to me and I wasn't willing to look elsewhere just to get pregnant. Adopting seemed like a wonderful opportunity, and I couldn't wait to get Shadow Wing out of the way so I could start my own family.

Later in the afternoon, Camille, her men, and Vanzir

showed up. They had brought Maggie with them, and Hanna took her to play in her room while we decked out the house. Camille sent Smoky and Morio out for KFC and other treats, while she, Trillian, and Vanzir helped Shade and me decorate the living room and kitchen.

"Does Iris know we're throwing her a party?" Camille asked.

I shook my head. "No, I just told her to come up for dinner. So she and Bruce will be bringing the children with them. They're leaving tonight, around eight."

"Good, that gives Menolly a chance to get here and see them before they take off. I can't believe Iris isn't going to be around anymore." Camille gave me a forlorn look. "Sometimes it's hard to believe that I don't live here anymore either. The Barrow is beautiful, and I wouldn't change my life if I were given the option, but even good change is stressful and takes getting used to. It's been almost four months since I took the throne, and I'm getting used to the life, but sometimes even a Barrow full of people can seem terribly lonely."

I set down the banner that I was tacking up and gave her a long hug. "I feel adrift too," I whispered. "Growing up can be awfully hard, can't it?"

Camille nodded, sitting down beside me. "I miss our father. Sephreh and I had our problems, but he came around at the end. Mostly. After the war is over… After we take down Shadow Wing, do you want to make a trip back to Otherworld to see Aunt Rythwar? I kind of feel the need for family right now."

"I understand what you're talking about. I've been feeling that lately myself. Maybe it's the stress we've been under the past few years, or maybe it's that we seem so close to the end now. Whatever it is, I'm feeling a little fragile."

"Are you two all right?" Vanzir asked as he passed by, a balloon bouquet in hand.

I nodded. "Just talking about sister stuff. How are you doing?"

In some ways, Vanzir had had one of the hardest transitions. When Aeval found out she was pregnant, it had come as a big surprise for him. It was even harder when she requested that he join her as her consort, out at the Barrow of Shadow and Night. The Fae weren't quite so quick to embrace a dream-chaser demon as their Queen's consort, but he was slowly winning them over.

Vanzir grimaced. "That question is debatable. Aeval is fine, and so is the baby, the pregnancy is coming along as it should according to the healers. It's difficult to know exactly how the genetic mix of Fae and demon is going to turn out, but everything looks okay. *I'm* having a hard time adjusting. I'm not used to people treating me with any sort of deference. And I keep thinking that they're mocking me, which is led to a few arguments that could have been avoided if I had just asked questions first. I guess everything's okay. This is not how I expected my life to turn out, I can tell you that. I'm not unhappy—it's better than I expected—but it's so sudden that I still don't how to deal with it."

It was just about the longest I had ever heard Vanzir talk about himself.

"You do have a choice," Camille said. "Make sure you want to be there, because having someone there who doesn't want to be around can be worse than being alone."

Vanzir shook his head. "I already know that I want to

be there. I never expected to fall in love with the Fae Queen—especially one like Aeval. I'm not sure what drew us together, but it seems to be lasting and she seems happy. It's just hard to wrap my head around everything that's happened."

"I think we all know a little bit about that," I said. "All right, someone help me get this banner up."

We were finished decorating an hour later and I had to admit, the balloons and the garlands and the pretty sparkling faerie lights that we hung up helped my mood immensely.

The men returned as Hanna called us into the kitchen to show us the three-tiered Black Forest cake she had made for the party. There were also platters of cookies covering the counters, and cinnamon buns, and bags of chips waiting to be opened, along with trays of lunch meat and cheese, and boxes of crackers. On the table were paper plates and several buckets of chicken.

"Early dinner before the party tonight," I said, motioning to the table.

We gathered around it, handing out pieces of chicken along with the biscuits, and Camille commandeered the mashed potatoes and gravy as Roz walked in, carrying a massive bouquet of pink roses.

"Do you think she'll like these?" he asked.

"I think she'll love them," I said, starting to look for a vase, but Roz stopped me.

"I bought a vase for her to take with her so she could carry them along." He pulled the crystal vase out of a box, and arranged the roses in it. After he finished, he carried them into the living room and then returned, joining us at the table. As he filled up a paper plate with chicken and mashed potatoes, he finally sat back, letting out a soft sigh.

"I know you all think I'm in mourning, but I'm not. Really. Yes, I fell for Iris pretty hard. But she's married to Bruce and I respect that, and she could never go for someone like me—not an incubus. And really, it was just infatuation. I'm over her, now. I love her, yes, but as a friend." He met my gaze, strong and steady, and I actually believed him. He looked calm, though sad around the edges.

As we began to eat dinner, Camille said, "So what do you think about this Joreal business? I can't believe we're actually going to meet Trytian's father."

"That's going to be an interesting little soiree," Morio said. "So what's the schedule for tonight then? Party here and then we'll head over to Menolly's mansion?"

"That's about the size of it," I said. "Menolly will be here shortly after dusk. And Iris and Bruce are supposed to show up around six thirty. We meet with Joreal at ten tonight."

"The Keraastar Knights will meet us at the mansion. Chase is arranging for transportation." Camille glanced at Hanna. "Do you mind if I leave Maggie here while we're over at Menolly's? We'll swing by and pick her up on the way home. I just wanted Iris to be able to say good-bye to Maggie too. I should have brought her high chair so she could sit in the kitchen while we eat."

"I think we have an old one in the storage room. Remember? We borrowed one at first, before we bought one for her. Let me go check," I said.

I hurried to the storage room and sure enough, there was the old high chair that we had forgotten to return to… I couldn't even remember who we had borrowed it from now. I hauled it out and dusted it off, carrying it back into the kitchen, where I set it up. Hanna hurried back to her room, bringing Maggie out and snuggling her into the high chair so she couldn't get away. The baby gargoyle still fit the high chair, and now she giggled, looking at the entire table and clapping.

"Maggie enjoys life out at the Barrow, but I think she misses this. We don't quite have the same type of dinners there," Camille said.

I nuzzled Maggie's fur, wishing I could keep her but once I got pregnant, it would be problematic. Maggie wasn't good with small animals or children, she was far too rough in her play, and could easily hurt another child or a cat or dog if she were left unattended with them. Keeping up with a baby gargoyle was hard enough, but adding children to the mix would make it even harder.

Maggie yanked at my hair, which had reached my shoulders again.

"Dee-ya-ya! Dee-ya-ya!" She stretched out her arms, the calico fur blending into surprisingly beautiful patterns. She pursed her lips and I reached down and gave her a kiss, wondering how long it would be before she reached the point where she could talk in complete sentences. Gargoyles grew very, very slowly and while they were almost as long-lived as the Fae, their childhoods extended through several hundred years. It would be at least two hundred years before Maggie was running around like a teenager.

"I love you too, munchkin. And I miss you. I promise to come out and visit you more often, and maybe Camille can bring you here to play more often." I gave Maggie another hug, then returned to my meal.

※

MENOLLY AND NERISSA arrived a few minutes before Iris, carrying a beautiful gift box that was about the size of a large dog. While both were incredibly strong, the bulk of the box made it difficult for them to get up the stairs and onto the front porch. They struggled through the front door while we were watching, Nerissa backseat driving all the way.

"Don't bump it against the door jam, be careful—the wrapping paper is sturdy, but it's not *that* sturdy."

"I've got it," Menolly said, giving her a roll of the eyes. "Everything looks intact." She glanced at me. "Where can we put this?"

"Why don't you put it in the living room? That's where the rest of the gifts are." I motioned for them to set it next to the fireplace, out of the way. While we hadn't explicitly said to bring gifts, we'd all been thinking along the same lines because there was a pile of very prettily wrapped presents in the corner.

"I hope they're going through a portal so they can take all of these gifts," Camille said.

"They can pile the rest in ours," Menolly said. "It's a double-twin stroller."

A tapping against the back door caught my attention.

"I think they're here. Everybody hide."

"Given the kitchen is filled with cakes and cookies and other goodies, I don't think the surprise is going to be much of a surprise." Camille gave me a shake of the head, laughing. "Let's just meet them in the kitchen."

I snorted. "Good point. Come on, let's go meet them."

We headed into the kitchen, just as Hanna opened the door. Iris and Bruce came through, pushing a double stroller with the twins in it. They were a year old and barely walking, but right now Iris had tucked them in securely. They were entering the phase where they were trying to get into everything, and she kept a close watch on them. She stopped short as she laid eyes on Maggie, and then everyone pouring through the entryway into the kitchen.

"I thought you might do this," she said, her eyes sparkling. "You're bound and determined not to let me get away without crying, aren't you?"

"We couldn't let you go without saying good-bye," Menolly said, her voice husky. "This is hard, Iris. You're part of our family. And though we want you to be safe, seeing you go isn't going to be easy."

"You too, Bruce," Smoky said.

Iris left the stroller with Bruce and moved forward, as Maggie held out her arms. The little gargoyle started to cry, calling for Iris as the house sprite accepted a footstool to stand on so she could see her better.

"Oh, hello, little darling. I can't pick you up, I'm sorry. But I'm glad to see you, too." She leaned forward and gave Maggie a kiss on the top of the head. "You're such a little love."

The twins gurgled on the stroller, and Maggie waved in their direction.

"Play? Play?"

"I'm sorry, sweetie, but no, you can't play with the

twins." Iris gave me a quick look. "I don't want her to feel bad. Maybe somebody should take her in the back room and play with her for a while?"

"Come here, little girl," Trillian said, swinging Maggie into his arms. "Why don't we go for a little walk outside? Would you like that?"

Maggie giggled and threw her arms around Trillian's neck. He glanced at me.

"She's taken a shine to me lately. We'll go for a little walk outside and I'll let her play. I won't let her get too cold." He turned to Iris. "Go ahead and start the party without me. I'll be back in a few minutes."

As he headed out the back door, I looked at Camille. "He's really good with her."

"I think Maggie's got a little crush on him—you know, the little girl–type crushes that all little girls get, even if they are gargoyles." She motioned to the table. "Why don't we get started? I know you've got a long journey ahead of you. When do you have to leave?"

"The Duchess is sending a couple of her men who are good at transportation spells. We're not going through a regular portal because we're not sure how that will affect the children, but the spells are pretty safe. We've got all our bags packed and ready down at our house. We'll lock up before we go. Bruce has a key for you, Delilah."

As we loaded our dishes and then moved into the living room to watch them open presents, for a moment it felt like old times. We were just one big happy family celebrating a milestone. But as the clock ticked on, Iris finally stood and glanced over at Bruce. He was sitting by the new stroller that Menolly and Nerissa had bought for them.

"I hate to break this up, but it's time," Iris said. "If you could help us back to our house with these gifts, we'd appreciate it. But…I just want to say how much you've all meant to me. How much your support has meant. There's no way to put it into words. I wish we could stay for this final battle against Shadow Wing, but it isn't safe. We'll be back, but… Things happen. Until then, please know how much the past years have meant to me. Without you… Without Camille and Delilah and Menolly, I wouldn't have met Bruce, and I wouldn't have my children. And I wouldn't have all of you as a family."

We were in tears then, all of us, even the men. We round robin hugged, and then Roz and Vanzir helped them down the stairs with all the gifts. Camille, Menolly, and I stood on the steps of the back porch and watched them as they traipsed back through the rain toward their house. At one point Iris paused, looking back. She raised one hand, then blew us a kiss, and then they disappeared into the thicket of trees around the house, and just like that they were gone.

CHAPTER SIX

Camille

SHAMAS AND I WERE WALKING THROUGH THE WOODS. THE forests of Talamh Lonrach Oll were far older than they had any right to be. Oh, the fir and the cedar were grounded in the history of the woodland, but the Fae had planted oak and maple and birch when they bought the land, and in the few years since then, they had worked their magic on the trees and the plants of the forest, increasing the growth rate by an exponential amount. The woodland was thriving, and if I didn't know better, I could swear the new trees were decades older than they were.

The magic permeated every root and branch, every speck of dirt throughout the Sovereign Nation, sparkling in the very air. I wondered what this forest would look like in a hundred years. Or in a thousand. And then it hit me. I'd be here to see it. I'd be wandering through these woodlands for as long as I lived, given I was the Queen of Dusk and Twilight. This was my home, forever and always, as long as I held the throne.

Shamas had asked me to come out with him so we could talk, and I welcomed the respite from the day's duties. We were due at Carter's shortly after sunset for the meeting with Joreal, but it was still afternoon.

"We haven't had much of a chance to talk since I…" Shamas drifted off, his voice hesitant.

"Since you returned from the dead?" I found myself far more blunt than I used to be. I used to think that being queen meant I'd have to be far more diplomatic than was my nature, but I had learned quickly that cutting to the chase had its benefits, and that diplomacy didn't mean pussyfooting around uncomfortable subjects.

He nodded. "I've been remembering more lately, from right before I appeared when you performed that ritual." He flashed me a sideways glance. "There are things I'd like to say, but I'm not sure how you'd feel about them."

I bit my lip. Shamas had been in love with me for years. When we were young, we had been secretly betrothed, but his family interfered and he hadn't had the courage to stand up to them. My half-human bloodline had offended their senses, and Shamas had broken it off rather than face their displeasure.

"I know you were still in love with me when you left to go back to Otherworld. Is that what you wanted to talk about?" I had tiptoed around the subject, but perhaps it was time to bring it out in the open and clear the air.

He sat down on a nearby nurse log, patting the trunk next to him. "Sit? Talk for a while?"

There were guards following us, but they were several paces behind us, as I asked them to be. They couldn't hear us from where we were. I let out a long breath. Maybe it really *was* time to get this over with. I brushed away a pile of fallen needles that covered the damp, mossy wood and settled myself beside him.

Shamas and I looked a lot alike. We were cousins and it showed. His hair was as dark as mine, though he wore it back in a ponytail, and his eyes used to mirror my own before he returned from the dead. Now, instead of violet, flecked with silver, they were almost blood red. He had died in battle—valiantly—after a convoluted life of making the wrong choices. But he had returned to take up the ninth and last spirit seal, and now the ruby gem hung around his neck on a platinum chain.

I waited for him to begin as the forest whispered around us, the trees telling tales to one another. Small animals crept through the fallen leaves, skirting us cautiously. They knew we were safe, but Aeval, Titania, and I had set a limit on interacting with the wildlife, in order to keep them from losing their natural instincts.

Shamas let out a long sigh. "I left because yes, I was still in love with you. I thought I could get over you when we broke up. I told myself I did, but when I escaped Lethesanar's dungeon and ended up here with you and your sisters, I realized that I had just been lying to myself. But you were married, and happy, and I couldn't do anything but watch. I'm so sorry I couldn't stand up for us back then. I'm sorry I let you down."

I leaned forward, resting my elbows on my lap, and stared at the forest floor. It was a cold day, but my cloak kept the worst of the chill at bay, and the rain had backed off.

"What's done is done. I'm happy, Shamas. I don't hold a grudge against you. Oh, for a while I did, but now? It's dust in our wake." I paused, then said, "That isn't what you wanted to say, though, is it? I can tell."

He shrugged. "It's one of the things. Camille, I don't know how to put this, but…I'm not back for good. I don't know how to explain it, but I know I'm living on borrowed time. I can't see the future. I'm here, and I know I'm here for a task, but…please, don't take it hard if I can't stay for the long run of things."

I closed my eyes, his words hitting hard. Even though I meant what I said, I would always love Shamas—in that way you love a treasured memory. The thought of losing him a second time hit deep. The Moon Mother had sent me out to sweep him off the battlefield, and that had been one of the hardest tasks I had ever had to face. I didn't know if I could do it again, even if she bade me. I couldn't bring myself to say anything, or I knew I'd start crying.

After a moment, he broke the silence. "Are you all right?"

"Getting over you was one of the hardest things I ever had to do in my life. But plucking you out of that battle, bringing your soul into the Hunt, was worse. When I realized that the Moon Mother was sending me after you… Well, it was almost as bad as the time I had to face Menolly after she had been turned." I stared at the ground for a moment. "I don't know if I can do it again, Shamas. What if she asks me…"

He wrapped an arm around me and I rested my head on his shoulder.

"I don't know if I can promise this, but when it's time, I'll try to keep you from being part of it. You brought me back, Camille. You gave me a second chance. I've been trying to redeem myself in your eyes and make you proud of me since the day you found out that I had taken up sorcery."

"*I* didn't give you a second chance," I murmured. "Fate did. But I'm glad that she brought you back into my life, for however long as you have." I paused, then added, "Somewhere, deep inside, I knew this. I knew you weren't back for good. But nobody truly knows how long they have in this world. Hell, I could step outside the door and get hit by a bus. Or get something caught in my throat and I could choke. How many times have my sisters and I come close to death over the years? How many scars do I have on my body from the fights we've been through? Life is precarious. Nobody gets out alive, regardless of how many years the Fates have spun out for us."

Shamas's shoulders slumped. "I didn't mean to bring you down. I'm sorry."

I turned to him, searching his face. "Shamas, I lost my naivete when my mother died and my father set me in charge of the household. I lost my trust when you ran off. I lost my belief in the innate goodness of people when Menolly staggered home after Dredge tortured her and turned her. I learned the hard way that you have to fight for what you want in this world, in this life. And when you get it, you grit your teeth and enjoy what you have because at any time it could be stripped away from you. I live in the present, and I indulge myself as much as I can, because as much as I love my sisters…as much as I love my husbands, when I die, I'll be the one to face the Moon Mother, and only I will know whether I truly let myself love life and embrace it, or whether I skulked through it, hiding because of fear. I understand reality all too well.

You didn't bring me down. You just confirmed what I've been feeling in my bones."

He took my hands in his, his eyes fixed on my own. "Camille, I have no right to ask this, but…will you kiss me? That's all I want. I promise I won't ever ask for more. But one kiss, in honor of the past we had together, and the future we're facing?"

I let out a long breath, running through the complications it could cause. But I was my own woman, and I had finally accepted that life was too fleeting to ignore the chance to bring a little happiness where I could. I nodded, slowly, leaning in.

Shamas pressed his lips against mine, and I was suddenly back in a field of wildflowers with Shamas by my side, kissing me under the glowing sun on a day when I believed we were each other's futures. A day before life had thrown more than a few curve balls my way.

But even as I kissed him, the memories swept by, and I realized that for me, the kiss was a shadow of the past. It was no more than a ghost of what we once had. Shamas slowly pulled away and hung his head.

"Thank you," he murmured. "You really do love them, don't you?"

I nodded. "Smoky and Morio, my beloved Trillian—they are my world, Shamas. I've given my heart to them, and they complement my life. They each bring something to me that I need. I don't believe that one person can give you everything you need, but together, they give me all that I could want. Love expands. But passion—there's only so much of that to go around. I will always love you, my cousin, but our day is long gone."

Then I stood and held out my hand. "Come, we should

get back. And Shamas, if the Moon Mother asks, I will be there for you when the time comes, and I'll do whatever I can to make it easier." Even as I spoke, the tears in my throat vanished and I heard the Moon Mother whispering in my head, and in my heart.

Have faith, Camille. I am always with you. I will walk with you until the end of your days on this world.

And right then, I realized that above all, my heart belonged to her, and she would forever be with me, even when all the shadows in the world had crept in to cover the light.

IN ADDITION TO SMOKY, Morio, and Trillian, I took Venus, Chase, Bran, and Shamas to the meeting. It was important that Joreal meet some of my Keraastar Knights, and these were my captains. That much I knew.

Joreal looked so much like Trytian that it made me catch my breath. As I settled on the sofa, I couldn't keep my eyes off him. Joreal was wearing a military duster with brass buttons, and there were stripes on the shoulder that I didn't recognize but I realized that they must signify his status in the daemon army.

Carter welcomed us in, and he grinned. "Nice wings," he whispered.

I blinked. I wasn't showing them, but then again, he was a demigod, so I shouldn't be surprised. I laughed. "Good catch. Are the others here yet?"

"No, but they're on their way." He motioned to the tea cart. "Something to eat?"

Carter had spread out extra chairs in the living room

to accommodate everybody. I sat between Smoky and Trillian, opposite Joreal. Smoky reached for one hand, while Trillian reached for the other. I had told them in private about kissing Shamas. I'd learned not to keep anything like that secret, even if it was something that had been unavoidable. Now Smoky glowered at Shamas a little, but when I explained why I had done it, he had relented and I wasn't worried that he was going to go off on my cousin.

It seemed weird to make small talk with a daemon general, but I was determined to try.

"I wanted to thank you again for your help, yours and Trytian's." I held Joreal's gaze, trying to read what lurked behind those impassive eyes.

He returned my look, steady and unblinking. "No thanks needed. Shadow Wing is a menace to everyone and everything. We must defeat him. My son was doing his duty, as were you." He shifted in his seat, then let out a soft breath. "I suppose we should dispense with standing on ceremony. You may call me Joreal. May I call you 'Camille,' Your Majesty?"

I was surprised he even asked. I had expected him to just dive in without asking permission. "Of course," I murmured.

"Once your sisters arrive, we should get right to the heart of the discussion. I don't have a lot of spare time." He shifted again, which told me he was uncomfortable.

"Please don't feel awkward—" I started to say, but Joreal arched his eyebrows and snorted.

"Uncomfortable? I think you mistake my impatience for discomfort. I have ten thousand troops waiting for me to give them marching instructions, and I cannot do that until we discuss the next step with you. I'm not feeling awkward. I just want this settled."

I stared at him for a moment, trying to stifle a laugh, but a snicker escaped.

Joreal stiffened. "You find my words amusing?"

I cleared my throat, forcing the laugh back. "No, not at all. Well…" I hesitated, then said, "You remind me so much of your son. He was always charging ahead, and so full of himself. He was also a pain in the ass—he couldn't keep his hands to himself." I hadn't meant to blurt that out, but there it was.

Joreal froze, looking like he was trying to decide how to respond. Finally, he relaxed, sitting back against the chair cushion. He crossed one leg over the other, his ankle resting on his knee.

"That sounds like my son. He had a good head, but he couldn't control his impulses. I tried to train him better than that, but you know how children can be. I apologize for his behavior. Demons may be grabby, but among our kind, we pride ourselves on our self-control."

It was my turn to look confused. I hadn't expected an apology from him, and I hadn't been fishing for one, either.

"Trytian was a pain, but he came to our aid. So I suppose in the end, it doesn't really matter," Morio murmured, deflecting the conversation for me.

At that moment, the doorbell rang, interrupting the conversation. Relieved, I cleared my throat and turned to Smoky, squeezing his hand. He looked like he was about ready to break out laughing, and I realized he had been following the conversation with amusement. Sometimes, his sense of humor was annoying as hell.

Carter returned with Menolly, Nerissa, Delilah, and Shade. They settled down, squeezing into the narrow living room with the rest of us. My Knights had kept quiet, and I realized they were waiting for my permission to speak. Bran had become bearable in the months since I had made him a Keraastar Knight, even though I was still leery of Raven Mother's son. But before I could say anything, Joreal spoke up.

"I received further news from my men today. Shadow Wing has totally gone over the edge. He's foraging on his followers, sucking the life out of as many of his soldiers as he can to increase his own power. Some have run off, but others are offering themselves to him willingly. His rule has become a suicide cult. But in the process, he's absorbing enough power so that he'll soon be able to break through the veils to enter either Earthside or Otherworld. We have to make our move."

Carter interrupted. "Joreal is correct. Before too long, he'll have enough raw power to break through any of the rogue portals, and I happen to know that a few have manifested over in the Sub-Realms. If he's aware of their location, all hell will break loose as soon as he feels strong enough to tear open the fabric that cordons off that world from ours. Or from Otherworld, depending on the portal."

When the Great Divide had occurred, the Great Fae Lords had created the Spirit Seal, which sealed the realms away from each other. Then they had broken it into nine pieces and sent them as far away from one another as possible. If they were reunited—as in touching one another—again, they would reverse the rips in time and space that they originally fashioned, and the resulting chaos would disrupt—and destroy—a vast swath of both Earthside and Otherworld.

But as time went on, the Fae in Otherworld began creating portals between Earthside and OW. In addition, because the Great Divide had never been meant to happen in the natural order of things, rogue portals began forming on their own, but they were unstable and flickered in and out. Eventually, the entire fabric of the Great Divide would fail, and when that happened, the worlds would merge again, amidst a natural disaster of epic proportions. We weren't sure how to prevent that, but we *could* prevent Shadow Wing from taking matters into his own hands.

Delilah spoke up. "Now that we know his secret about the soul receptacles, and we know that the only way to defeat him is through Camille and the Keraastar Knights, I guess—there's no more reason to wait, is there?"

I swallowed. Hard. "No, there isn't." Taking a deep breath, I said, "The Moon Mother is with me. She'll lead me in what I need to do. My power is strongest on the dark of the moon, so I suggest we wait till then to gate him over. Today is Thursday, and the new moon is next Monday night. Let's just do this. Get it over with."

Even as I spoke, I felt like I was sealing our fate. But this was what we had been aiming toward for four years now. This showdown. And it was time. I could feel it in my bones—it was time to take him on. Thanking the gods we didn't have to go down into the Sub-Realms to do so, I turned toward the others.

"Are you ready for this?" My voice was shaking, but oddly enough, my nerves were steady.

Delilah glanced at Menolly, who nodded. "The new

moon it is. But is Shamas powerful enough to cast the Demon Gate we need? We do have Yerghan's blade as an anchor. Shadow Wing gave it to Yerghan, so it has a connection to him."

I turned to Shamas. "Do you think you can do it?"

"I may need some backup," he said after a moment. "Do you know anybody who could help? What about Wilbur?"

"He's a necromancer, but he's strong enough to cast at least a demon gate of moderate size, so he can probably feed you energy." I paused, not wanting to bring Wilbur into it. But if Shamas thought he needed help, then we damned well better have backup there for him.

"I'll ask him," Menolly said. "I'll drop by there after the meeting tonight. Nerissa and I were going to head out to Grandmother Coyote's field so Nerissa can have some time in her puma form, anyway."

"Yeah, it's been awhile," Nerissa said. "We'll ask him and text you with the answer. If not, though, what do we do? I don't think we know any other sorcerers, do we?"

"I do," Joreal said. "I have a few in my army. If you can't get this…Wilbur…to help, then I can bring one over." He hesitated for a moment, then added, "But it would be better if you have someone you know you can absolutely trust."

"That still leaves us with one problem," Morio said, speaking up. "What to do between the time he shows up, and Camille and the Keraastar Knights surround him and do whatever it is they're going to do to him? He's a Soul Eater, and unhinged at that. He could easily take out several of us in that time."

"That's where I come in," Joreal said. "I will send you

twenty of my strongest fighters. They can keep him occupied while Camille and the Knights prepare. I have to say, the Great Fae Lords were stupidity incarnate when they thought up the whole spirit seal plan. It just insured that Shadow Wing is invincible without the Knights."

"We aren't disagreeing with you on that." I shook my head. "They didn't think about the long-term ramifications of their actions. You do realize, we're about to make history with what we're undertaking. If there are any details that set the tone for the future, we'd better think them over far more carefully than our forebears did."

"Camille's right," Smoky said. "This is why we dragons usually keep to ourselves."

"Dragon?" Joreal glanced over at him. "Oh, you're *that* dragon. Trytian had a grudge against you, though I doubt it matters now. No doubt over your woman."

I coughed. "I'm my own woman. I belong to no one but myself."

"Well, excuse me," Joreal said, but a twinkle sparkled in one eye and I had the feeling he approved. "No offense meant."

"None taken, as long as we understand each other." I leaned back as Smoky draped one arm around my shoulders. "So, strong warriors to keep him distracted? That might actually work. Where the hell are we going to do this? If we gate him into Otherworld, we have a better chance to keep him from destroying others. But there's also a better chance for him to escape."

"I think it's a good choice, though," Menolly said. "Gate him over there and we'll have more room to maneuver around. The population centers are less dense and less frequent. Let's face it, there are a lot fewer of people living over in Otherworld than there are here."

"True." I thought it over for a moment. "Not only that, but if we take the fight over there, we don't risk humans finding out about the demons. We've been able to quash most of the rumors here, but if we gate in Shadow Wing and something goes wrong, word would get out and that would be bad. Very, very bad."

"Yeah, the feds would take a nuke to him and just make him stronger." Delilah grimaced. "Demons eat uranium for breakfast. It's like a steroid for them." She glanced at Joreal. "What about the Daemonkin? Does uranium beef you guys up, too?"

Joreal stared at her like she had asked him if he had two heads. After a moment, he replied, "Not exactly." Abruptly changing the subject, he turned back to me. "So, now that you've decided to enjoin him in Otherworld, where exactly will you go?"

I thought about that. We couldn't, in all good conscience, take the battle near a city. And we sure as hell didn't want to take him down into the Southern Wastes where the ragtag remnants of sorcery still played out. Any sorcerers still living there would do whatever they could to help the Demon Lord.

"What about Thistlewyd Deep, the home of the Black Unicorn?" And right then, I knew I needed to ask both him and Raven Mother to help. I would be wearing not only the Keraastar diamond, but I would be carrying the unicorn horn and wearing the cape woven out of his hide.

As I spoke, a chill seemed to pass through the room and everyone fell silent.

A moment later, Venus the Moon Child spoke up. "You

intuit correctly, Your Majesty. They play a part in this as well."

I hung my head. The last thing I wanted to do was to put myself in debt to Raven Mother, but the moment the thought had popped into my head, I knew she and the Black Beast were to play a part in this battle.

"Do you need to use the Whispering Mirror?" Delilah asked.

I shook my head. "No." I turned to Bran. "Can you summon your mother?"

He gave me a long look, but whatever was running through his thoughts remained unreadable. Bran kept his feelings close to himself. He moved to one side and closed his eyes, his head raised toward the ceiling. A moment later, and a swirl of mist began to fill the room. It was so bright that I had to look away. And then, there was a subtle shift in the energy and I knew *she* was here.

"So, my lovely, you called for me? Let me see, who do we have with us this evening? Who indeed?" The cloying voice rang through the room, making me shiver.

Raven Mother stepped out of the mist, her long black dress fitting around the sweeps and valleys of her curves. Her breasts crested almost over the neckline, as though she were wearing the pushup bra from hell, and her lips were as black as Trillian's skin. She was pale as a vampire, though her eyes were masked, like those of a raccoon. Her eyes were ringed with red and her nails were long and sharp as talons.

"Well met, Raven Mother." I gathered my wits and stood. I'd need them about me if I were to make a deal with the devil, and frankly, making a deal with an

Elemental Lord—or Lady, as the case may be—was akin to just that.

She stroked her son's cheek as he stood unflinching, drawing her nail along the flesh, leaving a thin red weal to pop up. Bran merely nodded at her, not speaking. The two didn't get along well, though now that he was one of my Keraastar Knights, I wasn't sure how their relationship had shifted.

As she sauntered over to me, ignoring everyone else, my stomach twisted. Raven Mother had long tried to lure me into her service, away from the Moon Mother. Now that I was a Fae Queen, it was a lost cause, but I knew better than to put anything past her.

"Camille, oh my dear, dear Camille," she said, her voice spiraling around me. She spoke in rhyme and riddles, her words a swirl of energy that coiled like a snake. She taunted me, and yet I had the feeling that I mattered to her. Of course, since her lover—the Black Unicorn—had chosen me as the instrument of his death, I had become an integral part of their world, his reincarnation notwithstanding.

"My son summoned me, but it was you behind the call. What do you want, my delicious queen? What seek you from Raven Mother?" Her eyes were beady and grasping.

I forced myself to breathe evenly. "I have something I need to ask you."

"A favor, perhaps? Such a lovely young witch, but youth is fleeting and even now, the weight of the crown ages you. Such a pity, for you were delightfully innocent. We would have had such wonderful play in my forest, you and me, and my grand love. But now, you seek something dark. Something dangerous. Something only I can provide. You seek a boon, am I right? A favor you ask, and a favor I'll grant—perhaps." Her words spun a web that was difficult to follow, and even harder to ignore. "Tell me, Camille, what you want. Speak the words. Whisper them in my ear."

I glanced at the others.

Joreal was staring at her, transfixed, an open look of longing on his face. I almost snorted. He had no clue what he'd be getting embroiled with if she noticed and called his bluff.

The others bore cautious looks. They understood the danger with which Raven Mother cloaked herself. Bran, however, was staring directly at me, a look of warning on his face.

I gave him the barest of nods, and turned back to Raven Mother.

"Yes, I seek a boon. But for this, there is no repayment, save what you take from the actions."

Her eyes narrowed further, but her nostrils flared and I could tell she was interested. I wasn't sure what I could promise her in return if she insisted on a trade, but decided we'd cross that bridge when we came to it.

"We're going up against Shadow Wing. We need a safe place to where we can gate him. It occurred to me that your wood—and the woodland of the Black Beast—would be the right choice. Thistlewyd Deep or Darkynwyrd. Will you help us finish this battle? Will you allow us to gate him over to your forests so we can put an end to this?" I didn't bother explaining. She already knew what I was talking about.

Raven Mother paused before a feral smile spread to her lips, and she bared her teeth. They were needles of bone, terrifying in their jagged sharpness. She stared at me, and for a moment it felt as though she was looking deep into my soul. Then she slowly began to circle around me, so close I could feel her breath on my skin. She towered over me, so I was looking up, and so close that it made my wings tremble.

"Camille, Queen of the Dusk and Twilight. Camille, the witch. Camille the daughter, the lover, the mother to her sisters. Camille, the dark star, High Priestess of the Moon Mother. Your wings betray you. I make you shiver, don't I?" She reached out, stroking my face. "Tell me that I make you hunger for my wildness? For the feral paths of my forest."

As she spoke, I began to shake. She was chaos incarnate, feral and primal, and I recognized in her the core of what my nature aspired to be. It hit me that I feared Raven Mother because I understood her. I could never become who she was, could never mimic her, but there was a chord of madness inherent within her nature that I could feel on the outskirts of my own. And that made me terribly afraid. I could see myself following her, disregarding everything I had been taught, throwing off the shackles of responsibility and dancing into the mists with her, leaving everything and everyone I loved behind.

"Tell me the truth, and I will help you," she said, leaning so close that her lips were mere inches away from my own.

I slowly nodded. Whispering, hoping no one else could hear, I said, "All right, I'll answer you. Yes, I see myself in you. I recognize your energy. We're too much alike for my comfort, and I fear the chaos you bring, because there's a part of myself that would welcome the chance to shake the world off my shoulders and run free, without cares or responsibilities."

Raven Mother spoke in the same low tone. She pressed her forehead to mine as she clutched my shoulders. "You always pride yourself on being your father's daughter. A soldier's daughter. But you don't want that, do you? You never wanted that. Be honest with me."

I hated her. I hated that she was forcing me to look deep inside myself, beyond the platitudes I had mouthed for years. But she was right. I chafed at the restrictions. I had hated my father for making me take my mother's place and leave my childhood behind as I took up caring for my sisters. I hated that he had drilled it into my head that I owed everybody else my service except myself.

"Yes," I choked out. "I never wanted to be the one to carry the load." And then, I found my own tongue again and straightened my shoulders, shaking off her grasp.

"But whether or not I wanted it, I carried through. I did what needed done. I accepted the responsibility because nobody else was there to assume it. And that's what I'm asking from you today. I'm not asking for a *favor*. I'm asking you to step outside yourself for a moment, to do something that serves others. To back us up because it needs done, not because you're going to gain anything from it."

Abruptly, the buzz of energy died down and I held myself tall, gazing into Raven Mother's face with an oddly serene feeling.

Everybody was staring at us, but no one said a word until Bran stepped over to my side. He turned to his mother.

"I pledge my loyalty to the Queen of the Keraastar

Diamond, to the Queen of the Keraastar Knights. And I ask you, my mother, to give us your help. And I ask that of my father as well."

Raven Mother paused for a moment, her gaze darting between her son and me, and she finally stepped back and gave us a firm nod.

"Very well. Your father and I will help. You may use Thistlewyd Deep as the battleground. And we will be there to do whatever you need done. Contact me when it's time."

And with that, there was a flash so bright it hurt my eyes, and she vanished from the room.

CHAPTER SEVEN

Menolly

AFTER THE MEETING WRAPPED UP, NERISSA AND I DROVE over to Wilbur's, following Delilah and Shade into the Belles-Faire neighborhood.

"What did you think about Raven Mother?" Nerissa asked. "She scares the hell out of me."

"She should, she's one of the Elemental Lords." I clutched the leather-bound steering wheel. "I'll tell you this, I'm glad she picked Camille to fixate on. She would have staked me by now because I don't have the diplomacy to deal with her."

"Do you really think that Raven Mother and the Black Unicorn can help us? Or rather, *will* help us?" Nerissa glanced out the window as thunder rumbled overhead. A fork of lightning split the sky and hail began to pound down, bouncing off the windshield and the hood of the car.

I slowed down. Hail was slippery and it was covering the road in a sheet of white. The last thing we needed was to go skidding off into a ditch.

"Honestly? I don't know if they'll be more of a help or a hindrance, but I trust Camille's premonitions so I guess we need them there. At least we have a timeline."

Another rumble of thunder shook the air and again, lightning illuminated the sky. The flash was so bright it almost blinded me. Raven Mother had nothing on Mother Nature, that was for sure. But even as I navigated the dark road, I couldn't help but think that in just four days we'd be facing the end of the road. At least the road we had set foot on four years ago.

Nerissa's voice quivered as she said, "I can't believe what we're going to do. When the demons kidnapped me and carried me off to the Sub-Realms, I thought I'd never see any of you again. I guess, if we don't come out of this, at least I've had six more months than I thought I had left."

I paused for a moment, then said, "I've been thinking. What if you stay here? What if you don't come with us? Roman will look out for you if...if something happens to me."

Nerissa was silent for a moment, then the shit hit the fan.

"What the hell are you talking about? You want to leave me here while you traipse off to fight a Demon Lord? You expect me to say yes, *please, just ignore everything we've been through together and leave me behind*? I'm your wife, Menolly. I thought we got through this overprotective crap of yours. I'm just as invested in defeating Shadow Wing as you are, damn it. I won't let you put me on the sidelines. I'm in this relationship for life, and that means taking part in the good as well as the bad."

She sounded so pissed that I pulled off onto the

shoulder of the road. With the car idling, I turned to her and winced at the expression on her face.

"Love, I don't think you're weak or incapable. I just...worry..."

"Worry my ass. You're doing to me what you and Camille did to Delilah for so many years—trying to keep me in some sort of sheltered cage. From the talks I've had with Delilah, she wouldn't have had nearly the rude awakening she did about people if you'd given her the chance to be the strong woman she is instead of assuming she was incapable of holding her own. And you're doing the same thing with me. Oh, sure, I'm no vampire, nor am I a witch or a Death Maiden, but I've trained to fight, and I'm tougher than you like to think. If you force me to stay home, I might not be here when you get back."

She was pissed all right. Her voice told me that she meant every word and it cut me to the core. The thought of getting home only to find out Nerissa had left me was worse than the thought of facing Shadow Wing.

"All right," I said, giving up. "I won't fight you on this. I'm sorry. I won't be so overprotective. It's just...the thought of losing you is the biggest fear I have. It makes me want to lock you up in a tower to keep all the bad things in the world away from you." I stopped, realizing how ridiculous I sounded.

Nerissa stared at me for a moment, then snorted. "Menolly, you might as well put me in a glass casket and name me Snow White. The only protection we have in this world is that of the grave. Life is dangerous. Life is wild and unpredictable. People die *every day* from the stupidest things, never mind the more serious dangers. I can't guarantee you I'll come out of this alive—but you can't guarantee me that about you, either. We take our chances together, or we don't take them at all. Deal?"

As the storm raged overhead, I could only nod.

"Understood. We take our chances together, then. And we don't pull punches in battle out of worry over each other. We do what needs to be done."

"Whatever needs to be done," she said. "All right, now that that's settled, let's get over to Wilbur's before he hits the hay for the night."

As I pulled out onto the road again, the lightning flashed again. It occurred to me that Camille must be enjoying the hell out of the weather. She got a real charge out of lightning storms.

※

Wilbur's lights were still on when we eased into the driveway. Nerissa and I darted up the drive, trying to avoid getting pelted by the rain. Huge drops were pounding down so hard they weren't even soaking into the ground, just beading up and running in rivulets along the already-saturated soil.

I was surprised when Wilbur answered the door instead of Martin. His brother, the ghoul, was usually the one playing butler.

"I'm glad you're here," Wilbur said, leading us into the living room. Again, no Martin. Maybe he was off doing laundry for Wilbur or something.

"How you doing, Wilbur?" I stared at the necromancer. He looked like an old biker, with a long beard and shaggy hair that was gathered back in a neat ponytail. He was walking pretty good—it was hard to see even the glimmer of a limp. Wilbur had lost a leg sometime back, and it had taken some doing, but he was getting along pretty good with the prosthesis at this point.

"All right, I guess," he said. He didn't bother trying to grope either Nerissa or me, and I knew something was up. "What brings you girls here?"

"We have a massive favor to ask of you. In advance, you should feel to say no, because this is a doozy." We settled ourselves on the sofa. I glanced around. "Where's Martin?"

Wilbur paled. "Hold that question for the moment because that's a whole 'nother subject I'd like to talk to you about. What is it you need, Dead Girl?"

I paused. Wilbur had created the Demon Gate that had allowed me to go into the Sub-Realms, searching for Nerissa. And, he knew about the spirit seals from his own snooping, and he had paid a steep price for protecting that knowledge. As of this moment, he was the only human besides Chase to whom we had ever revealed the truth.

"Remember your journal? The one Van was looking for?"

He winced. "Yeah, though I'd rather not think about that clusterfuck. I still miss my leg, though I'm getting along fine without it, now. But...what about it, Dead Girl?"

"Then, you remember all the notes you took about us? About the demonic war we've been fighting?"

"Yeah, but I've never said a word. I swear on my honor."

"I believe you—it's not about whether you told anybody." I glanced at Nerissa, who nodded. "Okay, here's the thing. We're gearing up to open a Demon Gate to bring Shadow Wing over to Otherworld, so we can destroy him. We have the means to attack him now, and if we don't act now, there's a good chance his powers will be strong enough within a few months, maybe only a few weeks, to break through on his own."

He stared at me, his lips pressed together. Then, after clearing his throat, he said, "So, you need someone to open the gate."

I shrugged. "Not exactly. When our cousin Shamas was sent back from the grave, he was sent back with an increase in his own abilities. He can cast a Demon Gate but it's a good idea to have someone who can feed him extra energy. We need you to shore him up. I know it's a lot to ask and there's a good chance that some of us won't come out of this, but..."

Wilbur blinked, but a soft smile crossed his weathered face. "Are you kidding? I wouldn't miss this for the world. A chance to see a Demon Lord up close and personal? A chance to go into the front lines again? Say the word and I'm there."

He was dead serious. It had been hard on him, relearning to walk, learning to accept his limitations. He was able to go up and down the stairs now, and walk around and even run some, but in the long run, Wilbur's wild and free days had ended with the fire that had destroyed part of his house. There had been a difference in his nature that was tangible. He had lost some of the fire that he used to have, perhaps out of fear or out of perceived limitations. If we could spark that off again, so much the better.

I paused, then added. "There's one more thing. You'll have to go with us to Otherworld. That's where we're staging the final fight. We'll be leaving for there on Monday evening, shortly after sunset. That's the night of the new moon, when Camille's power is strongest."

Wilbur nodded. "Count me in. Tell Blondie and Busty that I'll be there, to do whatever you need me to." He stared at me for a moment and I sensed something was weighing heavily on his mind. "Now, Dead Girl, I have a favor to ask of you. A big favor." The look on his face told me he was serious. This wasn't any half-assed attempt to get in my pants.

"What do you need?"

He glanced around the room, then leaned forward, staring at the floor as he spoke in low, gruff tones. "It's about Martin."

I froze. What could have happened? Had somebody taken him out? Or was he just wearing down? Even ghouls and zombies had a finite 'lifespan', if you could call it that.

Wilbur glanced up at me and bleakly said, "I saw Martin yesterday. Then again this morning. He was...I think I saw his *spirit*."

Oh shit. We knew that Martin had been watching over Wilbur. Delilah had seen his spirit more than once, but we hadn't told Wilbur because he was convinced that somehow, Martin was still with him as long as he kept his brother's body around. But this changed everything. I wasn't sure how to approach this, but before I could speak, Nerissa was by Wilbur's side, one hand on his shoulder.

"That must have been traumatic, given the situation."

Wilbur frowned. "Thanks, Puddytat. I really don't know what to think. Am I going nuts, or did I really see him? I just want to know, because if his ghost is hanging around, what the hell am I doing keeping his body alive?"

Nerissa glanced at me and I gave her a nod. Best to have this out in the open, now that Wilbur had broached the subject.

"Do you want to know the truth?" Her voice was smooth and even, and I realized why she had become a victim's aid counselor at the FH-CSI. It also hit home just how much her talents were being wasted as my secretary.

"Please, if you know anything." Wilbur didn't often say *please*, and when he did, it meant he was desperate.

Nerissa took a deep breath and then said, "Delilah's seen Martin. He's watching over you, Wilbur. He's happy, and he wants you to be happy and to forgive yourself. You didn't kill Martin. You didn't let him down. He misses you, but he can't contact you as long as you cling to the belief that he's locked inside that corpse."

Wilbur stared at her mutely, then a tear streaked down his weather-worn face. He blinked, then buried his face in his hands. "What have I done?"

I joined Nerissa, sitting on Wilbur's other side. "It's okay, Wilbur. You just missed your brother and you convinced yourself that as long as his body was here, so was he. But his spirit doesn't need his body to be near you. He's been with you since he died, regardless of whether his body has been around."

Wilbur was sobbing, now, his shoulders heaving in silent jerks. I wasn't good at comforting others, but Nerissa was. Finally, I stood.

"I'm going to make you some tea. I'll be back in a moment." I headed into the kitchen to put the kettle on the stove. There was a noise from the broom closet and, cautiously, I opened it, only to see Martin standing inside, staring at the door. He didn't make any attempt to exit the closet, or to lash out at me, but simply looked mildly confused. *Crap*. What the hell were we going to do with him now? I closed the door, not knowing what else to do.

I fixed two cups of tea and found some gingersnaps and carried the tea tray with mugs and cookies into the living room, setting it down on the coffee table. Wilbur was clutching a handkerchief, staring straight ahead.

"Why didn't Kitten tell me about seeing Martin's spirit? I'm a necromancer. Hell, I should have known better. How could I have been so blind to the truth?" He hacked up what sounded all too much like a hairball and spit it into his hankie.

Nerissa gave me a quick look that said, *Time for you to take the helm on this*.

I licked my lips, trying to think of the best way to word things. "Wilbur, you've had Martin's…corpse…with you for years now. He seemed like such an integral part of your life that we were worried what might happen if you found out that his spirit was hanging around. We didn't want to make you feel guilty over keeping his body with you."

He stared at me for a moment, cocking his head, then snorted.

"Dead Girl, you were trying to protect me? From myself? You might as well try to stop a dog from worrying a bone. Ah hell, I made a right mess of things, didn't I? Well, it's time for this to end. If Martin *has* been hanging around, trying to communicate with me, and I've interfered with that by keeping his body around, I have no doubt he's pissed as hell." He turned his head, glancing at the television. "I'll miss having somebody around, though. It's not always easy being a curmudgeon when you're alone. *Jeopardy* won't be the same without him."

I pressed my lips together. There was nothing that Nerissa or I could say to make this any easier on him. Finally, I reached out and took his hand. "You have friends. Maybe it's time you started dating? Or found some necromancer group to meet up with?"

Wilbur grunted. "Easier said than done, chickadee. I'm set in my ways, you know. No woman worth her salt would put up with me and I know it. But that brings me back to the favor I was going to ask you, and it cements my decision."

"Yes?" I had a horrible feeling that I knew what he wanted me to do. The fact that he had shut Martin up in the kitchen closet told me where this was leading.

"Since it seems that Martin's spirit is hanging around and wants to talk to me, and that I've been keeping his shell alive for years without any reason, can you—will you —" His voice dropped to a whisper. "*Take care of him for me?*"

I shivered. "Can't you just undo the spell that brought him back as a ghoul?"

He shook his head. "It's not that simple. I wish I could, but I used some pretty potent magic that I learned from a Jaguar tribe down in South America. There's only one way to stop the ghouls they create. You have to destroy them—either hack them to bits or burn them to ashes. And even knowing what I know now, I just can't bring myself to do the deed."

I didn't really have a choice, not given the circumstances. Wilbur had done a lot to help us, and he had just volunteered for what could be a suicide mission. I couldn't let him down.

"All right. I'll…put Martin to rest for you." I closed my eyes, not wanting to see the confusion and hurt on his face.

"Don't tell me anything about it, other than it's done, please." He hiccupped, and for a moment I thought he was going to start crying again, but after taking a deep breath, he shook it off. "I wouldn't ask anybody else, Dead Girl. You understand more about these things. Your sisters wouldn't really get it, but you actually crossed over to live on the other side of the fence. You can tell when there's sentience and when there isn't. Vampires still have their souls. But I guess, somehow, I deluded myself into thinking a ghoul would still understand me. That Martin would still be with me, even though…"

I stood. "You want me to take care of this now?"

He nodded. "Might as well get it over with."

"Nerissa, stay here with Wilbur while I take Martin for a walk. Don't worry, Wilbur. You won't find anything to remind you." I headed for the kitchen while Nerissa took up the conversation, her voice soothing over the rough edges of the night.

⚔

Martin willingly followed me out the kitchen door and down the ramp to the backyard. Wilbur's house was on about an acre of land, so I decided it might be best to take the ghoul over to our house—Delilah's house, now. We had far more space, and that way Wilbur wouldn't find signs of a fight. Because like it or not, I knew Martin wouldn't go that easily. I called Delilah to tell her what I was planning.

"You're kidding? Martin's spirit appeared to him? I suppose it's for the best, though. I think that because Wilbur kept Martin's corpse around, he actually prevented Martin's spirit from being able to move on, but for the sake of the gods, don't tell him that." Delilah sounded just about as flabbergasted as I felt.

"Can Shade help me? I was thinking with his Stradolan magic, he might be able to make this easier on all of us." Given Delilah's husband was half shadow dragon and half Stradolan—a shadow walker—it only made sense that he might be able to give me a hand.

"I'll ask. Hold on."

I waited while she talked to Shade. Martin stood behind me, placidly, and I wondered briefly whether he had any sense that he was awaiting his execution. A moment later, Delilah came back on the phone.

"Shade says to meet him out back by the rogue portal. He'll help. After you finish, how about coming up to the house?"

"I need to let Wilbur know I'm done, and pick up Nerissa. She's staying with him while I do this. But Shade can tell you everything that goes down." I slipped my phone back in my jacket pocket, then turned to the ghoul. "Well, come on. Let's get this over with."

As we headed across the street and toward the house, Martin slogged along behind me. The first time I had seen him, I'd almost destroyed him. That was when we had first met Wilbur—he had come looking for Martin when the ghoul had wandered off. Wilbur managed to stop me right before I had torn Martin to pieces. I *had* broken Martin's neck, hence the neck brace he continually wore, but that was about the extent of damage I'd managed to inflict.

Shade was waiting around back of the house. He was wearing a pair of dark jeans and an indigo blue sweater, and when he saw me, he gave a little wave.

"So, Wilbur found out the truth about Martin?" He walked over to the ghoul, sizing him up.

"Yeah, and now he knows that by keeping Martin's body around, he's been blocking Martin's spirit from contacting him. He feels guilty as hell. I just hope to hell Martin actually attempts to talk to him again, so that Wilbur doesn't feel like he's been duped." I stood back, folding my arms across my chest. "Is there an easier way than tearing him apart? I really don't want to do that, but I will if there's no other choice."

Shade swept his shoulder-length hair back into a ponytail. The amber locks set off his dark skin nicely, and while he didn't have Smoky's intense charisma, Shade could be pretty charming on his own. He had a gentle sense of humor and wasn't as blustery as Camille's dragon-boy.

"There are two options. One, I can turn into a dragon and flame him down. Dragon-flame is searing hot, and I can muster up a good lungful without, I hope, torching the trees and plants."

"Good choice. What's the other option?" I was leery of flame, simply because it was also one of the best ways to destroy a vampire.

"There's a spell I can use—a karmic death magic—to turn the undead to dust. It unmakes them. But it's got a few potential side effects that I'm not sure either of us want to see happen."

"Like what?"

Shade tugged on his collar. "Um, if it goes the least bit astray, well, you're undead and it might just hit you. Small chance, but still—a chance."

I blinked. "Let's *not*, then. I like my life, vampiric or not, and I'm not looking to leave it just yet. I know you're not Camille—your magic doesn't go kerflooffy as often as hers, but… How big of a chance?"

Shade grinned at me. "That's the problem. I don't know. I haven't cast the spell since before my powers vanished and then returned, so I have no clue on how well I can perform it."

"It's settled, then. Dragon flame it is. I can take cover away from fire. Are you sure you're willing to do this? I could just start the process of taking him apart limb by limb."

Even though the words came tumbling out of my mouth, I realized that it wouldn't be that easy. It wouldn't be easy at all, since we had gotten to know Martin over the years and thought of him as Wilbur's pet.

"I'm good with it. Okay, I need space for this, so let's head out into the clearing." Shade motioned for us to follow him.

I took Martin's hand and gently dragged him along behind me. The backyard was huge, with forest surrounding it. One path led to Iris's house, and on the other side of the yard, a path led down to Birchwater Pond. There was enough space for both Smoky and Shade to comfortably shift into dragon form.

"At least it's been raining a lot, so the grass should be

soaked through. Lead Martin into the center, would you? And you'll want to tether him so he can't wander off. I know that ghouls don't move quickly, but we don't want him running around in flames." Shade paused. "Are you sure about this? Once he's toasted, there's no coming back."

"I think if Wilbur kept Martin's body around now that he knows the truth, he'd feel guilty every time he looked at it. And as much of a pain in the ass as Wilbur can be, I don't want that. So let's do this and get it over with." I glanced up at the house. "I'll find a bit of rope and a stake to tie him to." I handed Martin's leash to Shade and zipped up to the house.

Delilah was standing on the back porch. "I thought I'd come out and help. What do you need?"

I gave her a quick hug. "Thanks. We need a piece of rope and a stake to tether him with. Shade's going to use his dragon fire to toast him to ashes." I paused. "Wilbur was pretty shook up. He really had no clue that Martin's spirit was around him all these years. Odd, for a necromancer."

"Sometimes all it takes is a little denial. You don't want to see something? You don't see it." Delilah sorted through a pile of garden tools and brought out a length of rope and an aluminum stake. "These should work," she said, handing them to me.

"Why do you think Wilbur hid the truth from himself?" We crossed the lawn to where Shade waited with Martin.

"Because he had already turned Martin into a ghoul. Let's put it this way. Suppose I died and you were able to raise me again. You thought you had given me a second chance at life, when actually, all you did was to animate my body?"

"Are you talking about Erin?"

She shook her head. "Not at all. This has nothing to do with you turning Erin. Erin is Erin, regardless of whether she's human or a vampire. She still has her soul. Martin's spirit is still Martin. But his body? His body is a monster, when you think about it. The form has no soul, though it has some sentience and cunning. All this time, Wilbur's been thinking that his brother is still with him—albeit in a slightly skewed manner." She shook her head. "Seeing Martin's spirit must have been incredibly traumatic, and yet, I'm glad he did. This way, it can put things to rights for both of them."

"Do you really think Wilbur effectively grounded Martin's spirit? That Martin wants to move on and can't?" There were a lot of ghosts who had been locked into the physical plane for one reason or another.

Delilah considered my question for a moment.

"I think Martin has things he wants to say to Wilbur, but he can't until his body is given rest." She stopped beside Shade, staring at Martin. "It's really the end of a stagnant period for Wilbur. He'll be able to move on from here and let go of the past, I hope."

"Letting go and moving on seems to be a theme in our lives right now, doesn't it?"

"Yeah. But Wilbur's made strides. Remember when we first met him, he claimed Martin was a transient whom he had claimed at the morgue? It took us reading his journal to figure out the relationship between the two. I think even then, he was regretful over what he had done, but he wasn't able to face it yet." She glanced over at Shade. "Are you ready? Do you need anything else?"

He shook his head. "No. Just tie him to the tether and then get behind me, especially Menolly."

I walked over to Martin, who looked vaguely suspicious and a little afraid.

"It's okay, Martin. You'll be fine. You're going to be just fine."

I gently attached the tether to his leash ring that Wilbur kept on him, and then, with one giant thrust, hit the ground with the end of the aluminum stake, driving it deep enough for it to hold firm. Then I tied the tether to the stake and turned back to Martin.

"It will all be over soon. There's going to be just one bright flash, Martin. Brighter than anything you remember. Then you'll be free and...nature can take her course." I paused, then reached out and hesitantly patted him on the shoulder.

He tilted his head, as much as the brace would allow, and stared at me with unblinking eyes, looking for all the world like a confused dog. Then, a glint seeped in that made me wary, and I found myself seeing him not as Martin, Wilbur's slightly demented Jeopardy-watching-partner, but as a ghoul, who needed to devour flesh and energy to live. And with that, I backed away.

I joined Delilah, standing well behind Shade and to his left. He glanced at us.

I nodded. "Go ahead."

In a billowing cloud of smoke, Shade began to shift form. He rose out of the dark fog, a massive skeletal dragon, with dark brown vertebrae running down his spine, towering over us like some behemoth dinosaur skeleton. His wings spread wide, the bones shimmering with a nimbus of purple light. He craned his neck, winding down to stare at Martin.

The ghoul tried to back away, but the tether held. Even though I knew this was necessary, part of me didn't want to watch—didn't want to see what Shade was about to do. But I forced myself to stand vigil, if not for Martin, then for Wilbur.

Delilah reached for my hand and I wound my fingers through hers, holding tight. We steadied ourselves as Shade pulled back and took aim, his massive head targeting Martin. Unlike Smoky, his skull was a frightening visage of bone, the eye sockets blazing with light. Once again, it struck me how brave my sister was, loving someone who could easily squash her with one step. Shadow dragons were the Death Maidens of the Dragon Reaches, and Shade wasn't afraid of his power.

He opened his mouth and a spray of fire shot forth. The ghoul let out a howl, but it was cut short as the flames caught hold of him, burning swiftly.

Delilah clutched my hand tighter and gasped, but before we could even say a word, the fire grew so hot we could feel it from where we stood.

White hot and blistering, the flames crackled over Martin, who tried to pull away. But other than the single howl, the only sound in the night was the roar of Shade's fire.

A moment later, Martin's form flaked into ash, and then the bones followed. Another minute, and Martin's body had returned to the earth, cleansed by dragon's breath.

Delilah shuddered, but then straightened her shoulders. "It's done, then."

I nodded. "Yes, it's done. I'll be able to tell Wilbur it was quick. He doesn't want to know the details but I will tell him Martin didn't suffer."

"He didn't," Shade said, returning to his human form. "He burned clean and quick. Dragon fire's so strong that the shock numbs the victim for a moment, and then destroys them before the numbness is gone." He walked over to where Martin had stood. "Nothing left as a reminder. It was a quick and clean kill."

"Good, then," I said, trying to process how I felt. But there was just an empty void where the thought of Martin was concerned. It hadn't been his spirit—it hadn't been *him*, really. Just his shell, turned into something that he wouldn't have even recognized or wanted.

After saying goodnight to Delilah and Shade, and telling them that Wilbur would be going with us to Otherworld, I headed back to his house, to pick up Nerissa, and to tell Wilbur that his brother was finally free.

CHAPTER EIGHT
Delilah

I blinked, yawning as I rolled to a seated position. The other side of the bed was empty and I could hear Shade in the bathroom, whistling as he took a shower. I thought about joining him, but I had taken a shower the night before and, after all these years, I still didn't like getting wet. Sniffing my armpits, I decided I could wait till tonight, and pushed my way out of the bed, yanking on a pair of jeans and a long-sleeved top. I threaded a brown leather belt through the belt loops, then slid my feet into my bunny slippers and headed downstairs. The smell of bacon and eggs drifted up from the kitchen, where Hanna was preparing breakfast.

As I dashed down the stairs, the house echoed around me. It was too empty. After talking to Tim and Jason, I had decided it was time to approach Shade with a discussion about adoption. Whenever the Autumn Lord decided to father my child was up to him, but that wasn't going to prevent me from starting our family now. Only one thing remained as an obstacle: Shadow Wing.

Realistically, I knew that some of us might not survive facing him, but I was running on faith. The Autumn Lord wanted me to bear his child. I held onto that as hope that there would be a future for us after the battle. And my sisters would make it through, too, because I needed them to. Holding tightly to my optimism, I headed into the kitchen.

As I slid into a chair, flashing Hanna a cheery "Good morning," she handed me a plate with eggs, bacon, and pancakes on it. I poured a waterfall of syrup over the entire breakfast, much to her look of dismay, and dug in, biting into the soft, fluffy cakes.

"Mmm, you outdid yourself this morning." I waved my fork in appreciation. "These are fantastic. Blueberry!"

"Thank you. I tried a new recipe." Hanna paused, then sat down beside me, a cup of tea in her hand. "May I ask you a question?"

She had become fluent in English since she came to live with us, her sentence structure becoming less stilted with each day. She still had her Northlands accent, almost Norwegian in nature, but she seemed much more relaxed than she had in the beginning.

Hanna wore her hair in two braids. She had let it grow long since she had come over Earthside, and had finally settled on a style that seemed to fit her—jeans and pretty floral tops. Some days she wore long skirts instead of the jeans, but she had never taken to makeup and she reminded me of a retro-hippie, albeit a tidy one. She had also discovered cowboy boots and wore them constantly. She still looked weatherworn, and every year of her age, but her face had acquired a softness to it that she hadn't had at first.

"Of course. What is it?" I asked through a mouthful of bacon.

"Don't talk with your mouth full," she said, sounding for all the world like Iris. "I'm wondering if you'd like me to stay on after you face Shadow Wing. I'd like to, but I realize that you and Shade may want to bring in your own choice of a nanny and housekeeper, especially now that Iris has left."

I blinked. I hadn't even thought of hiring a nanny, and Hanna had become as much a part of the family as Iris had. I wiped my lips with the napkin.

"Hanna, you're part of our extended family. If you want to leave, we wouldn't try to stop you, but as long as you want to stay, you're welcome. I'll need someone to help me with the baby—babies—however many we end up with. And the gods know, I suck at playing housekeeper. Hell, it took Iris dumping my litter box on my bed to teach me to tend to myself. If you want to stay, Shade and I would be happy to have you. If you need a raise, just ask."

She nodded. "I thought as much, but we never really formally talked about it. I came home with Camille, and when I offered to move to the Barrow with her, she told me you'd probably have more need of me than she would because she has all nature of servants out there. But...you just never know in these situations."

"Have you ever thought of going back to your home?" I asked, cautious because I knew that was still a sore subject, and probably always would be.

Hanna pressed her lips together, silently regarding her cup of tea. I went back to my breakfast, thinking she wasn't going to answer, but then, after a moment, she began to speak.

"When Hyto kidnapped Kjell and me, he killed my husband. He carried him high into the air and dropped him on a quarry of sharp rocks while I watched. I had managed to sneak my daughters away safely—girls were disappearing from the area and I was smart enough to realize why—but they were the only ones from my family who escaped."

I leaned back, taking a deep breath. Hyto had tortured Camille, and even though he was dead, hearing about what else he had done gave a real scope to how sadistic Smoky's father had been.

"Do you know where they are?"

She shook her head. "No. I have no idea where they escaped to, or if they even still survive. I'm afraid to find out, to be honest. As long as I don't know, I can imagine them happy and healthy, with families of their own. Hyto destroyed my world. In the end, I destroyed Kjell to release him from the torture. I killed my son to save him from the dragon. I don't think I could withstand finding out that my daughters fell into a bad end. Sometimes, ignorance truly *is* a saving grace. Do you understand?"

She glanced over at me.

I nodded. "Yeah, I think I do. If you don't know what happened to them, then they're still alive in your mind and heart."

She took a sip of her tea. "Yes. And that way, Hyto didn't strip *everything* from my life. I will be forever grateful to your sister, Camille. She gave me the courage to stand up and say, "No more." And for that, I bless her. But going back to look for my daughters? No. If something happened to them, it would mean Hyto truly did devastate my life." Carrying her cup back to the sink, she glanced at the ceiling as we heard Shade clattering around overhead. "Staying Earthside is best for me. It's a different life. I don't want my old one back. There are too many heartbreaks in Otherworld—in the Northlands—for me."

I left Shade at home—he and Roz were planning to start winterizing the house and land—while I headed for the Supe Community Council meeting.

Frank Willows, a werewolf, was the president and when I checked my email before bed, he had put out a call for an emergency meeting at eleven AM. I wasn't sure what was going on, but the memo had been brusque. Frank was a good guy with a level head, so when he sounded worried via an email, I knew there was something up.

As I passed the Wayfarer, I felt a pang. I knew Menolly missed working there, but Derrick made an excellent acting manager and I had my suspicions that eventually the portal in the bottom of the bar would be disabled, and then Derrick would buy the store outright.

I arrived at the Supe Community Council early enough to help set up. Frank was standing in the corner. I made my way over to him, touching him lightly on the shoulder.

"Hey Frank, what's up?" I could smell the worry on him. Weres had a way of exuding a certain set of pheromones when they were agitated. Something had definitely triggered Frank.

He blinked. "Thank you so much for coming, Delilah. Can I talk to you alone for a moment?"

I nodded. "Of course. Your office?"

He led me back to a small office which was neater than I could imagine keeping it. But Frank was meticulous. He shut the door behind us, motioning for me to sit down.

"I was hoping you'd arrive early."

"What's wrong? I can smell you across the room." I took the chair, accepting the candy bar he tossed me from his desk. Frank knew my weakness for sweets.

"I have a favor to ask. Well, it's a little more than a favor. I know you're likely to say no, but please think it over. Talk over your concerns to me, because I really want you to say yes."

An urgency in his voice made me straighten up. He really *was* worried.

"Okay. Ask."

Frank took a deep breath. "I need you to accept my post."

"What do you mean?"

He frowned, fidgeting in his chair. "I need you to take over as president of the Council. Effective today."

Surprised by the request, I sat there, candy in hand, uncertain of what to do or say. Finally, I cleared my throat and leaned forward. "What's going on, Frank?"

He cast his glance down. "My family and I are leaving Seattle. My grandfather is the Alpha of the New York Bright-Eyes Wolf Pack. He's been feeling poorly lately, but everyone thought it was a bug. Then yesterday, he fell into a coma. Come to find out, he's been keeping a life-threatening heart condition secret, even from Gammy. My father can't leave here, he's too busy with farming. He owns the farm I manage, plus five others. Since I'm the eldest son, I'm the one who's expected to go back to New York and take over as leader of the pack when my grandfather dies. Which could be any day. And if he dies without me there, it could mean trouble among the alpha contenders."

I blinked. "Oh Frank, I'm sorry. I didn't know your father owns your farm."

"It's a family business. My father will assign one of my brothers to take over management, and he's funding my family's trip and relocation. We'll move into Gammer and Gammy's house, and take care of Gammy while we're at it."

"At least you have a place to go."

"Yeah, and we'll be fine. It will require some adjustment, but we should be able to handle it. But I have to leave tomorrow morning. I want the person to take over this post to be someone who fully understands this agency. You and your sisters are the ones who pretty much founded it, so I think it's time for you to take the role you've long deserved, Delilah. The Council loves you. They respect you."

I didn't know what to say. We hadn't told Frank about the demonic war so he wasn't up to speed on what what we were facing, and I didn't want to add to his worries by doing so now. He had been the leader of the Supe Militia, a branch of the Supe Community Council, but I could easily find someone to take his place. We had plenty of warriors who I could trust, but Frank was right. Nobody knew the organization like I did, given that I had been the driving force behind it. I couldn't very well start something this important, then abandon it when I was needed.

Frank had served us well, but he deserved to go with an easy conscience about the Council.

"I'll do it." I stared at him, thinking that this was the last thing I needed to add on my plate, but I'd work out the logistics later. "We'll announce it today."

He let out a long breath and leaned back, a look of relief spreading across his face. "I was so worried I was going to have to argue you into it. I admit, I was prepared to guilt trip you if necessary." With a wolfish grin, he wearily rested his elbows on the desk.

"That rough, huh?"

Frank nodded. "That rough. We've lived here in the Seattle area for over a hundred years. We love the woodlands here, and the atmosphere. My wife and the children aren't happy about the move, but there's no real choice in this matter. They'll adjust. And I have to do my duty."

"Duty," I said softly. "That's something I understand all too well." At his querying look, I shook my head. "Don't ask. You don't want to know. Just do what you have to and I'll manage here. If I can't run it by myself, there are plenty of people who can help. Now, let's get out there and help them set up."

As he followed me out of the office, I thought, *this feels right*. Not easy, not something I would necessarily choose, but *right*. I'd figure it out as I went.

⚔

BY THE TIME I got home it was near four. I had stopped for groceries and caved at the pizza counter in the store, ordering three large meat-eaters pizza. By the time I got home, it was pouring again and the parking space in front of the house looked like a massive mud puddle. At least we had had the driveway paved some time back, so there was no trouble getting into and out of the house.

I no sooner had opened the door, heavy bags in hand, than Shade was there, taking the groceries from me.

"I'll run back and get the pizzas," I said, dashing down the steps before he could say a word. When I returned, he was back at the front door.

"I need to talk to you *now*," he said, gently maneuvering me over to the porch swing.

"Not you, too? Everybody seems to have something urgent to talk about today." I laughed, but then stopped. Shade looked serious. *So* serious that I began to think that the day had a monopoly on bad news. "What's happened?"

"We have company and I wanted to prepare you before you stumbled in on them." He shook his head again as I started to speak. "Quickly—if I take too long they'll be out to find out why. I told them I was going to help you bring in the food."

"Who? Who's here?" If Shade was nervous than our guests were worth caution.

He licked his lips and then, sitting beside me on the swing, said, "My sister, Lash is here."

"I like Lash." I wasn't sure where the problem was. "Did your mother come, too? She's a little intimidating, I admit."

"Not my mother. Honey, my father's sitting in our living room right now."

His words dropped like lead. I stared at him.

"You've got to be kidding me! *Your father*? What the hell is *he* doing here?"

Shade's father was full-blooded Stradolan, the only

race who could interbreed with shadow dragons, but the children of such unions were sterile. And only Stradolan men could breed with shadow dragon females.

Shade's father had effectively disowned his son for refusing to follow in his own footsteps. He was known as the Enforcer, and he punished wayward spirits in the Netherworld. Because Shade had taken a different route, his father had shunned him. So the fact that he was sitting in our living room either foretold one hell of a turn-around, or trouble. Or maybe, both.

"My father is here with Lash. I'm not sure why—they just got here. But he wants to meet you. So, let's get in there. And please, don't offer them pizza. Lash could eat it and she probably would out of courtesy, but the Stradolans eat energy, not food. My father would be terribly offended. He doesn't have a good sense of humor." Shade grabbed the pizzas out of my hand and hustled me inside.

"I'm not dressed for meeting him—" I started to protest, but Shade vanished into the kitchen with the pizzas and food while I leaned back against the wall, holding my breath.

I could hear the murmur of voices coming from the living room, but I wasn't about to go in there by myself. If Shade wanted me to meet his father, he was jolly well going to be by my side to deflect what I imagined was going to be a painful scrutiny. With a name like the "Enforcer," my father-in-law didn't exactly inspire confidence.

Shade was back in a flash. He took a deep breath, wrapping his arm through mine.

"Are you ready?" he mouthed.

I nodded. "As ready as I'll ever be. Do we *have* to do this?"

"I'm afraid we don't have much choice."

And with that, he swung me through the arch, into the living room.

※

Lash was as I remembered her, tall and elegant with rich brown skin. Where Shade's hair was amber, hers made me think of caramel, done up in a chignon of braids that looped down to her shoulders and up again to catch beneath a dragon-shaped cloisonné barrette. She was wearing a mustard colored chiffon gown, shimmering with layers of orange and flame red woven into the skirt. The dress floated around her as though it had a life of its own.

Next to her stood a man who looked vaguely like Shade, but he was almost a blur, as though he had his own personal shadow surrounding him. He was around six feet, shorter than his son, and it was difficult to get a read on his expression because his face seemed cloaked in shadow. I could see his features if I didn't look directly at him. His eyes were white, with brilliant plum colored irises, and there was a murkiness about his appearance that I suspected was the Stradolan energy coming through.

Lash moved forward, lightly embracing first her brother and then, me. As she leaned in for a hug, she whispered, "This wasn't my idea, please believe me."

Lash and I had gotten off to a bad start but Smoky had helped win her over, and she had come to our wedding, along with her mother, Seratha. They had both been cordial and made me feel that—if I didn't *fully* belong in their family—they were willing to be patient and give me a chance. I didn't expect that from Shade's father. In fact, Seratha had warned me never to interfere in the relationship between the two men, nor to hope for any sort of blessing from him.

As she backed away, Shade turned to his father.

"Welcome to my home, Sir."

The Enforcer—I had no idea what his name was, nor whether he would even give me a name with which to refer to him—stared at his son, silent for a moment. Then he turned his gaze to me. I felt like he was looking at me inside-out and had the sneaking suspicion he could see far more than I thought he could.

"So, this is where you've come to rest," he finally said, turning back to Shade. "You've fully dedicated yourself to the Harvestmen, then? And you won't change your mind?"

Shade lowered his gaze, but he kept his shoulders straight. "Yes, Sir. This is my life." He still hadn't introduced me, but I wasn't broken up over it. In fact, I thought that perhaps I was better off just keeping my mouth shut and trying to get through the visit as unnoticed as possible.

"Mind your manners, boy. Introduce me."

Great. So much for that hope.

Shade inclined his head. "As you will, Sir. This is my wife, Delilah D'Artigo. Delilah, this is my—" he paused, looking confused. I wondered what was wrong until it hit me. The Enforcer had disowned his son, so if Shade referred to him as 'Father' it might only cause a deeper rift.

The Stradolan turned to me. "I'm sure he's told you that I sired him. I no longer claim him as my son, but that doesn't remove the biological connection. You may refer to me as "Sir" as he does. Or as Your Honor, for I am a judge in my world, another fact I'm assuming he has mentioned?"

"Yes, Sir." I tried to steady my voice, not wanting to sound afraid, even though I was petrified. The energy coming off the Stradolan was intense, and I could feel it in my core. It was the energy of the Netherworld, of death and the harvest. It was the energy of the end of all things, and it also was wrapped up with pain and harsh judgment. The "Enforcer" fit Shade's father as a name, and it was hard to imagine Seratha living with this energy day in, day out. She seemed a rather cheerful sort, as far as shadow dragons went.

"Delilah. You are a Death Maiden."

It was a statement, not a question, and I wasn't sure whether he expected me to answer, so I merely said, "Yes."

"You wear the energy well. It cloaks you. We are not dissimilar, then." He sounded almost pleased.

I blinked, wanting to shout, *Oh hell, no!* but I kept my mouth shut. No way in hell would I accept that I had anything in common with him. He wasn't sneering at me, nor was he sounding sarcastic, but the complete sense of detachment made me fear him. He simply *didn't care*—he had truly let go of any feelings for his son, that much I could tell. He had written Shade off, like he might toss out a used tissue.

The Enforcer must have noticed my expression, for he

grunted out a laugh that held anything but mirth within it.

"You disagree with me, but look at what you do, Death Maiden. You mete out death. You can make that death painful, and I can feel that you have done just that. You may not be the judge, although I suspect you've taken that role on yourself at least once or twice, but you are the executioner. You're an assassin for the Harvestmen. You're a weapon and you never think to disobey. You are an avatar of death, as am I. You're more like me than my own son is."

His words bit deep and I grimaced, not wanting to admit that he was right. I wasn't sure what to say, in fact, and glanced at Shade for help.

"Don't needle my wife." Shade looked wary, but he pulled me to him, wrapping his arm around my shoulders.

The Enforcer paused. I wished I could read his expression, but the shadows around his face grew deeper and I had no clue what he was thinking.

"Father, remember, you came to them. They did not come to you," Lash said, keeping her tone respectful but firm.

He glanced at her, then back at us. "True. I just hope that Shade realizes he's married the very nature he sought to distance himself from. Let this be a lesson: You cannot escape your essential self, boy. It will find its way to you through one path or another."

After a moment, Shade let out a long breath. "Why did you come? You seem set on continuing our estrangement."

That brought a swift response.

"I came to make this formal. I will never accept your

choice to turn from our birthright. By choosing to bind yourself to the Autumn Lord, you've placed yourself in a position of subservience. And my lineage has *never* been subservient to another, in all our history. Therefore, unless you recant and rejoin the family business, from this day forward, I will never acknowledge you as my son." And with his words, there it was—the reason Shade had been disowned. Pride and caste, both so important in the dragon world, but apparently even more so in the realm of the Stradolans.

Shade hung his head, then softly said, "Sir, I respect you. I have always respected you. But I will not live the life you want me to. Delilah and I are bound to the Autumn Lord. He is our master and we willingly embrace the destiny he's set forth for us. I cannot return to your side and take part in a job that I consider cruel and unnecessary."

"Is this your final decision?"

My husband seemed to flare, a nimbus of energy forming around him.

"You've made your stance abundantly clear and I accept it. I've chosen my path and I stick by it. I've married the woman I love, just like you chose to marry Mother. If you don't approve of me, then fine—I am no longer your son. But hear this: you're never to return to my home, you're not to hound my wife and me. You will forfeit that right when you cast me out of the family. Either I remain your son and you accept my path even though you don't approve of it, or I'm no longer your son and out of your life forever. *But make your choice and stick by it.*"

Lash gasped, stepping back. I had to force myself to

stand steady beside Shade, given both of us were in the direct line of fire.

The Enforcer stared at Shade for a moment, the anger receding behind the shield of disinterest. "I came to give you a second chance. To invite you back into the family, to offer you the chance to take up your life in the Netherworlds again. Your wife would be able to manage it, being a Death Maiden. But you're a stubborn fool, and I see now that you never will admit your folly." Somehow, in his indifference, he was almost more frightening.

"And you will never understand my reasoning. We're too far across the divide to ever meet and agree," Shade said softly.

Something big was about to happen—the room was practically crackling. I glanced at Lash, who looked like she wanted to weep, but stood stoic, witnessing the interchange.

Shade's father straightened and in a cold voice, said, "Then let it be noted in the history of our family, as of this day, I officially erase you from the family tree. You will never enter our domain again. You will never refer to me as your father again. If your mother and sister choose to visit you, they do so on their own, without any official recognition. You are dead to me. I have no son."

He turned to me. "I do not blame you for Shade's missteps. He made his own choice. May you go easy into your destiny, Death Maiden. It's a heady responsibility. Learn to corral that impulsive nature I sense within. As for you and me, we will never meet again." Without waiting for an answer, he turned to Lash. "Come, my daughter. My only child. We return to our world. We have business to attend to."

Lash started to turn back to Shade, but her father took her arm, forcefully directing her to follow him. She silently obeyed, and within seconds, they vanished from the room, disappearing in a cloud of smoke.

Shade stared at the spot where they had stood. "Well," he said after a moment. "It's official. I no longer have any legal status in the Netherlands."

"What do you mean?" I wasn't sure of what to say or of how to comfort him.

"When one of your parents disowns you, officially, your very status of existence is erased from the roles. It doesn't matter which parent. All it takes is one to blot out your life. At least your life on paper, so to speak."

"Does this mean you can never go back to the Netherworld?" My heart hurt for him. It had been bad enough when his powers were stripped away, and I had rejoiced when they returned. But this— This felt gut wrenching. And there wasn't anything I could do about it.

"No, I can come and go without a problem. But it means I have no official standing there. I'll never be able to go back to my home. If Mother and Lash want to visit me, they'll have to come here, and I can't send messages to them. They'll be turned away at the door."

I thought for a moment. "Can *I* send messages for you? He didn't forbid me from showing up at your house."

Shade wrapped his arms around me and leaned his forehead against mine.

"My sweet love. Don't worry your head over this, truly. I knew my father would never come around and I've been preparing for this day. It had to happen at some point. My mother and Lash will figure out ways to communicate with me. I made my choice long before I met you—long before I knew you existed. So don't think you were a part of his decision. If I had gone back to the fold, you would have been a welcome addition. In fact, I think he would have liked you better than me, once he took the time to get to know you."

I believed him—Shade didn't lie—but I couldn't help but feel bad. When my father had turned away Camille for staying with Trillian, whom he had hated based on Trillian's heritage, it had been so hard to handle. At least they had made up before Sephreh died, but I had the feeling that Shade's father would never compromise.

"Come on," Shade said. "Let's go warm up the pizza, curl up in front of the TV, and talk about your day. You can tell me what the big hurry with the meeting was."

I followed him into the kitchen, trying to push the Enforcer's visit out of my mind, but I couldn't help but wonder what kind of ruthless world view it took to write off your own son just because he chose to pursue a career path other than the one you wanted him to. And that thought haunted me the rest of the evening.

CHAPTER NINE
Camille

"Camille? Where are you?" Morio's voice echoed from the other side of the room.

I was sitting on the bed, cross-legged, preparing for my ritual. Since the upcoming New Moon was going to be spent in the fight of our lives, I decided to perform a ritual drawing on the power of the Moon Mother, to prepare myself and my Knights.

"I'm over here." I was naked, staring at the clothes I had picked out for the evening. The gown was a deep indigo blue spidersilk dress, long and warm, with a low-cut neck, and a lace overlay sparkling with crystals that looked like stars. But I had yet to put it on.

Morio frowned as he approached. He was wearing a long black robe over a karate *gi*. Both pants and jacket were black, fastened by a black cotton belt. His hair was drawn back in a long ponytail and his mustache had managed to achieve truly awesome proportions. He had a true Fu Manchu mustache now, neatly trimmed, with the ends reaching down to where the goatee, also neatly trimmed, accented his chin. It made him look even more roguish.

"Shouldn't you be dressed yet? The others are waiting."

"I know," I said. "I'm just thinking. I've been thinking a lot the past couple of weeks." I slid on my panties, then fastened my bra, shifting my breasts to fit in each cup. "Do you realize that in two nights we're going to summon Shadow Wing? *Two nights*? This war feels like it's dragged on forever and then, suddenly, it's right here, in front of us. How did that happen?"

Morio sat down beside me, handing me my dress. I slipped the gown over my head and fastened it at the waist with a silver cord. Then I slipped the lace kimono over the top and moved to the vanity. I had a maid, but for rituals I dressed myself. I took off my circlet, then picked up my brush. Morio moved behind me and took the brush from me. He began to brush my hair in long, even strokes while I closed my eyes.

"How did it happen? It's the way of any major life event. Anytime there's something big going down, that you know is coming, the waiting seems long and stretched out. It doesn't matter whether you're anticipating it with joy or dread, the waiting is always the hardest part. And then it's as though time telescopes and you're suddenly there in front of it, staring it straight in the face. I think it's worse when it's something you're dreading. You get used to thinking it's going to be sometime in the future, but there's always a point where the future becomes the present, and boom, there it is."

He pulled my hair back, tugging on it just hard enough

to make me lean back. As he bent over me, pressing his lips to mine, I drifted into the warmth of his kiss, thinking about what he said.

"And now, my lady, how would you like your hair tonight?" He nuzzled my ear, then straightened up again.

I would have much rather crawled into bed with him, but I let the thought drop away. I had magic to work.

"I think a braid. I don't want any distractions tonight, and that way, it won't fly in my face." I waited while Morio finished plaiting my hair and tied the end with a beautiful bow, then reluctantly slid my feet into the ankle boots I had chosen. They were low-heeled, with silver buckles and chains draping across the sides.

"Ready?" He held out his hand.

I let out a long sigh, but nodded. "As I'll ever be. Let's go see what happens this time."

And so we were off, to a secret grove near my Barrow that was reserved for only me, my Keraastar Knights, and Morio, my consort and High Priest.

※

Wisteria Grove, as I had named it, was a secluded clearing near my Barrow, and it was guarded day and night to prevent anyone from wandering in. In the middle of a thicket of cedar and fir, the clearing was a good forty yards in diameter, with four gates—four tall arches—to guard and mark each of the elements.

The earth was in the north, air in the east, fire in the south, and water in the west. Each arch was made of a different wood—the north gate was oak, the east was birch, the south was holly, and the west was yew. Each arch was ten feet tall, and decorated with ribbons to match the colors of the elements—green for the earth, white for the air, red for fire, and for the water, blue.

The outside borders of the grove were defined by a ring of rose bushes, mums, and ferns. In summer, the roses would bloom a deep burgundy. As they faded, the mums burned to life with a coppery rust color, and when winter's chill put them to rest, the Charity Mahonia's yellow flowers cheered up the gloom. The ferns were large enough to withstand the winter weather, dying back to a degree but still impressive, and they blossomed out with new growth in the spring.

About two feet inside the ring of flowers was another circle, this one composed of fly agaric, their brilliant red and white caps forming a true faerie ring. The mushrooms were ever growing, new ones coming up to replace the old year round due to the magic inherent within the land.

In the center of the ring was an altar table, compact in size but big enough so that I could lay a ceremonial blade across the top. I was still using my silver dagger, but I knew the time was coming when I would replace it with something more suitable. I wasn't sure what that blade would be, but I'd know it when I saw it.

"Can you move the table? We won't need it tonight."

Morio obliged, moving the table to one side, leaving enough space for me to form a circle with my Knights. Morio took his place by the eastern gate. Ever since the Moon Mother had taken him in and made him my priest, we had worked together in Circle, doubling the power of our rituals, but he could not enter the web that I wove with my Keraastar Knights, and so he stood vigil as a magical guard.

As I waited, a rustle sounded from the woods to the east and the Keraastar Knights began to emerge, in a single line. First came Venus the Moon Child, whom I had appointed the leader. He wore the seal of fire opal around his neck. Every day, the crusty old werepuma delved deeper into the fiercesome force I expected him to become.

Second in line was his captain. Bran, the son of Raven Mother and the Black Unicorn. He wore the smoky quartz seal, and his eyes were dark and unreadable, but we had set aside our mutual antagonism when he had taken the seal and pledged himself to my service.

Third was Amber, wearing the topaz seal. Followed closely by her brother, she moved silently, eyes focused ahead. She was proving to be far stronger than we thought she would become. In training, she could bring a man down without breaking a sweat. Both she and her brother Luke—who wore the aquamarine—were werewolves, and by now, their seals had taken them fully over, and they were the walking embodiments of the magic itself.

Fifth in line was Chase, wearing the amethyst seal. He was composed, gliding along behind them. Over the past few months, Chase had thrown himself into his training, and I was worried that he was rapidly heading down the rabbit hole along with Amber and Luke, but that was the nature of the spirit seals. The seals changed their guardians as the nature of the stone blended in with the essence of their host. The Keraastar diamond would do the same to me, over time. That much I knew, though where it would lead, I had no clue.

After Chase came Tanne, wearing the emerald seal, and then Clyde and Lisa, hosts for the citrine and sapphire seals, respectively. Bringing up the rear was Shamas, with the ruby seal draped around his neck. He glanced at me, then focused his gaze on the back of Lisa.

The Knights spread in a circle around me, shifting position until their outstretched hands could clasp. We had been meeting at least three times a week since I had taken the throne of Dusk and Twilight, working to attune our energies and to bring our focus in line, all in anticipation of the day we would face Shadow Wing.

I walked the circle, gazing into the eyes of each Knight in turn. The energy had already begun to cycle and I could feel it building.

Fast, I thought. *This is faster than any time before*.

We were a powerful group, but it had always taken a few moments of guided meditation to prepare them. However, today it felt as though our link from last time held. Walking the Circle simply reinforced that bond and made it stronger. Each of my Knights stared steadily back at me, and I caught the flashes of lightning in their eyes, the sign of building magic. When I was done, I returned to the center and drew my dagger.

"Seal the gate," I said, motioning to Morio.

He stepped outside the gate, standing beside the arch as he wove a magical seal across it to keep in the power, and to keep *out* anybody who might be spying on the astral.

"Done." He took up position.

I smiled as the power began to rise.

A veil of flames, a veil of shifting shadows danced in and around us.

I withdrew my blade and walked outside the ring of the Keraastar Knights, holding my dagger directly out to my side with my left hand as I faced the north and began to circle deosil. I walked the Circle three times, once for each verse, as the power built in the wake of my blade and song.

> *Lady cast this Circle white, weave a web of glowing light,*
> *Earth and Air and Fire and Water, Bind us to thee.*
> *Lady cast this Circle red, weave the strands of glowing thread,*
> *Earth and Air and Fire and Water, Bind us to thee.*
> *Lady cast this Circle black, weave the wisdom that we lack,*
> *Earth and Air and Fire and Water, Bind us to thee.*

When I finished the invocation and returned to the north for the third time, I drew a sweeping pentagram in the air, and the only sound was the whistling of the wind. I paused, letting the energy settle, then turned to the north. All of the Knights, as well as Morio, turned with me, facing the northern gate.

> *Spirits of the North, I call you forth!*
> *Spirits of the elk and the wolf and the*
>   *bear, be with us.*
> *Satyrs and Nymphs of our sacred Grove,*
>   *be with us.*
> *Spirits of the Earth,*
> *You who are bone and stone, crystal and*
>   *soil,*
> *You who are the highest mountain tops,*
> *You who are the deepest caverns,*
> *I call to you.*
> *Spirits of Earth, join our rites,*
> *Welcome and Blessed Be.*

The grass rustled in the wind, and in the distance, a wolf bayed long and low, and the sound settled around us, sending a ripple of energy up my spine. I turned to the east and they followed in unison.

> *Spirits of the East, I call you forth!*
> *Spirit of the raven and hawk, the owl and*
>   *eagle, be with us.*
> *Sylphs who dance on the wind, be with us.*
> *Spirits of the Air,*
> *You who are breath and gale,*
> *You who are hurricane and gentle breeze,*
> *I call to you.*
> *Spirits of the Air, join our rites,*
> *Welcome and Blessed Be.*

A sudden gust swept up, and a chill raced through me

as the winds hit full force. Shivering, I turned to the south.

> *Spirits of the South, I call you forth!*
> *Spirits of the salamander and snake, be with us.*
> *Eye catchers and the Rising Phoenix, be with us.*
> *Spirits of Flame and Faerie Fire,*
> *You who are bonfire and hearth,*
> *You who are Faerie fire and boiling lava,*
> *I call to you.*
> *Spirits of Flame and Faerie Fire, join our rites,*
> *Welcome and Blessed Be.*

As I spoke, a dozen globes of light began to dance around the grove. They were eye catchers—it was dangerous to invoke will o' the wisps—and the shimmering balls of light spread out, their illumination gentle against the night. I turned to the west.

> *Spirits of the West, I call you forth!*
> *Spirits of the salmon and shark and whale, be with us.*
> *Sirens, Naiads, and Undines, be with us.*
> *Spirits of the Water,*
> *You who are the Ocean Mother and the raging rivers,*
> *You who are the gentle pools, and the tears of our body,*
> *I call to you.*

Spirits of Water, join our rites,
Welcome and Blessed Be.

As my voice fell away, a mist began to rise in the grove, thick with the moisture of the air. I let the invocations settled and then started to replace the dagger into the sheath hanging from my silver belt, but my fingers slipped and it dropped to the ground.

I bent over to pick it up but beside the dagger was another object—hard and cool—hidden in the grass beside it. Frowning, I picked up my dagger, and then the other object.

Another blade, unlike any I had ever seen.

The dagger was double-edged, a long, thin, obsidian blade that looked to be razor sharp. It was made out of some metal, but was lighter than aluminum. The hilt was sparkling silver, with etched filigree encircling it. The moment my hand touched it, I knew it was mine.

Another sign of the approaching battle, the Moon Mother whispered to me.

I sheathed my regular dagger and, not questioning—going on faith—I held the new blade up in the air.

The rain stopped as a break in the clouds let the slim crescent moon overhead shine down. Her light fell on the dagger with a charge that ricocheted through my body.

I dropped my head back as the energy circulated, spiraling up my arm, to circle out and around through my muscles, my bones, into my bloodstream. It was the energy of the Moon Mother at her sternest and most deadly, and it whispered to me, a force that I couldn't resist if I had wanted to.

. . .

FEEL ME. Know me. I am the core of courage, the strength of the doomed who still press forward, knowing they are marching to their deaths in battle. I am the spirit of the brave, the strength of the legions who have entered Valhalla, the heart of those who have been washed in the Cauldron of Rebirth. I am the spirit of Mother Bear, who risks all to protect her cubs. I am the battle cry, rallying the troops. I am the cornerstone of war and the banner of those who resist all tyranny. I am the armor that protects your body. Wear me into the depths of hell, and I will carry you forward even unto certain doom.

THE WHISPERS SURROUNDED ME, swirling inside my thoughts as I let them in. They ate against my fear, they ate against my doubt and worry, and the strain of knowing that my Knights and I alone were destined to bring an end to Shadow Wing. As they fused into my being, my shoulders straightened and my wings unfurled.

I opened my eyes, startled to find that I could now see a web of light surrounding me. It emanated from the diamond, violet flames flaring out in all directions to touch each Keraastar Knight. The energy raced from Knight to Knight, and we formed a wheel of power, a wheel of death, a wheel of force that burnt all it touched to a crisp.

Each of the Knights began strengthening the force, returning it back to me as I gathered it and wove it into a bright mass, filtering it into the Keraastar diamond.

I could feel all of them—all of my Knights. I could feel their fears and their hopes, the unsettled turmoil as they allowed their seals to take control of their lives. It was as though I could see into the dark corners of their hearts and their memories—all they had hoped for, all they had surrendered, and the fierce loyalty they held to the cause. Each one had melded tightly with their seals, and they were all strong links in the chain. And now, they were using the energy I fed them to rebound back on me, to strengthen my own will and nerves. To help me become the true Queen of the Keraastar Diamond. We were becoming a hive mind, and I, their queen, would lead them into the thick of the battle.

I thought, "Move two steps to the right," and as a single entity, they did, each taking two steps and no more, to the right.

We played all night, with me giving them directions by thought and the Knights responding. And all through the night, the energy kept flowing through the dagger, into me, into the Knights to cycle around and return. The diamond around my neck was now glowing with a light brighter than I had ever seen it, and I felt like I could fly. I directed the energy to lift me up, and it spiraled beneath me, buoying me up into the air. I hovered there, arms spread wide, realizing that I had just taken all the energy we had built and directed it into a single command. Cautiously, before I grew too tired, I lowered myself to the ground.

As my feet touched the grass, a great weariness swept over me. I gently broke the chain, not severing it but allowing each member of the Knights to return to their own thoughts as I withdrew from their energy fields. Another few minutes, and we were standing there, absolutely exhausted.

I dropped to the dewy grass and closed my eyes as I rested. I hadn't known what to expect, but this was the strongest we had ever bonded, and now I knew how to bring their power together, within myself. And how to direct it out. Which meant I could take our combined powers and attack Shadow Wing, aiming for his soul receptacles. The Keraastar Knights had their weapon, and *we* were it.

I SLID into the bath Trillian had prepared for me, closing my eyes as the bubbles sucked the tension out of me. I was shivering, feeling for all the world like a light that had flared too brightly. I felt singed and crisped around the edges. The scent of cinnamon and spice and apples rose from the water and I surrendered to it as it drained the tension out of my muscles. He had engaged a few eye catchers, which gave off a dim, pleasant light that rested easy on my head.

Trillian was sitting on the floor by the tub and he reached for my hand. "Are you all right, babe?"

I winced as I shifted. My stomach was queasy and I felt one step away from puking. Running strong magic could do that, especially when I was the focus of it.

"Yeah, I will be. I was overwhelmed by the amplitude of the energy we raised tonight, but now I can prepare for it. At least I know what we're capable of, and how we're supposed to focus our attack on Shadow Wing. We aim the energy for the soul receptacles. And then we hope it's enough. And we hope we can keep him in one place long enough. At least Joreal will have his soldiers there to help us." The very act of speaking made my stomach churn and

I groaned, wanting nothing more than to curl up in bed, not moving, and sleep for a week.

"It really hit you, didn't it?" He reached out, stroking my hair away from my face.

"Um-hm. I felt exhilarated afterward, but then on the way back to the Barrow, it hit. A magic migraine, you might call it." I paused, then slowly shifted to where I was sitting upright. My back hurt in ways that I hadn't felt in a long while. Every muscle in my body felt pummeled. "I'm going to need a gentle massage tomorrow, and to rest up for Monday night. I have to be at my strongest then." Pausing, I sought for the right words. "I want you to know how much I love you," I finally said.

He tried to press his finger to my lips but I gently pushed his hand away.

"Let me speak, please."

"I'm sorry. I just know you feel like crap and I didn't want you to stress yourself." He sat back. "Besides, I don't want to hear it."

"How do you know what I was going to say?"

He snorted. "Any time you start saying how much you love me, it only means you're afraid we're not going to make it. Camille, I *know* very well just how much you love me. And you know how much I love you. Years ago, we bound ourselves together. The ritual of Eleshinar doesn't fade. It doesn't vanish as time goes on. It's beneath our very skin, etched in silver, binding us together for as long as we wear these bodies. It means that neither you nor I can ever walk away for good."

I paused, then leaned back into the thick of the bubbles again. "I know. I tried once and it didn't work."

"I chased you down because we're meant to be together. I may share you with the lizard and the fox-boy, but you and I, we have something unique. I'm your Alpha, and you're my queen, Camille." He took my hand in his, the jet of his skin a startling contrast against my pale fingers. As he pressed his lips to my palm, he whispered, "Until we cross the veil to the Land of the Silver Falls, I will be with you. I will stand with you. I will be your champion, my love."

I cupped his chin in my hand and forced him to look at me. His eyes were clear, his love so strong I felt it wrap around my shoulders like a soothing cape.

"Promise me something. You, most of all, know how important it is to see Maggie grow up strong. If somehow I don't come through this—and don't tell me there isn't a chance because we're facing goddamn Shadow Wing—promise me that you'll take care of our baby gargoyle. She's the closest we'll ever have to children, and I want to know that you'll watch over her." The thought had weighed heavily on my mind the past few days.

Trillian held my hand, pressing his lips to it again. "I give you my promise, as your husband, bound to you by both the ritual of Eleshinar and the ritual of Soul Binding, I will guard her and take care of her as long as I'm alive."

Relieved, I let out a breath I didn't know I'd been holding.

"Thank you. It's not that I don't trust Smoky or Morio or my sisters, but when you give your word to me, I trust it more than I trust anybody else's. You have always been an honorable man, one I'm proud to call my husband." I felt myself getting a little teary. "I'm sorry, I'm just so tired, and my head is pounding."

"Come then, let me get you to bed." He helped me out

of the tub and gently carried me into the bedroom after I dried off, tucking me beneath the covers in the giant bed I shared with all of my men. "Are you hungry?"

I was about to say no, but then realized that my stomach was clenching partially because it was empty. "Yeah, but something simple, please. Some toast and broth or applesauce?"

As he headed out to call one of the servants, I realized just how lucky I was. And I hoped to hell that after Monday night, I'd still have my family intact.

⚔

SMOKY WOKE me up early Sunday morning. "How are you feeling?"

I blinked, realizing that all three of them had slept on the lounges. Serving as both sofas and spare beds in case one of us was sick and the others needed to give them space in the bed, they were comfortable and wide enough to really stretch out on.

Morio and Trillian were still asleep, so I slipped into a warm robe and slippers and tiptoed past both them and Maggie's crib where she was snoring like a stuffy-nosed cat. I followed Smoky out into the main sitting room of our chambers. We had more room in our suite than we had had back at the house, including a kitchenette that had been installed at my insistence. I didn't want to have to ask the servants to get me something every time I felt hungry.

"I'm all right. Still aching but my headache has lifted and I'm actually hungry." I frowned. "What's wrong?"

"Nothing. I was hoping you'd feel up to a flight." He

shrugged, his hair moving around him as though there were a draft. "I thought we could go out and fly for a while."

I realized that he was feeling as restless as I was. "Sure. Let me get dressed."

I slipped back into the bedroom, then into the walk-in dressing room. It was far more than a closet, with plenty of room for all our clothes, and a vanity and bench, a large ottoman, and enough mirrors to see from any angle. I changed into my black cat suit, then laced up my patent leather witchy boots, and shrugged into a heavy jacket, zipping it up. I still loved my corsets and skirts and stilettos, but I had learned the hard way over the years to dress for the occasion. And flying on the back of a dragon during autumn? *Cold*. Hence: dress warm.

I sat down and slapped on a quick but effective face of makeup, then back through the bedroom and into our living room.

"Ready," I said, making certain my circlet was firmly seated on my head. I wasn't allowed to take it off unless I was in bed or in the bathtub. One of the rules of being a queen, it turned out.

Smoky hustled me out the door, grumbling as the guard followed us. But even he hadn't been able to convince Aeval and Titania that I didn't need a contingent of bodyguards with me at every moment. They hung back, though, as we had agreed, and followed at a distance.

As one of the conditions of taking the throne, I had insisted that, near the private garden, they set up a landing field. It had to be big enough for Smoky to change shape on, take off from, and land on. It was on a knoll, with a large stone fence around it. And the knoll, too, was guarded, to prevent any would-be dragon slayers to sneak in.

As we approached the center of the field, the guards hung back. Smoky glanced over his shoulder at them, then looked back at me.

"I got a phone call this morning, around six-ish." His voice was soft, so low that I could barely catch what he was saying. "It was from Estelle Dugan."

I froze. It had been a long time since I had heard that name. Estelle Dugan was a nurse and a health care worker, and she was in charge of taking care of St. George. Georgio Profeta had once seen Smoky turn into a dragon, and the poor man, who had never fully been right in the head to start with, had snapped. After that, he fancied himself St. George, and for a number of years he had sought out Smoky, determined to slay him. But a plastic sword and a garbage can shield bore no damage against a dragon, even in human form.

Before long, he slid so far into his delusion that Smoky had arranged for someone to watch over him, given St. George had no family left. Estelle Dugan had been his caretaker for almost two years now.

"What did she want?" I asked, though I knew in my heart what the answer was. Georgio's health had never been good.

"He died peacefully shortly after midnight. Estelle was with him. She said he seemed to clear for a moment, and he looked at her and said, 'Tell him I said thank you for everything. And that I could never kill such a magnificent beast.' And with that, he turned his head to the side, took one last breath, and died." Smoky squinted, staring at the sky.

I slowly sank to the ground. "Oh, poor St. George. I don't know why, but this hits hard. He never meant to hurt anybody, really."

Smoky squatted beside me, tipping my chin up. "Love, it was bound to happen sooner or later. At least he's had a good life the past couple of years, safe and protected and free to roam the halls of his imagination."

I let Smoky pull me into his arms and hug me until the tears began to lessen.

"I'm just on edge. Monday is looming in my thoughts and all around, it feels like change and separation and death are constantly dogging our heels." I sniffed back my tears, accepting the handkerchief he offered me and blowing my nose. "Georgio was—he was and always will represent those who are lost and cannot fend for themselves. At least in my heart."

"But he's free now, to recuperate and renew himself, and hopefully he'll find the part of him that got lost along the way. He went easily and free from pain, with someone there who cared. That's all any of us can hope for, really."

Now I understood why Smoky needed to go flying. He needed the freedom to mourn in his own way, and I felt honored that he wanted me with him. I stood back as he shifted form. He looped his long, sinuous neck down, staring at me with those brilliant blue eyes, and I swung myself aboard. I held onto his mane as a long strand of hair wrapped around my waist to hold me steady, and then we were up and into the air, flying toward the mountains.

We flew long and hard, and when I glanced down I

realized we were on the way to Mount Rainier, where Smoky had his own Barrow. He swept down, toward a house near there. It was where Georgio had lived, with Estelle. Smoky tipped his wing, saluting the ground, and then we caught an updraft and soared again, sweeping back toward Talamh Lonrach Oll, away from the past, and back toward our present.

CHAPTER TEN
Menolly

"You've got to be kidding me," I said, staring at the desk.

"I wish I was," Roman said. "There's no way I'll make it back before next month, and maybe not even then. Things are so screwed up over here that it's going to take us weeks to sort out what the hell Harriman was up to. I have no clue what he was thinking, but the accounts and ledgers are a total mess. It looks like he's been embezzling money owed to my mother, and from what I can tell, he's been encouraging vampires to go out hunting for humans, which means we have a nightmare on our hands."

"This is not good," I said, shaking my head. Harriman was lucky he got off with being staked. Although I had a feeling Roman had prolonged the end.

"That's an understatement. Public relations for this thing is going to be insane, and I've asked Mother to fly me over the best handlers we can find to take charge of this situation. The humans in this country are ready to make vampire slaying a national sport. If we don't find a way to make amends, all I can say is that our kind won't be welcome here much longer."

He stopped abruptly, as though he'd suddenly run out of steam.

I cleared my throat. "So, basically you're doing major damage control."

"That's about the size of it."

"What about Harriman himself?" I was pretty sure that I already knew the answer.

"Dust. First thing we did when we got here. Actually, I took care of it to make sure it was done right. Now, I wish I still had him alive, so I could make him realize just what a fuckup he was." Roman's voice darkened and I found myself thinking that I never wanted to get on his bad side.

"That's about all you could do, I guess. There's no bringing them back when they go over the line into their predator." I had seen that myself, when I had to stake a good friend.

"What about you? How are things going?" Roman sounded lonely.

I didn't want to worry him even more than he was already was, but he had to know. I glanced around my office, making sure nobody else was around to hear me.

"We're gating Shadow Wing to Otherworld tomorrow night. I'll be over there and so will Nerissa. It's time to finish this war and be done with it."

There was a silence on the other end, and then, his voice ever so slightly uncertain, Roman asked, "You're actually going to do this?"

"We have to. He's eating his way through a battalion, adding to his power with every kill. If we don't do it now, we may never be strong enough. It's only a matter of time before he'll be able to gate himself through the worlds without anybody else's help." I paused before I added, "Roman, you knew this day was coming."

"Yes, but I thought I'd be there to help. Or that you'd— Maybe somebody else would take care of matters." A mournful note hung in his words.

"Did *you* ask somebody else to go clean up after Harriman?"

After a moment of silence, he said, "I understand. Truly. But Menolly, there's so much danger there. Please be careful."

"Of course we will, but you know there aren't any guarantees in life. This is something we can't just walk away from." I glanced at the door as a rap on it caught my attention. "Somebody's here. I have to go. Nerissa and I send our love."

He paused, then softly said, "My love to both of you. Call me when it's over. I need to know that you—and Nerissa—are all right."

As I hung up, I thought that we'd be lucky to stagger out alive. But as long as we took down Shadow Wing, that was all that mattered.

⚔

When I answered the door, it turned out to be a messenger. The youth was dressed in a black, sleek suit and dark sunglasses, Roman's standard uniform for his servants.

"Message from the Queen, Your Majesty. She asks that you meet her in the observatory in half an hour. She bids you to dress appropriately." His voice was smooth and unflinching, but I could feel the respect. He stood at attention, waiting for my reply.

When Blood Wyne asked for your presence, you showed.

I nodded. "All right. Follow me." I headed down the hall, with my guide in tow, stopping at my suite. Turning, I motioned for him to wait in the hall. "I'll be out in a moment."

Blood Wyne wasn't as locked into the past as her son was. Dressing for an audience with her meant wearing impeccably clean clothes, nicely tailored, with neatly brushed hair. I quickly changed into a pantsuit, dark blue linen with pressed creases down the front of the pants. Beneath the blazer, I wore a white sweater beaded with delicate sapphires. I added a gorgeous sapphire pendant that Roman had given me, pulled my braids back into a ponytail, and put on stiletto ankle boots. Then, satisfied that I was about as prepped as I was going to get, I followed the guard to the observatory.

The observatory was at the top of the mansion and was really just a room with a retractable roof from where we could watch the stars or have a rooftop party. The guide hurried up the stairs, glancing behind me to make sure I was following him as we approached the door.

"Are you ready, Your Majesty?"

I nodded. "As I'll ever be. Go ahead and announce me."

He tapped on the door, then opened it and stepped inside. I could hear him announce me, and that was my cue to greet Blood Wyne as he withdrew, shutting the door behind us.

"Greetings, my daughter," Blood Wyne said.

The Queen of the Crimson Veil was standing by a

picture window that looked over Roman's estate. She was taller than I was, but then most people were, and her hair rose in a chignon, with a diadem of rubies and diamonds tucked in front of the elaborate coiffure. Her skin was as pale as cream, she had been alive so very long, and her eyes were the color of hoarfrost. She was regal, elegant, and oozed royalty with every movement. Blood Wyne's features were refined, and her lips bore no color. She was wearing a Victorian dress in crimson brocade, and the train swept out behind her. But most noticeable was her power.

I knelt in front of her, bowing my head as was expected. "Your Majesty."

"Come." She motioned for me to follow her over to the leather sofa and chair that sat in front of the picture window.

I obeyed. Outside the window, the city lights sparkled in the cloud-laden night. Beyond the walls of the estate, traffic flew by, far sparser than in the day, but still—the comings and goings of people everywhere kept the city alive.

Blood Wyne walked over to the window and stared out into the night.

"I remember when the lights of a city were measured in torches, and candles lit the village houses. I've been alive for an incredibly long time, Menolly. I've walked the outskirts of the Crimson Veil many times, but I've never fully given myself over to it. Kesana, the mother of all vampires, may have created the Veil, but it has a life of its own now. It thrives, even as vampires thrive. The day none of us exist within this world is the day it will fade and vanish."

I wasn't sure what she was trying to say, but I had learned to wait and listen instead of jumping to conclusions.

She turned, pressing her back against the window as she stared at me. "When first we met a year and a half ago, you were repressing your nature. Running from it. You've come a long way since then. You still resist certain aspects of your life as a vampire, but you've opened up." Pausing, she turned again to stare out of the window.

"I've learned a lot over the past eighteen months." I hesitated, wondering whether I should tell her about Shadow Wing, but since Roman knew, his mother probably should. "I have news you should be aware of."

"Well, it can't be that you're pregnant," Blood Wyne said with a chuckle. "What is it?"

I licked my lips. She had promised not to interfere with our war against Shadow Wing, but I still didn't trust that she would be on board with me putting my life on the line.

"Tomorrow night, my sisters and I are facing the Demon Lord. We've figured out how to fight him, and we're taking the war to Otherworld to finish it."

Her gaze fastened on me, she remained silent.

"Nerissa and I will both be going. I hope we'll both be coming back, but given the nature of our task, I can't guarantee it." It was my turn to wait.

She didn't fidget, or shift, or look away. Instead, she just stood silent for what felt like an eternity, but in reality it was probably no more than a couple minutes.

Finally, she inclined her head. "And so you come to the end of this battle? Do you anticipate victory?"

Surprised by the question, I stopped to think. "Do I

think we can win? Honestly? I think so, but I don't know what costs we'll incur. But if we don't attack now, while we know what to do while he's still vulnerable, then we pave the way for Shadow Wing to gate over here. He's gaining power daily, eating the souls of his followers in the Sub-Realms. Soon, the spirit seals won't be able to guard against him. Portal or not, he'll find a way to rip through into this world. We can't let that happen."

Blood Wyne inclined her head again. "Do you know why I picked you to be my son's wife?"

I nodded. "You wanted to cement my powers with the Vampire Nation, and you don't trust your other children to take up the crown, should something happen to you and to Roman."

She glided over to my side and sat down next to me. "True, but it was more than that. You are true to your causes, Menolly. You don't back down and you don't renege when you've given your word. You're bound by your duties, and you take your oaths seriously. I knew that you would make an honest queen, one who was willing to put her life on the line for what needs to be done. And so, you prove me right yet again."

I felt flattered, though it was daunting having the queen of vampires putting so much faith into me. "I thought you might be angry at me for chancing my life over this."

At that, she laughed, and a rare smile spread over her face. "Oh, my dear, I am not my son. As much as I am proud of Roman, he carries too much of his hopes and dreams from his youth, from his days when he still breathed and walked in the sun. He hasn't learned to put them aside, not enough to be an effective ruler. If something were to happen to me, I hope you will help him learn how to rule with his head, not his emotions."

I didn't want to argue with her, but I couldn't help myself. "Don't you think that carrying those emotions into his current life makes him stronger? It keeps him in touch with humanity, and that makes him more effective as a leader in this current day and age. With the Vampire Rights bill locked in the mire of hate groups versus our advocates, we need to show the people we're not so far different than they are."

Blood Wyne frowned, but she didn't look angry. "On one level, I would agree with you, but we can't allow them to view us as their equals. We're predators, Menolly. We're their superiors in so many ways."

"Then, do *you* want to take over? Pretend to be their friends but actually become their rulers?" I shook my head. "We may be superior in strength and lifespan and powers, but we're no better than they are intellectually, and we're a little subpar when it comes to controlling our urges, I think. Our inner predators push us harder, which is why we must resist their power. It's harder to resist the thought of being somebody's overlord when your inner nature is urging you to drink their blood—and when you know you can do it."

"Would you have us neuter ourselves? Do you *truly* believe vampires should have rights?" Blood Wyne's eyes narrowed, but she sounded truly curious.

I let out a grunt. "I'm not certain what the answer is, to be honest. Yes, I think we should have rights—the right to be counted as individuals. The right to vote? Yes. And when a vampire is killed—one who hasn't done any real harm—then I want the murderer to be brought up on charges if the authorities can prove it. Obviously, it's harder to prove murder when we turn to dust and nobody knows if we're actually still alive. But if we insist on lording it over the living, on rubbing their noses in the fact that we're stronger than they are, then we're setting ourselves up as demagogues. And that's asking for trouble."

Blood Wyne considered my words for a moment. "I told you there were reasons I chose you for my son's wife. This is just another example. While I don't feel comfortable with your analysis, I think I agree. You see, we've been asked to send a speaker to Washington, DC, to speak before Congress about the Vampire Rights bill at the end of the month. I want you to go."

I fell back against the seat cushions. "Me?"

"Yes. You are good at making a case for our people. You understand both sides. You're close enough to the days when you were alive to remember what it was like. You'll be able to relate to the fears that the humans have." Blood Wyne nodded. "It's settled. Provided you come out of your battle alive, and *I trust you will* because we need you here, you'll journey to Washington, DC, at the end of the month to put in an impassioned plea for the Vampire Rights Act. If we don't win this year, we most certainly shall next year."

I didn't know what to say. The last thing I had expected was to become a politician, though I supposed that went along with being royalty. But preparing a speech for Congress in the next couple weeks? The very idea seemed insane. Then things got even more surreal.

"In fact," Blood Wyne said, "I like the idea so much that I propose to send you and Nerissa around the country on a nationwide goodwill tour. Roman can join you at several major functions. We'll stage vampire-hosted soirees for top community leaders in a number of major cities, and you and Nerissa will co-host. Seeing the pair of you—with her still alive, and you a vampire—will only reinforce the concept that vampires and the living can coexist in peace."

She sounded so satisfied with her idea that I wasn't sure what to say. Any protests would fall on deaf ears, that much I already knew.

"How long do you think this tour will last?" I finally asked.

She shrugged. "We won't rush it—and this will give the two of you a chance to see the country. I have the feeling neither one of you would mind getting out and doing some traveling, am I right?"

I cleared my throat. This was a good time to bring up another subject.

"To be honest, I don't think we would mind, but… Your Majesty, Nerissa and I haven't been exactly happy here. It's not because of Roman or you," I hurried to add, "but we feel cooped up. We feel as though we're prisoners in an ivory tower."

Blood Wyne's gaze settled back on my face. "Do you regret your choice to marry my son?"

That was a hard question, given she had given me no choice in the matter.

"I respect you as the queen of vampires. Therefore, when you required it, we married him. Don't get me wrong. I *do* love Roman, but not the way he wishes. But Nerissa and I…we aren't royalty at heart. We prefer a more private life. However, we gave our word, and we'll stick to it."

I stood, pacing over to the window. It was easier to talk when I wasn't facing those ancient eyes. "I understand why you picked me for your son. I truly do. I just wish he had the chance to find someone who made him happy—who could give her all to him. Roman is exciting and he fits a part of my nature, but Nerissa won my heart, and her happiness is my highest priority."

Then, Blood Wyne did something she almost never did. She rose, joined me at the window, and put her hand on my shoulder—about as close to a hug as I ever expected to get.

"Things have a way of working out. I think, perhaps, the national tour would be good for both of you. You'll have to take guards, of course, but that can be worked out. It will give you time to yourselves."

"Will Roman understand, though? I truly don't want to hurt him." I glanced up at the ancient queen.

"Oh, he will understand. I'm sure of it. But tell me this, if he does find someone who speaks to his heart and who loves him back, how will you feel? What would you think if he eventually takes a mistress?"

I thought about her question for a moment. In a way, I supposed I might be hurt, but then again, I wanted him to have what Nerissa and I had. He deserved it, and I knew that I wasn't the woman to give him that.

"I think, it might be hard in some ways, but I would bless them both and wish them the best of joy and happiness. Because if he can find someone who loves him the way I love Nerissa, then he'll never feel alone again."

Blood Wyne nodded, then turned as we went back to

staring out into the night, two disparate women bound by similar fates, sharing so many commonalities.

※

BY THE TIME I returned to my office, Blood Wyne had given me the task of choosing one major city from each state that Nerissa and I would like to visit. I was about to call Nerissa in to tell her the news when my phone rang. It was Roman again.

"Hey," I said, answering. "I just spent over an hour chatting with your mother."

He sputtered. "*Mother? Chat?* Well, that's a new one. Was she in a good mood or a bad mood?"

"Neither. More…a thoughtful one. She's made some interesting decisions, but they can hold if you're in a hurry." I wasn't sure what Roman would have to say about Blood Wyne's decision, but I knew he wouldn't fight it.

"Actually, I am in a hurry. I just wanted to ask you if you could have Ernie forward every email we got from Harriman in the past six months." He sounded exasperated.

"More trouble?"

"Yeah, there is, but I really don't have the time to go into it now. Thank gods I've got help over here. Harriman's captain of the guard—her name is Valentina—is amazing. She disagreed with his policies and she kept an eye on him, suspecting this was going to happen. She's walking me through all the fuckups the idiot made. And there were plenty of them."

"Good. I'm glad you have help. I'll tell Ernie as soon as we get off the phone. Wish me luck tomorrow night."

Roman's irritation seemed to drain out of his voice. "Of course I do. You and Nerissa be careful. Come back in one piece. It's important. I mean it."

"Your mother agrees with you there. We'll do whatever we can to stay as safe as we can. I'll call you when it's over. Or…on the outside chance something happens, I'll ask somebody to call you for me." We murmured our goodbyes and then hung up. As I went to find Ernie—Roman's chief of communications—it occurred to me that maybe Blood Wyne had a psychic bone to her. Things were changing—I could feel them in the wind. Maybe things would work out for the best, after all.

⚔

Nerissa and I hadn't been out on a date in ages, just the two of us, so I rescued her from her desk after I talked to Ernie, and we went to the Wayfarer, more out of a need to touch a piece of our past rather than anything else. Derrick set us up in the best booth, and we ordered a steak and lobster dinner for Nerissa and a bottle of flavored blood for me. Apparently, Morio's trick had caught on in the magical community and now was spreading as a business.

"Morio should have patented this spell. He could have made a fortune," I said, staring at the bottle.

"I think he'd see it as a form of open-source magic, rather than proprietary," Nerissa said, leaning back in the booth. She was wearing a gorgeous hot pink mini-dress, and her hair shimmered, hanging down around her shoulders. She was hot beyond hot, and every time I looked at her, I was reminded of why I had fallen in love.

"I've got some news for you. How would you like to go on a trip around the country with me? We'll stop in a major city in every state." I took a long sip of my blood, relishing the taste of clam chowder. It was a small bottle, appetizer size, and I was looking forward to the fish-and-chips flavor for dinner.

Nerissa blinked. "You're kidding? I think that would be a blast. But we'll never be able to get away."

"*Au contraire*, my dear. Blood Wyne herself suggested it. She wants me to speak before Congress at the end of the month on the Vampire Rights Act. While neither she nor I expect it to pass this time, we discussed what might help for next year, and to that end, she plans on sending us out as goodwill ambassadors around the country to stir up support for it. She thinks by seeing you—a werepuma, alive and breathing, with me—a vampire, not so alive and breathing—that people will feel more at ease and provide a groundswell of support for the next election."

Nerissa's eyes flashed, and her lips spread into a wide grin. "What if, by some miracle, the bill *does* pass this year?"

"Then we can just strengthen it with a tour like that. I thought you might like it, and since Blood Wyne thought of it, there's really no way to say no." I paused, hoping she would jump aboard the idea. I hated trying to convince her to do something she wasn't thrilled with. Nerissa had already compromised so much for me.

She clapped her hands. "I can hardly wait. I've always loved traveling, and this way we'll be able to really see the country. Can we stay for a few days in each city?"

"I'm sure we can," I said, relief pouring through me. "I'm so glad you like the idea."

She paused. "What about Roman, though? Will he be coming?"

"Blood Wyne said he could fly out for several of the actual meetings—we'll be giving speeches and hosting events for notables who support our cause. But he won't be coming on the actual tour. So it will be like an extended honeymoon. Fifty cities, if we spend two or three days in each city—that's four or five months of travel. You're sure you don't mind being away that long?" I suddenly realized just how long that was, and how much I'd miss my sisters, but I pushed aside the thought. This was a chance we might not have again.

Nerissa shook her head, her cheeks flushed. She reached across the table, taking my hand. "I don't mind. Not at all. In fact, it sounds like a dream. I'm so excited." She suddenly stopped, staring down at her plate. "First, we have to make sure…" Her words drifted off.

"Shadow Wing?" I asked.

She nodded. "Yes."

"Tomorrow night decides it. But for tonight, let's just hold onto the thought that we get a trip around the country. You know Blood Wyne will spring for the best accommodations. Where should we start? Blood Wyne is going to leave it up to us to decide the itinerary, as long as it coincides with cities that have a high vampire population."

And so we pushed aside the worries over Shadow Wing as we made plans for the trip. We sat in the booth for three hours, nibbling on our food, chatting with Derrick, and looking toward a future that seemed brighter than it had for a long time.

CHAPTER ELEVEN
Delilah

TRENYTH WAS THERE TO GREET US WHEN WE SHIFTED through the portals shortly after dusk, with a surprise by his side. Standing next to him was Feddrah-Dahns, the prince of the Dahns Unicorns. Mistletoe, his pixie servant, was straddling his horn.

We were standing on the northern border of Thistlewyd Deep, on the outskirts of the Windwillow Valley. The grass plains spread out behind us, the knee-high blades whispering in the constant susurration of wind that played through the area. Travelers could take days on end to plow through the never-ending grasslands.

We were probably one of the largest groups that had ever gated over together from Earthside. Besides my sisters and Nerissa, we had all the men with us, the nine Keraastar Knights, and twenty of Joreal's daemon soldiers.

Wilbur looked around, his eyes wide. "What the hell..." The look on his face said it all: for once, we had shocked him speechless. He just kept turning, looking in all directions.

The sky was clear, which meant it would be cold tonight. The moon wasn't showing—she was at her darkest tonight, and our only light at the moment was the glimmer of the unveiling stars. I closed my eyes, drifting in the quietude. Even with a party as large as ours, the lack of noise from traffic and appliances and the hurried scuffle of human interaction was calming. As nervous as I was, I also felt a sense of peace surround me.

The thicket that spread for hundreds of miles was made up of mostly conifers, very much like at home, dark and overgrown with vegetation. To the northeast was Dahnsburg, home of the Dahns unicorns, and the westernmost port on the edge of the Wyvern Ocean. To the west and southwest, the Deep spread out, buttressed along the way by Dahnsberry Lake and Willowyrd Glen. Eventually, Thistlewyd Deep blended into the forests of Darkynwyrd, where Raven Mother also roamed, and then out into the Ranakwa Fens—dangerous marshes that spread on for hundreds of miles. Over to the west of the Deep, the Tygerian Mountains split through the world, a long, trundling mountain range that was impossible to cross other than through the high mountain passes that were covered with mist and fog, and during the winter, with snow.

Camille ran over to Feddrah-Dahns. The two were good friends, and she threw her arms around the unicorn's neck, hugging him tightly. I looked around, hoping to see Sharah. Chase was looking too.

"Well met," Trenyth said, stepping forward to greet us. "Although I can't say that I'm glad for the circumstances bringing us together this evening."

Camille turned around, her face taut. "We feel the

same way, trust me. But circumstances are pointing toward now and we can't wait any longer. Joreal predicts that Shadow Wing may be able to break through the worlds within a month's time, possibly sooner."

That brought a resounding frown to Trenyth's face. The elf had been Queen Asteria's advisor when she was alive, and now he played the same role for Sharah.

"Then we'd best move forward with the plan."

"Trenyth, excuse me, but is Sharah here?" I didn't want to interrupt, but I knew Chase was champing at the bit to see her.

But Trenyth shook his head. "No, she was required back in Elqaneve. Official business. She sends her best blessings to you." He paused, turning to Chase. "And her love."

Chase acknowledged the message with a brief nod. "Understood. It's just as well. All our focus must be on the mission."

I glanced at him. He sounded different—a little stilted. But he saw me looking and gave me a faint smile, and I turned my attention back to Trenyth. "Raven Mother was supposed to meet us. Do you know if she'll be here?"

I knew just what Trenyth thought of Raven Mother, but he had centuries of practice and he didn't even bat an eye as he said, "She'll meet us as we enter the woodland."

"*We?*" Camille asked. "You're coming with us?"

He nodded. "Sharah asked me to attend. Queen Asteria was there at the beginning of this journey. Sharah and I felt that she would have wanted me to join you, to bear witness. You are about to make history—either way the cards fall. The elves will be there to watch."

I caught my breath as a shimmering form rose up

behind him. Queen Asteria was there, watching over her unrequited love. She had fallen hard for him, and it had been equally apparent how much he loved her, but her position stood in their way. They had never come together. I wanted to tell him that she was there—she was with him—but stopped myself. Sometimes, there were reasons people didn't know the dead followed them. If she wanted him to know, she'd find a way. Nobody had been more stubborn than the Elfin queen.

"Derisa and some of the priestesses from the Moon Mother's Grove are supposed to be here, too, but they seem to have been detained," he added.

"We can't wait for them, they'll have to catch up," Camille said. She turned to Feddrah-Dahns.

"I, too, shall come with you. My father gave me leave to come witness and do whatever I can to help." Feddrah-Dahns hoofed the ground, shaking his silky white mane. It shimmered under the darkening evening.

I shivered, zipping up my jacket as Shade handed me my cloak. I had brought it in case the night proved too cold, and now the temperature began to plunge as the skies darkened overhead, clear and panoramic.

Camille and her men took the lead, followed by four of her guards from the Barrow. Then came the Keraastar Knights. Menolly and Nerissa, with Wilbur between them, swung in beside the ninth Knight—Lisa. Then Roz and Vanzir and Shade and I fell in behind them. Trenyth, Feddrah-Dahns, and Mistletoe followed us. The daemon guards closed in behind and we set off, into the woods, toward the final showdown.

The Deep closed in around us almost immediately, and the woods were alive with the scuffle of animals, the rustle of tree and branch and bush and plant. The smell in these woods was pungent, thick with old magic and mushrooms and mildew and the tang of soil, sour from the decay of the detritus. The ground vibrated with the heartbeat of the Deep, a resonance so ancient it predated everyone and everything. It was feral, wild and untamed, and filled with the magic of the Fae and of Elementals and all things living between worlds. It made me uneasy, but I noticed that Luke and Amber didn't seem fazed by it, nor did Clyde, and they were Weres as well. The spirit seals must have attuned them to magic in a way most Weres never experienced.

Ahead, Camille wore the hide of the Black Beast and carried in one hand her new dagger that she had been so mysteriously gifted. In her other hand, she carried her yew walking staff. I knew the unicorn horn was deep in her cloak pocket, but she wisely kept it hidden. While we were grateful for Joreal's help, the thought that one of daemons might decide to run off with the horn was daunting, and too much a possibility for comfort.

As we worked our way into Thistlewyd Deep, I wasn't sure where we were going, but Camille seemed intent on a direction. Though we passed several forks in the road, she kept us in a straight direction, heading southwest into the heart of the forest.

Shade, who was walking by my side, took my hand as we crept along in the darkness. The only illumination we had were the eye catchers that floated around Morio and Camille, and I had the feeling they had learned to either summon them, or to create them. Nobody was entirely sure what exactly the lights were, but they were all over Otherworld.

We were about an hour into the Deep when Camille stopped, looking around. Another moment and there was a swirl of smoke in front of her, and then, a brilliant ruby flash and a raucous laughter that I recognized all too well.

"Well met, my friends, and welcome to the Deep. Thistlewyd awaits you, and so do I."

Raven Mother stood there. She made me antsy. Neither Menolly nor I understood how Camille put up with her, even though she had helped us in the past. I didn't trust her, but that could be because she was the very nature of the raven, and cats and birds weren't meant to mix.

When I looked at Raven Mother, the word *garish* came to mind. She was flamboyant to a degree that unsettled me, and she was as dangerous and crafty as the forest we were standing in. But her fate seemed inexorably linked to our own, so I kept my misgivings to myself.

"Well met," Camille said, dipping into a curtsey. "Thank you for helping us."

"Lovely lovely Fae Queen, of course I would help you, Camille, whom the Moon has claimed and brought into the dark shining realm. You hold my heart in your hands," Raven Mother added, looking at Bran.

The pair had not been on speaking terms as of late, but when he entered Camille's service as a Keraastar Knight, it seemed to forge a new respect between mother and son.

"I will do my best to keep him safe, but being your son, he will survive." Camille glanced back at Bran, who merely nodded.

The Elemental Lords were the only true Immortals,

and Bran was the son of not only Raven Mother but the Black Beast as well, which meant he was one of the few walking in the world who would never face death. And when I thought about that, it actually soothed me. He was one of the Keraastar Knights, and was also Immortal, which meant he could stand there forever and beat on Shadow Wing till Shadow Wing was dead, if it came to that. I was about to make a joke about sending him in on a non-suicide mission but then bit my tongue. I was learning to be diplomatic, and it occurred to me that wouldn't go over as well as it had in my head.

Raven Mother glanced at Feddrah-Dahns. "So one of the young comes home to nest."

Feddrah-Dahns dipped his head with a whinny. "Raven Mother, my father sends his regards. Do you think the Black Unicorn will mind my presence?"

She shrugged. "Why should he? You are one of his descendants. You were there when he went through his last cycle. Just don't attempt to correct him and you should be well, well indeed you should. *But keep the pixie in line.*"

Feddrah-Dahns murmured a soft agreement and edged away.

"Where do we set up?" Camille asked.

"Come, a little farther into the Deep. The Black Beast has prepared an arena." Raven Mother turned and, taking the lead, began to lead us into the undergrowth.

Pushing through the heavy brush seemed a trial at first, but after about ten minutes we found ourselves on yet another path, one that couldn't be seen from the main trail. We wove around bushes and ferns, and the occasional boulder, and all along the path, the sides were alive with the sound of creatures snuffling through the woods. I wasn't what they were, but they kept to themselves, not daring to come out against such a sizable force.

I glanced behind at the daemon guards. They looked uneasy, but they were minding their manners, and I slipped back to talk to the captain. His name was Welbourne, and he seemed to have a good command over his men.

"Thank you for coming on the mission," I said, walking along beside him.

He shrugged, the leather of his armor squeaking slightly as he did so. "If we can help defeat Shadow Wing, then we've done our duty. None of us expects to return to our home. We consider this to most likely be our last stand, and we will fight to the death against him, as needed."

The daemons looked incredibly human-like, except for the glow in their eyes and the energy that surrounded them. They were charismatic rogues, where very few demons were, but they were willing to work with others, also unlike most run-of-the-mill demons. In fact, Vanzir was one of the few demons that we had found who wasn't just out for himself.

I felt a chill run down my back. He was deadly serious. At that moment it hit me, we were all potentially walking to our doom. Shadow Wing wasn't a god, but he wasn't just another run-of-the-mill demon general. And who knew what kind of power he had absorbed?

"You're right. This could be our last stand." I paused, then asked, "So why did you volunteer?"

He shook his head. "We were chosen as the brightest and best among the army. We're from Joreal's personal guard. We're battle-ready, and used to pressure. If we can't help keep Shadow Wing surrounded until your crew can take him on, then nobody can." He cleared his throat. "Now, please allow me to return to my thoughts. I'm making my peace with this life."

I nodded, then moved back to Shade's side. We followed Raven Mother in silence until the path gave way and opened out into a large clearing. Surrounded by the blasted trunks of ancient trees, the ground was compacted and hard—I couldn't tell whether it was mostly stone or dirt. The trees looked like they had been blasted by lightning, their trunks rising into the sky, black skeletons that had been scorched into charcoal.

We spread out around the clearing. Menolly and I joined Camille, who was standing next to Raven Mother.

"What is this place?" I asked, glancing around. I could see spirits walking through the clearing, taking no notice of us. They weren't only spirits of Fae, but of creatures, too, and birds. "Something happened here, didn't it? Some terrible war?"

Raven Mother's smile slid away and she nodded. "Yes, this was the site for a renegade group of sorcerers who were hiding out after the Scorching Wars. They thought they could hide in my forests, they did, but they were wrong. The elves sought leave to track them down, and there was a terrible fight. Rather than surrender, the sorcerers destroyed the area with one mighty spell, killing themselves and their attackers. Nothing has grown in this spot since then, and it remains haunted and deserted by all save for the spirits who walk this forest."

I glanced around, suddenly in awe of the vast history of this place. The Scorching Wars had changed the face of our home world, and destroyed hundreds of thousands of lives over a long period. If we failed to kill Shadow Wing, he could easily bring another reign of terror to the land.

I took a step closer to Menolly, who glanced at me, nodding as if she could read my thoughts. "It seems fitting to stage this battle here, then."

"A blighted land for a blighted enemy." Raven Mother paused before adding, "And I bring one other card to the game." She stepped back, turning toward one of the large trees. Out from behind the tree stepped a woman who looked like she was made of silver. I blinked, but Camille gasped and stepped forward.

"Lady Pentangle," she whispered, kneeling.

Pentangle was one of the Hags of Fate. The Mistress of Magic.

Pentangle was shorter than I was, but she felt *oh so incredibly powerful.* Dressed in a silver-beaded silver and ivory corset over a long flowing ivory skirt, she wore a headdress that shimmered like ice and was crowned with crystal antlers. Her eyes were deep black, sparkling with silver flecks, and she held a glowing wand in one hand while her other hand trailed a wake of sparkles as she gestured.

I glanced over at the daemons, who were watching her with fear in their eyes, then back at the Mistress of Magic, wondering what she was doing here. It seemed odd to me that she would keep company with Raven Mother.

"I come to help balance the worlds, but my help is limited," Pentangle said. "I can offer you one gift, but it comes with a steep price."

"What is it?" Camille asked, rising to stand before the mother of all magic.

Pentangle waited till we were all silent, listening to her. "You must all agree, or I cannot grant the boon. Raven Mother will be exempt from this, of course, given her nature. As will her son and the Black Beast."

Smoky nodded. "Understood."

I sucked in a deep breath. Whatever her gift was, it was bound to be a doozy, especially if we all had to agree. The entire clearing felt charged, like a live wire, and I had the sudden image of a clock with a timer, and the minutes were counting down. Which, I supposed, they were.

"I can cast a Circle that will prevent Shadow Wing from leaving the area. He will be trapped in here, but so will all of you. You will have twenty-four hours to fight him before the barrier vanishes. I hope you will not need to use all of that time."

"Why can't you just trap him in a Circle and leave him? Do we even have to fight him?" one of the daemons asked.

Pentangle turned a cool eye to him. "I could, but at some point, he would find a way to emerge. Time continues to run in this world, and while the Hags of Fate and their kin are immortal, our magical creations are not. I could try to freeze him within a magical circle, but there would be no guarantee that it would last. Especially when he wields powerful magic himself."

"We can't just leave him for future generations to deal with. We will not bequeath this monster on *our children*, or their children in turn," Trenyth said.

Something about his words struck me as odd. I looked at him. The emphasis on "our children" had been strong—too strong. He glanced up to see me staring at him, held my gaze for a moment, then looked away.

"Trenyth is right," Camille said. "We came to destroy a

threat to all worlds. I suggest we focus on that. And if Pentangle can give us the gift of a twenty-four hour trap to keep Shadow Wing from bolting, I suggest we willingly accept. It means we're all in more danger, given we can't get away from him, but it means he's within attack range for that long."

"Put it to a vote. You must be unanimous before I will create the barrier." Pentangle walked over to Raven Mother's side. "Remember: while someone may enter the barrier, no one will be able to leave it."

"Do we need to debate this?" Camille turned to her husbands. To a man, they straightened and put on their game faces.

"All right. Let's hear it," Menolly said. "I'm in." She pointed to Nerissa.

"I'm in," Nerissa echoed.

Wilbur spoke up. "I'm in it to win it." He sounded steadier than he had in a long time.

Menolly pointed her way around the Circle. When she came to me, I glanced at Shade, who nodded.

"Accept Pentangle's offer," I said.

No one disagreed, not even Trenyth. When we had taken our vote, Camille went over to talk to Pentangle. I motioned to Trenyth, who frowned, but joined me.

"Can we talk privately for a moment?" I asked, glancing over my shoulder to make sure Chase wasn't in earshot.

He didn't look happy about it, but nodded. "All right, how about over by that tree stump?" He pointed a few yards away to where a broken stump jutted out of the ground.

I followed him. When we were away from the rest of

the group, I took a deep breath and decided that directness was called for. We didn't have time for small chat.

"*Our* children? Why did that feel personal?" I tapped him on the arm as he started to turn away. "Tell me, so that if we come through this, I can help prepare *him*." I knew, as sure as I knew my name, what was going on.

Trenyth cast his eyes toward the ground. "You surprise me. Usually, you're… Well, never mind that. All right, though truly, you have no business knowing this."

"I have every business knowing it, since Chase is my friend and blood-oath brother." I leaned in. "You're fathering an heir to the throne, aren't you?"

He stiffened, then behind those ancient, unreadable eyes, I saw a spark glimmer.

"Yes, even now, Sharah carries my child. But I will never become king to her queen. I honor Chase and respect the man, but my first duty is to Elqaneve and the Elfin race. Sharah understands her duty as well."

"What about Astrid?"

"You know that my race will never accept an heir who is not full-blooded elf. It's been this way since time began, and it will be the way far longer than you or I will tread this soil."

I shook my head, staring at my feet. "I never would have thought you capable of this, Trenyth."

He let out an exasperated sigh. "This was not *my* idea. Sharah asked me to father her child. She truly loves Chase, and she didn't wish to bring someone to her bed who would demand the right to share it after the child is born. I agreed. My heart will always belong to one who no longer walks this world, and Sharah knows this. She also knows I won't ever seek to supplant Chase."

I fell silent for a moment, thinking. Trenyth was an honorable man. He would obey Sharah's wishes, and he was still—and forever would—hold a torch for Queen Asteria. But how would Chase take the news?

"If the pregnancy holds—will she be required to give birth to more than one heir?"

"Two, three would be preferable. Chase will just have to accept that's a part of her life. Her heart belongs to him, but she is subject to the laws with which she governs." Trenyth nodded at Camille and Pentangle, who were talking. "This is neither the time nor place to discuss this. Leave it till after the battle. Focus on the immediate need. Control your emotions, Delilah. We all have to be at the top of our games."

I wanted to argue, but he was right. I closed my eyes, focusing on my breathing as I brought my attention back to the present. We had a battle to win, and in the long scheme of things, perhaps Sharah knew best. Perhaps Chase would understand. And this way, she was free of marrying someone for the sake of birthing a child, and perhaps Chase could join her as her consort.

"I'm sorry. You're right, this isn't the time to discuss this." I turned to go.

Trenyth stopped me. "Delilah? Please, don't think ill of me."

"I don't. But why is your race so freaking stubborn?"

He chuckled. "We wouldn't be elves if we weren't. This is our way. It's our custom."

As I returned to where Menolly and Camille were, Menolly gave me an odd look.

"What's up?" she mouthed.

I shook my head. "Best leave it for later."

Camille finished with her meeting and now she called out, "Shamas, I need you and Welbourne over here."

As the two men moved toward her, another shuffle in the bushes alerted us and then, out stepped the Black Unicorn. He was massive. Even though he had been reborn only a couple years ago, he already outstripped the biggest horse I'd ever seen. He was vibrant, thoroughly alive and in his prime. He was black as night, black as pitch, black as the darkness of an empty soul, yet his horn was crystal, with strands of gold and silver running through it. Once every thousand years, like the phoenix, the Black Unicorn shed his body and was reborn. His hide and horn would then go to someone chosen to bear them, powerful magical artifacts.

Camille stepped forward, wearing her robe made of his hide, and she withdrew her unicorn horn. Then she knelt by his feet.

"Stand, Queen of the Dusk and Twilight." He didn't speak, but his voice echoed within our minds. "I am here. I will stand with you over this battle."

He said no more as Raven Mother moved to his side.

Shade was beside me then, wrapping an arm around my waist. "Can you feel it?" he whispered. "The forest feels like it's watching in anticipation. The world knows that we're standing at a crossroads in time."

I looked up at the sky. Overhead, the stars were twinkling down, an icy backdrop to the night. The moon was silent, hidden in her shadows, cloaked in her mystery. The temperature was dropping, and I shivered as I realized how cold it was getting. Shade snuggled close and then he turned me to him, and pressed his lips to mine. We kissed, ignoring everyone around us, locked in one last desperate kiss.

And finally Camille spoke. "It's time to begin. Shamas and Wilbur are preparing to cast the Demon Gate. It will take them a couple of hours, so I suggest we spend the time in meditation, to steady our nerves and prepare."

"I will cast the barrier as soon as the Demon Gate is ready for use," Pentangle said.

Shade and I moved off to one side, sitting in silence on a log. Smoky was lighting a fire to keep us warm until then. Camille and the rest of the Keraastar Knights formed a circle, with Morio and Trillian guarding them, and while I couldn't tell what they were doing, I had a feeling they were merging their energies, blending their powers.

Menolly and Nerissa had wandered to one side as well, and they were doing much the same as Shade and I were —spending the last couple hours we had until battle, with each other. Wilbur was helping Vanzir and Roz, and the daemons were keeping guard around the clearing. Feddrah-Dahns and Trenyth were holding quiet conversation with Raven Mother and the Black Unicorn.

Shade pulled a thin blanket out of his pack, draping it around our shoulders. We didn't speak, merely held each other, as the night wore on and we learned whether we would have a future to look forward to.

CHAPTER TWELVE

Camille

THE GATE WAS READY. It stood twenty feet tall, a construct made from two of the charcoaled tree trunks from the surrounding area. Smoky and Shade had helped to build the structure, carrying the trees as if they were toothpicks, and planting them in the ground in the southern quadrant of the clearing. Shamas had spent the past three hours covering the logs with runes, drawn in his own blood. Wilbur had helped him. Each time he cut his arm to gather blood, Wilbur bound up the cut.

"Let me put antibiotic salve on it," Wilbur said, but Shamas shook him off.

"No, it won't matter, not in the end." Shamas pointed to the gauze. "Just bind the rune, and give me another shot out of the bottle."

I knew what was in the flask. Shamas had prepared a

mixture of herbs from my magical herb garden, steeping them in 151-proof rum. The mixture smelled deadly, and could probably blind you if you drank enough. But it gave him the steel nerves he needed tonight.

Wilbur handed him the flask and Shamas took a slow pull on it, then handed it back and went back to the next rune.

To reach the upper part of the poles, Menolly carried Shamas on her shoulders, flying him up and holding him steady as he deftly drew them out. By the time they had finished, the poles were covered with the symbols. I could see the faint glow of magic outlining them, even though Shamas hadn't cast the spell yet.

"Do you need time to recharge before opening the gate?" I asked, trying to calm my nerves.

He shook his head. "No, we can't let too much time lapse or the energy from my blood will fade. Pentangle should cast the barrier now."

I nodded, holding his gaze. "Do you think—"

"Don't even ask. I'm trying to focus on one step at a time. Our future—the future—will come on its own, regardless of what we do, or not do, this night. We'll either be there to meet it, or we won't. Gather everyone. It's time."

I headed over to where Pentangle was standing. "We're ready, Lady."

She reached out and took my hands in hers. "This was destined from before your birth, Camille. Understand that Fate chooses who she will to create history, and the Hags of Fate weave her wishes into being. In the end, you and your sisters would have always come to this moment. There was simply no other path open to the three of you."

She picked up her wand. "I will cast the Circle now, and then I will stand back and keep vigil. I will not be able to help you once the circle is cast. You understand this? No matter what happens, I cannot change matters."

I nodded. "I do. You intervene but only where you're allowed to."

As I made my way back to my Knights, Smoky swung in by my side, then Morio and Trillian. I stopped and we formed a tight huddle, our arms around one another.

"Whatever happens tonight, we're soul bound. Together, forever. If one of us falls…the others carry on," Trillian said. He looked up at Smoky. "Iampaatar, you and Morio are the only other men I'd ever willingly share my wife with. We are, and always will be, a family."

Smoky's hair rose on the wind that gusted past, and he encircled us all with it. "We are bound, by choice as well as by ritual. I will lay down my life for you, all of you."

Morio let out a slow sigh. "Let's do this, and in a year, we'll look back and celebrate victory. There can only be one option. Entertain no other thought."

Tears were threatening to surface, and I pushed them back. They could come later, when all was said and done. For now, I needed to be the queen I was. I needed to be my father's daughter once more—ready to take on the world.

"I love you. Each one of you, more than anything in this world. Don't hold me back tonight. Let me do what I was born to do. Protect whoever you can, but don't fear for me. I will be at the mercy of the Fates, my loves." I looked at each one of their faces in turn, holding the vision tight to shore me up.

"Camille?"

I turned to see Raven Mother and the Black Unicorn standing there. "Yes?"

"Pentangle is almost finished."

I nodded, turning back to my husbands. "It's time. Get ready to rumble, boys. Shadow Wing's coming to town."

***

We were in place, with Shamas and Wilbur directly in front of the poles. The rest of the Keraastar Knights were circling me, ready to sweep Shamas into our group the moment the gate began to open. Joreal's daemons were surrounding the gate. They would help pass Shamas through their ranks, back to the Keraastar Knights, when it was time, while attempting to keep Shadow Wing at bay. The others stood behind the daemons, readying whatever they had to volley at the Demon Lord when he came through.

"Are you ready?" I called out to Shamas.

He glanced back at me, nodding.

I closed my eyes, holding the unicorn horn in one hand and my new dagger in the other. Focusing on the horn, I projected myself into the center of it.

***

When I opened my eyes. I found myself standing in the room I had been in so many times before, with Eriskel in front of me.

The jindasel bowed. "What may I do for you, Your Majesty?"

I swallowed hard. "It's time. I need all your powers to bear. We're facing Shadow Wing, and I need the Lady of the Land, the Master of Winds, the Mistress of Flames, and the Lord of the Depths to give me everything they've got when I call for it."

Eriskel sobered. "As you command, Lady." He stepped back, waving his hands toward the four massive screens in the room. "They are yours for the summoning."

I stepped up to the north screen and raised my hands. "Lady of the Land, I summon thee forth to do my bidding."

As I waited, a deep throbbing resonated through the room as a woman with skin as dark as the land appeared. Her hair was spun corn silk, and her eyes were the color of lemon chiffon. She was wearing a dress that flowed like vines from her shoulders, and she knelt, bowing to me.

I turned to the east screen. "Master of Winds, I call upon thee. Come forth, to do my bidding."

The screen began to glimmer, and mountains appeared—the highest peaks of the world. A leather-clad man, with hair the color of spun flax, appeared. He was carrying a sword that flashed with lightning, and he dropped to one knee, lowering his head.

Another turn, and I faced the south. "Mistress of Flames, creep forth from your lair and attend me. I command your presence to do my bidding.

On this screen, a rolling river of lava appeared and a woman with skin the same color emerged. Her hair flowed down, blending with the molten rock, obsidian locks grounding her into the flaming channel. She knelt, her eyes alight with anticipation.

Once more I turned, this time to the west. "Lord of the Depths, rise and hear my call. Come forth to do my bidding."

And once again, the screen cleared, and out of a churning sea rose a man with cerulean skin and a shimmering scaled tail. He was carrying a bronze trident and he thrust it overhead with a shout.

I turned to Eriskel. "Old friend, I don't know the end of this battle, but if I fall, let us hope who next wields the horn will be an ally."

The jindasel regarded me with solemn eyes. "The world will move as it will. I have hopes, my Lady, that you will continue to be my mistress. The Elementals of the Horn will do their utmost for you. We all await your command.

Reluctantly, I withdrew. It would be easy to stay, to take time and rest, to put off the inevitable, but in the end, everything had its season, and it was time to finish this chapter in our lives.

"Thank you, for all you've done," I said, hugging him. He felt misty, insubstantial, and yet the energy surrounding him was more powerful than just about anything I had ever felt. Another moment, and I waved softly before I closed my eyes and withdrew.

⚔

I BLINKED, back on the battlefield. Everybody was poised, waiting, focused on me. I held up the horn in one hand, my new dagger in the other, and let out a loud ululation.

"It's go time, boys. Open the gate."

Shamas stepped back away from the poles, Wilbur

behind him. Wilbur placed his hands on Shamas's back and the energy began to swell, kept concentrated by the barrier that Pentangle had created around us.

We watched in silence as Shamas held out his hands, and a crimson light began to emanate from them. It filled the night, surrounding the poles, clinging to the symbols on the charcoaled wood. A low roar began to fill the clearing and it rocked beneath our feet as the runes began to writhe with fire, lighting up like a Christmas tree, brilliant and flaming symbols of power. As each one caught hold, the clearing quaked yet again, and the roar grew, reverberating through the air like the drone of a low-flying airplane.

The hair on the back of my neck rising, I focused on controlling my fear, concentrating on Shamas and the gate. He was in thrall of the magic now—shaking as he continued to feed the ethereal rune-fires. Wilbur was, in turn, pouring as much energy as he could into Shamas. Then, as the last rune caught fire, there was a loud shriek as the veils separating the worlds began to split, wedged apart by the magic.

"The sword!" Shamas called, and Delilah raced to his side, holding Yerghan's sword. It was our anchor, as Shadow Wing had possessed it and it carried his energy.

Shamas motioned for Wilbur to take hold of it, and then pushed Delilah away. She darted back behind the daemons. As soon as she was clear, Shamas held his hands over the sword and called out in a loud voice.

"I open this Demon Gate. In the name of the gods, in the name of all that is powerful, I command thee, Shadow Wing the Unraveller, Demon Lord of the Subterranean Realms, to appear before me. Come forth now!"

As soon as he finished speaking, he motioned to Wilbur, who threw the blade through the Demon Gate, where it vaporized in a flash of fire. The next moment, Shamas turned and vaulted toward me, the daemons shifting to let him pass. As he raced into his place in the Circle, the daemons closed up the passage again, facing the gate.

As Shamas clasped hands with Chase and Lisa, forming the Circle around me, the Knights immediately slid into trance and I felt them beginning to raise the energy that I would need. The diamond around my neck was glowing, and I could feel every single stone making up the Spirit Seal vibrating with a low, deep resonance. I faced the gate, horn and dagger ready.

The Demon Gate let out a shower of sparks, and then a deep keening split the air as a thick cloud of smoke began to pour out from between the posts. Sparks flew everywhere, sizzling as they hit the daemons, but the guards neither shouted nor responded. They held their ground, weapons ready, as the posts began to crumble and a figure began to emerge.

He was massive, fifteen feet tall, with rust-colored skin and wings that spread out like a bat. He was bald, with a troll-like face, and horns that spiraled into the air. In one hand, he held a whip, and in the other, he cradled a ball of flame. He was wearing a loincloth that looked to be made of numerous skins, and his eyes were glowing with the light of ten thousand suns.

I found myself beginning to waver as the sheer power of the Unraveller washed through the clearing. At that moment, he froze, as if suddenly realizing that he wasn't in Kansas anymore. He let out a bellow that shook the clearing and then he turned his head. As he caught sight of me, he let out another shriek that almost broke my eardrums and pointed at me, his fingers ending in massive talons.

"*You. Die,*" were the only words he said that I could understand, but there was no mistaking the bolt of lightning that came sailing out of his palm next. The jagged fork split the air, and it was aimed directly at me. But in a split second one of Joreal's daemons launched himself into the air in front of the bolt. The lightning hit him square in the chest, exploding, and the daemon let out a shriek as his chest split wide. The guard's body hung suspended for a second, then fell to the ground, lifeless.

Smoky backed up away from the group to one side, where he began to change shape. Shade did the same, and the two dragons were there, crowding the edges of the clearing. Shade let out a massive belch and showered a flame strike toward Shadow Wing, but the Demon Lord just seemed to absorb it, laughing as the fire washed over him. The next moment, Smoky followed suit, but instead of fire, it was a shower of ice pellets, launching like bullets as they peppered the Demon Lord. Shadow Wing roared, trying to wave off the frozen projectiles.

Raven Mother vanished in a wave of smoke, turning into a massive raven. She flew up, letting out a series of long calls, and out of the darkened trees around us, an unkindness of ravens appeared. They were large, with glowing eyes. These were no ordinary birds, I thought as they rose and, with Raven Mother in the lead, began to dive-bomb Shadow Wing. They couldn't do much damage, but they *could* keep him distracted.

As the daemons launched an attack with jagged

swords, I narrowed my attention to the exclusion of the chaos going on around me. The Keraastar Knights had joined hands, and a loud humming began to emerge from the energy that was rising around us. I could feel it, seeping from the spirit seals into their hands, and as the seals touched without touching, the circle of power began to build. The diamond around my neck was drawing on it, feeding it through my body into the blade, into the unicorn horn, into my soul. I tilted my head back, and let it sweep me under even as it built me up.

Menolly

Camille and the Knights were preparing their attack. I glanced over at the circle, feeling almost queasy. The power they were raising was palpable. It was ancient and frightening and for a moment, the look on Camille's face made me freeze. It was as though the power possessed her, and I wondered what kind of force was manifesting through her body.

I turned back to gauge what was going on with Shadow Wing. Raven Mother had led an attack with her magical ravens, and while they had managed to distract the Demon Lord for the moment, it wouldn't last long. A group of five of the daemon guards had taken him on, attacking him with their swords. But Shadow Wing swept at one with his massive hand, grabbing the daemon up into the air. As we watched, Shadow Wing brought the daemon to his face and then, like motion blur in a movie, he began feasting on the daemon's life force. The daemon began to scream as Shadow Wing devoured his energy, sucking it deep.

Smoky let out a second blast of ice magic, slinging another rain of ice pellets toward Shadow Wing. The Demon Lord stumbled forth, bellowing again, as he stepped on yet another one of the daemons. He flung the body of his other victim to the side, and the daemon landed on the ground with a wet splat.

I wanted to run in, to attack him, but we were to hang back as long as possible and let those who had distance attacks use them first. I glanced over at Nerissa. She had shifted into her cougar form and was pacing the edges, looking for a way to edge in toward the demon.

"No," I yelled at her. "Not yet."

She glared at me for a moment, but backed down. I glanced around, looking for a way to help. Then I saw that the daemon Shadow Wing had stepped on was still alive and I motioned for Nerissa to follow me and circled around to his side.

At that moment, the Black Unicorn stepped forward and lowered his horn. He pawed at the ground with his front hoof and tipped his head up so the horn was aimed at the face of the Demon Lord, and a stream of crimson light flowed out of his horn like a laser, hitting Shadow Wing square on the nose.

Shadow Wing shrieked, his great wings fluttering in the air, and he clawed at his face, trying to drive away the light. I wasn't sure what the force was doing to him, but one thing was certain: he didn't like it.

Smoky suddenly rose into the air and flew at him, raking at him with his front feet as he swept past the

Demon Lord. He managed to rip a long gash on Shadow Wing's chest, but before he could fully fly away, the Demon Lord reached up and, with his own talons, slashed at Smoky. He landed a hit and as I stared, unbelieving, he managed to sever Smoky's leg at the knee joint. Smoky bellowed, flailing back, his great wings beating frantically as he lurched away to collapse on the ground at the far edge of the clearing, trailing a massive shower of blood in his wake.

"Smoky!" Delilah screamed, running toward him. Shade was on her heels, flying high enough to avoid knocking anyone over.

I was torn—I wanted to run over to help, because Camille sure as hell couldn't—but we couldn't just drop the attack on Shadow Wing. I turned to Nerissa.

"Go, see if you can help him." As she loped off, I motioned for Vanzir and Roz to flank me. The daemons renewed their attack on Shadow Wing, whose face looked horribly burnt from the strike the Black Unicorn had managed to make. The three of us spread out in front of Camille and the Keraastar Knights, joined by Trillian, trying to protect them as they built their power.

As the Black Unicorn moved in for another attack, Raven Mother returned with more ravens, and they swept down to focus on the Demon Lord's face. I glanced back at the circle of Knights, but from what I could tell, they needed more time. If we could just keep him occupied long enough, we might still have a chance.

Delilah

. . .

As Smoky lurched away from Shadow Wing, I saw the trail of blood pouring out of his severed limb. He'd bleed out if we didn't do something. I turned to Shade and screamed for him to follow me, then raced over to where the massive dragon had fallen.

I reached his side just in time to see him open his eyes and let out what sounded like a massive moan. As I knelt to examine the wound, I realized that this would be his right arm when he was in human form. I glanced up at Shade.

"Can you do something to stop the bleeding? Please?" I couldn't let Smoky die—Camille would never forgive herself if he died.

Shade waved one giant skeletal paw at me and I moved out of the way, leaning against one of the nearby charcoaled tree towers that stood within Pentangle's barrier. As he landed on the ground next to Smoky, Shade took one look at the wound and then leaned in close. The next moment, he began to breathe a concentrated stream of fire onto the stump of Smoky's arm, using careful control to make certain the flames didn't land on any other part of the white and silver dragon. The wound bubbled up, sizzling, and Smoky let out another scream and then collapsed. Within seconds, he reverted to human form and lay there, unconscious and unmoving.

Shade transformed to human form and knelt on one side of the dragon, examining him. He looked up at me. "He needs help."

"We can't get him out of here—remember? Nobody can cross out of the barrier for twenty-four hours." Frantically, I looked around, but then a thought hit me. "Wait here."

I raced over to the edge of the circle, to where Pentangle was watching. Sure enough, a force field prevented me from crossing the barrier, but I frantically waved my hands overhead, shouting at her.

"Pentangle! Please, I need to talk to you."

She approached the outer edge of the circle, her face impassive. "What do you need?"

"We need medical help. Shadow Wing severed Smoky's arm. There's no way we can bring him out?" I figured she'd say no, but it was worth a shot.

"No, I'm sorry, there isn't. But you can bring someone into the circle, if they're willing to help." She retreated to the side of the tree against which she had been leaning.

I turned, returning to Shade, where I saw Wilbur. He was on his knees beside Smoky, wrapping up the remaining stump of the arm with a handkerchief. He looked up at me.

"I was just telling Shade here that if Smoky was human, he would probably be dead by now—he's bled out a lot. But he's still breathing." Wilbur glanced over at Camille and the group. "I've got to get over to Shamas. He may need me again." He pushed himself up off the ground, looking back at the fight.

The Black Unicorn had taken another shot at Shadow Wing and this time, it looked like he had managed to put out one of the Demon Lord's eyes. The ravens were continuing to encircle his face, and on the ground, four of the daemons were busy hacking at him with their swords. They were injuring him, but it was obvious they weren't making much headway. Smoke filled the clearing, and the sounds of battle rang in my ears, echoing. I suddenly found myself back in Elqaneve, during the siege, watching the fires burn and hearing the shouts and screams. I shook my head and the images cleared, but the feeling was the same. We were in a war zone, and as I took another look at Shadow Wing, I wondered if we had made a huge mistake.

"Delilah? Delilah!" Wilbur's voice cut through my thoughts.

I shook my head. "Sorry—what were you saying?"

"I need to be ready to help Shamas if he needs me, Puddytat. And Shade's going to have another go at Shadow Wing." He paused, then clapped my shoulder with his hand. "Wake up, Kitten. Be here. Stay in the present. It's the only way to get through the fight. Take it from a war-weary veteran." And then, he was off, heading over to Camille's side of the clearing.

I turned back to see Menolly and Nerissa trying to help another daemon get back on his feet. They were cannon fodder, I thought, the daemons. Joreal knew that when he assigned them to us, and they knew it when they had come on the mission. Wondering what it felt like to be viewed as expendable, I slowly turned and numbly made my way back to Smoky's side.

※

Camille

THE POWERS WERE ALMOST at their peak, mixing and churning through my body, flowing through the

Keraastar Knights, into the diamond, blending with the mother-force, and then into me where it formed a living web through every cell of my being. The Keraastar diamond pulsed with a deep, deadly heartbeat, throbbing against my chest.

My hive slowly circled around me, chanting in low tones as they moved one sure step at a time, creating a living wheel that turned ever onward, spiraling through the years, through the decades, through the centuries, through the eons. Different bodies in different times, but we had done this before—that I knew for sure. *We* were the weapon that the ancients had hidden for times of crises, when nothing else could stop the demonic powers from rising up and breaking through.

And sure as I knew this, I knew that this had happened before. Unwritten in the history books, unsung in the songs, the Keraastar Knights had rose and fought, then fell into hiding until the next time they were needed. The prophecy first given by Grandmother Coyote had not been about *us as people*, but had been about *our force*, and the prophecy had covered more battles through the millennia than would ever be remembered.

I tried to remember my name, but it vanished on my tongue, as did the names of the men and women who circled round me, building the power as they chanted, building the force as they wheeled in a widdershins motion. For we were mere instruments now, unwinding the coils that constrained the powers into the gems. We were removing the barriers to their use, letting them shine through for an instant before once again burying them in obscurity.

My gaze was on Shadow Wing. *Shadow Wing the Unraveller.*

I could see the soul receptacles now, on either side of his horns. They were my targets, and they shone brightly, like signal fires. All my fear drained away and now there was only the push to finish the destiny to which I was born. Nothing else mattered and I paid no attention to what was going on with the rest of our allies.

Shadow Wing sent another daemon flying through the air, and I heard a scream from across the clearing, but I couldn't afford to look, I couldn't afford to feel *anything* but the drive to fully open myself to the power and let it flow through me.

And then, like flipping a switch, I knew it was time. I called out, and my Knights swept back into a V-formation, with Chase at their lead behind me, and Shamas and Venus behind him. We began to move forward, toward the Demon Lord.

There was blood on the ground, and I thought I saw a hand but I ignored it as we moved through the smoke. A few of the daemons were left, doing their best to distract him, and Raven Mother sent one last volley of ravens toward his face. The Black Unicorn was resting near the edge of the circle and I could feel from where I stood that he had exhausted his energy. I caught glimpse of someone in white on the ground across the circle but I forced myself to look away. There was no space for fear.

Moving forward I held up the unicorn horn and the dagger, readying them as we marched toward the Demon Lord. Images of the past four years tried to flicker through my mind but I pushed them away, focusing only on my target.

And then, we were there, in front of Shadow Wing. He let out a roar, his face bloody, with one eye missing. He was covered with wounds, but he was still on his feet. And then, I leaned my head back as the powers began to rush through me.

"This is your time," I whispered to them as I gave myself over, letting them sweep through and take control of me.

I brought up the unicorn horn and the dagger, and aimed toward his soul receptacles.

The force of the lightning that swept from my weapons rattled my teeth, frying my senses and my sight. The flare was blinding, and as the ground rocked beneath my feet, I found myself in the center of a war of elements, a whirlwind of power that threatened to overwhelm me.

I gave up my last resistance, thinking, *"Do what you will, this is my fight, and I will surrender to it."*

With one terrifying shriek, the forces that we had built rose up, and I opened my mouth, letting them rush out on my breath, toward the Demon Lord, and then…I knew no more.

Menolly

THERE WERE ONLY five of the daemons left as Camille began making her move. The Keraastar Knights followed, spreading out into a V. Chase was directly behind her, then Shamas and Venus, then Tanne and Bran, Amber and Luke, and finally, Clyde and Lisa.

As I watched in horror, they approached Shadow Wing head-on. The magic was so thick around them, it was difficult to tell what was happening, but Camille was holding up the unicorn horn and her dagger. Sparks were spiraling around both, a nimbus of crackling blue and purple. In fact, her entire body seemed to be surrounded by a web of magical threads that wove and rewove themselves. A wail of wind rose up, gusting by with so much force that it almost knocked me off my feet, and the skies clouded over, unleashing a torrent.

I wanted to run to her, to push her out of the way, but I couldn't move. *This was it*. This was our chance. And whatever happened, I had to let happen. Trillian joined me as Morio and Wilbur stood to the side, waiting to help in whatever aftermath was to follow.

And then, amidst the massive storm, a jagged fork of lightning shot out of both the horn and the dagger, aiming for Shadow Wing's soul receptacles. I tensed, waiting and watching as the attack landed square on. A massive web of light began to spread out as the receptacles shattered, and then, as though fueling a giant internal furnace, Shadow Wing's body began to crack. It was as though he were porcelain, hit by a hammer. Tongues of flame emerged from between the cracks and I realized what was going to happen.

"Run! Get out of there!" I screamed at Camille,, but my words were drowned by the gale storm that the unicorn horn had summoned. The ground was still trembling beneath our feet, and as I tried to run forward, a tremor hit hard and knocked me down. I forced myself to my hands and knees as the ground rolled beneath me.

The lights emanating from between the cracks on

Shadow Wing's body grew so bright I could barely watch. I shaded my eyes, thinking that it was as bright as the sun, and then I realized that my skin was blistering. I had to find cover. I looked around for anything behind which I could shield myself and saw one of the giant charcoal stumps that was in the circle. It was wide enough to protect me from the light so I made a mad dash for it, sliding behind it just in time.

Delilah

Shadow Wing's soul receptacles were gone, but it wasn't over yet. His body was breaking up. I saw Menolly scrambling for cover as I stood, turning away from Smoky, but Camille and the Keraastar Knights were in the direct path. Frantic, I began to run toward her, but Shade caught me, twisting my arm as he pulled me back.

"You can't survive that. Let me go," he said, thrusting me behind him. I screamed at him but he just shook his head and, running, he headed for my sister. I wanted to follow him, but I knew better—he'd just worry about me. I held my breath, watching, and suddenly felt someone beside me. Glancing down, I saw a leopard by my side.

"Arial!" My twin had come to help. She could only appear in her spirit leopard form, but she was here with us at the end. She bobbed her head, then bounced after Shade.

The light from Shadow Wing had grown too bright to look at, and I saw that Camille and the Knights were trying to scatter. Shade was almost there, but he wasn't going to make it in time. The next moment, Chase grabbed Camille and threw her out of the way as a giant explosion rocked the clearing, setting off yet another quake. The massive pillars of the Demon Gate rocked precariously and then began to fall as the Demon Lord exploded into pieces, fire pouring out from his core. He was a creature of fire, and fire was his blood and life force.

Camille rolled to the ground, pulling the unicorn hide cloak over her body. The Knights scattered, but with all the smoke and flames roiling through the area I couldn't see if they'd all made it to safety. The ground rocked again, toppling trees around the clearing, and then... everything was still except for the sounds of the torrential rain beating down on the flames as they crackled under the sodden night.

⚔

Camille

MY HEAD WAS STILL RINGING with the sound of the explosion. I blinked, trying to sit up, but everything felt catawampus. I managed to push myself to a sitting position and shoved the hide away from where I'd covered my head. It was covered with a fine ash, and I stared at that, wondering where it had come from. Then I glanced over to where Shadow Wing had been standing, and I realized that the ash was from him.

He was gone. He was truly gone. I had expected to feel victorious, to jump up and scream with joy, but all I could feel was a hollow ache inside. I blinked, looking around, trying to figure out what was going on. Delilah was coming toward me, saying something, but I couldn't hear her. I pointed toward my ears and shook my head, and she paused, then nodded and reached down, grabbing me up by the arm. Tears were streaming down her cheeks and I knew something was wrong.

"What happened? What's going on?" I glanced around, wondering if I had been wrong about Shadow Wing. Was he still alive? But then she was leading me over toward the edge of the Circle. The area was far too reminiscent of Elqaneve during the siege, and I shuddered as we passed body after body of the daemon guards.

As we approached Trenyth, he was kneeling on the ground, and beside him was Smoky. For the first time since I'd met my dragon prince, he was covered in blood. Then I realized the blood was his, and part of his arm was missing. I began to scream, falling to my knees in the mud-laden clearing as the rain pounded down around me.

Trillian was there, and he grabbed me, shaking me.

Delilah said something to him that I couldn't hear, and he took my hand and put it on Smoky's wrist, where I could feel a faint pulse.

"He's still alive?" I asked.

Trillian nodded, and I burst into fresh tears, hanging my head. He was alive, and that was what counted. Then Delilah tapped me on the shoulder. I was loath to leave Smoky's side, but I let her lead me over to where Menolly was standing with a somber expression on her face.

Shade was tending to Venus, who had burns over the left side of his face, and Nerissa was tending to Tanne, who was also wounded. At that moment, out of the forest surrounding the clearing, I saw Derisa appear, several of the priestesses from the grove behind her. They entered the circle and immediately began helping to tend to the wounded.

But Delilah turned me around. She was still crying as she led me over to one side where Shade's duster was laid out open on the ground. On the coat were Chase and Shamas, both still, heavily burned. I looked back at Delilah and she shook her head.

They were dead.

An image flashed into my head. Shadow Wing was looming over me, the light from his wounds blinding me, and then somebody had pushed me out of the way before the explosion.

Chase— Chase had saved my life.

I began to shake, the numbness cracking, and the tears turned into a torrent, and then into silence as I dropped to my knees between the two men, staring up into the rain as it pounded down, extinguishing the flames. After a long moment, I began to speak. I couldn't even hear if I was actually talking aloud or just mouthing the words, but tradition held true and I would honor it for my cousin and my dear friend.

But as I began to speak, Delilah and Menolly were kneeling beside me, taking my hands as we recited the prayer to the dead.

"What was life has crumbled. What was form, now falls away. Mortal chains unbind and the soul is lifted free. May you find your way to the ancestors. May you find your path to the gods. May your bravery and courage be remembered in song and story. May your parents be proud, and may your children carry your birthright. Sleep, and wander no more."

As I fell silent, the only thing I could think was that we had defeated Shadow Wing, but we had paid with blood and with loss.

CHAPTER THIRTEEN

Menolly: One Year Later

I looked around the Wayfarer at the bustling crowds filling the booths and tables. I missed the place. I missed the smell of the booze, the smell of the food being grilled, I missed greeting people and hanging out and even the occasional bar fight. But those days were long gone, and it was time to move on. I turned back to Derrick, who was watching me expectantly.

"You're finding it hard to give this up, aren't you?" The werebadger understood how I felt. He had been with me several years now, and he had become a friend as well as an employee.

I nodded. "Harder than I thought it would be. When I first came over here, I didn't know what to expect. And they stuck me in the bar, which was run by Jocko at the time. And then he was killed, and everything snowballed from there. It's been a whirlwind, especially since the bar burned down and had to be rebuilt."

I looked around again. "You're doing a really good job of keeping her up. She looks wonderful, Derrick. I trust you to take care of her for me." I pulled the documents to me, scanning them once more. Once I signed these, the Wayfarer would belong to Derrick, lock, stock and barrel, including the portal in the basement. My sisters and I had pulled some strings and he now worked for the Otherworld Intelligence Agency, which had undergone a great deal of change since the war in Otherworld. But he would do a good job, and we could trust him.

He handed me the pen. "Are you *sure* you want to do this? I know this is your baby. And I know how many memories you have here. I don't want to take those away from you."

I took the pen, staring at the sleek black barrel of it. "You can't take them away from me—nothing can. It's stupid of me to keep it, when I can't even get down here most days. The Wayfarer deserves better than that. She deserves someone who can love her and watch over her on a daily basis. And you're the only one I really feel comfortable handing it over to."

I scribbled my name across the bottom line, and then on the next page. The woman sitting next to me was a notary public. I had brought her with me for this express purpose. She watched as he signed, and then she put her signature to the deed as well, indicating that she had witnessed the transfer. And then it was done. Derrick owned the Wayfarer.

My heart hurt, but I also was happy. I was happy for Derrick, and I was happy for the bar. I slid off the stool, waving at him as I headed for the door.

"Don't you want one last bottle of blood for the road?" he called after me.

I shook my head, glancing over my shoulder. "Nerissa

and I leave for the UK in a few hours. We need to finish packing for the trip." I saluted him, forcing a smile to my lips that I didn't feel. "Take care of her for me, I'm counting on you."

"You can drink me dry if I don't!"

As I headed out into the night, I took one last look at the bar, and then straightening my shoulders, I headed for my car.

⚔

NERISSA WAS WAITING FOR ME. I was grateful to see that she had packed for both of us. She was good at those sort of things, whereas I wasn't. She gave me a kiss, pulling me into her arms and snuggling me.

"Was it so very terrible?"

I shrugged. "It wasn't easy, but we've been through worse. Far worse." I closed my eyes, trying to rid myself of the images that still played from that fateful night. We had killed Shadow Wing, destroyed him for good, but the aftermath was still settling. There was no telling when things would feel back to normal. If ever.

"Roman's waiting for us in London. He won't be able to meet us at the airport, because it's going to be about 1:00 P.M. when we get there, but I'll make sure you're protected as they take you out of the plane, and he's arranged for several of his werepuma guards to meet us. They'll arrange to drive us to the hotel." She glanced through the stack of travel documents. "I think we're good to go. Did you have a chance to say good-bye to Delilah and Camille?"

I hefted the suitcase off the bed and sat it next to the

others. "Yes, we met out at Delilah's. I cannot believe how big she's getting. Not long, now. I wish I could be here for the birth—though frankly, I have no idea what kind of niece to expect, given she's the daughter of an Elemental Lord. The gods know, Delilah's going to be running ragged after her, I'll bet."

Nerissa nodded, then bit her lip. "How's Astrid doing?"

I gave her a bleak look. "Astrid's rebounding remarkably well. She was only about a year old when Chase died. She's toddling around like a moppet now." I leaned on the edge of the bed. "You know, when I first met Chase, I used to tease him. I'd scare the shit out of him because hey, it was easy and fun. And he was such a lecher at the time, chasing after Camille's skirts. He's lucky we didn't beat his ass black and blue. But he came around. He actually grew into being a man I could respect and enjoy spending time with."

Nerissa grinned. "Did you two ever…"

I stared at her for a moment, clueless, till she gave me a little wink. "Oh, hell no! No, Chase was not my type. I did sleep with Roz once, though it wasn't nearly the sparks and fireworks we hoped for. Speaking of Roz, he's supposed to drop by. He had something to tell me—apparently he already told Delilah and Camille."

At that moment, I stopped when someone tapped on the door. Nerissa answered it, and Dolph escorted Rozurial in. After assuring Dolph that we would be just fine left alone, he retreated.

Roz sat down on the loveseat, his long hair pulled back in a ponytail. He was sans his walking armory status. "They swiped my duster at the door. They'd better not pilfer through it."

I laughed. "You'll get your duster back, doofus. They can't let you into the 'Princesses' Palace' when you're wearing more ammo than anybody needs."

"True that." He paused, glancing at the suitcases. "So, you're headed out soon?"

"Yeah, we'll be touring the UK. Since our Vamp-Human mutual appreciation gig went over so well in the US, and since it's almost a guarantee that the Vampire Rights Act is going to pass this year, no small thanks to our efforts, Blood Wyne asked us to take on Europe. First stop: the UK for two weeks, visiting ten cities around England, Ireland, and Scotland. I want to make a stop at Stonehenge. Camille asked me to take something over to the Merlin for her."

This was going to be my first trip overseas and I was excited about it. Which actually seemed silly, given I had traveled between worlds to get to Seattle in the first place. But I was looking forward to the trip.

Nerissa and I had spent five months on the road over the past year, and it had been good for us, and good for our connection with Roman. He had found a girlfriend who had fallen hard for him—Valentina, his assistant when he was dealing with the Harriman issue. While Blood Wyne forbade him to marry a third time, she had no objections to him seeing her on the side. And neither did Nerissa nor I. If she could make him truly happy and feel truly loved, then we were all for it.

"You have news for us?" I asked.

He nodded. "Yeah, I know you're in a hurry to get to the airport. I tried to get here earlier, but the traffic was nuts. So…I'm going back home to Otherworld."

I stared at him. He had been part of our life for five

years, since he had stumbled into us on the hunt for Dredge. He had fought alongside us in every battle. And now…

"You're leaving?" I swallowed the lump rising in my throat. "Why?"

"Because there's nothing left for me to do here. Everybody is moving on with their lives, and it's time for me to do so, as well." He looked like he was about to burst. "I've got incredible news."

"What?" I was ready for just about anything, given all that had happened.

"I talked to Pentangle the night of the siege on Shadow Wing. She agreed to put in a request for an audience with Zeus and Hera. After all these hundreds of years, they've agreed to remove the curse they laid on Fraale and me."

I stared at him. Roz had never expected to ever be able to reunite with his wife, even though she had longed for the day since they were first swept apart.

"You're kidding?"

"No. In a few days, I'll be back to the Fae farmer I once was, and so will Fraale. And we're going to return to the hills of Otherworld and buy a house and settle in. We'll be together again." His voice cracked and he hung his head. "I never thought this day would come. I kept telling Fraale to get over me, that there was no hope. But finally, hope has come. And so we're going to give it another chance."

I sat down on the bed, stupefied. "You're joking, right? I mean, it's been hundreds of years. How can—do you really want to go back to who you were? How can you, after all this time?"

Nerissa poked my arm. "Menolly, what kind of question is that?"

Roz raised his gaze to meet mine. "Look, I never *asked* to be an incubus. I learned how to cope with it, but it's not who I am by birth. It's not my nature. Fraale was my heart, until we were cursed. Now, we're getting a do-over. We get another chance to make it work. How can I *not* try? And if it doesn't work out, well, we'll cross that bridge when we come to it. Life's too short to be afraid. Any moment, a Demon Lord can pop out of the woodwork and lay you flat."

I knew he was thinking of Chase, and how he had never gotten to be with the woman he loved. "Yeah, all right. I get it. I don't want to lose you, Roz, but you need to follow your heart. Don't be a stranger, okay? Bring Fraale over to visit. If you have kids, bring them along."

We hugged, Nerissa murmuring her best wishes, and he headed out. As the door shut behind him, I felt one more surety in our lives vanish, off into the future.

"Our lives are shifting right before our eyes," I said, staring at the door.

"New adventures, new friends, new enemies. You know that it's not really an ending, Menolly. We're growing up and moving on. Just think—we get to spend six months traveling through Europe. And look at what Erin and Wade have done—the Vampire Rights Act isn't passing just because of our tour, but thanks to the incredible amount of work they've done on it."

"True. And stagnation isn't a pretty state."

Nerissa held out her arms and spun around. "The world is growing, and with the Church of the Earthborn Brethren dismantled as a hate group, and the Freedom's Angels going bankrupt, we're paving the way for a better tomorrow. *For everybody*. Human, Were, Vampire, Fae… we're making a difference."

I swallowed a wash of tears that had risen in my throat. "You're right. We're making a difference, and this time, it's out in the open, and a hell of a lot more pleasant."

She opened her arms and I slid into her embrace and she kissed me soundly. Her lips were warm against my cool ones, and I could hear her heartbeat, whereas mine was still. But we were in love, and married, and we were happy. And that was all that mattered.

"You know, I bless the day that we got involved with the Rainier Puma Pride, because it brought you into my life," I murmured.

She leaned down, resting her forehead against mine. "Shut up, woman, and kiss me again."

And I did.

CHAPTER FOURTEEN

Delilah: One Year Later

"Stop chasing Freeto, Astrid!" I had no more finished balancing bread and milk and sandwich fixings in my arms when Astrid waddled past, chasing the puppy we had gotten for her. The puppy was carrying her pull-up pants and she was stark naked.

I juggled the food over to the counter and then dashed after her as she ran into the living room, but Shade was quicker than me and he caught her up, tickling her tummy.

"Enough of that, Miss Priss," he said, bringing her back into the kitchen. "No more playing nudist." He glanced at me. "I'll put another pair of pull-ups on her while you finish making lunch. When's Hanna getting back from the store?"

"She said in an hour or so. I was going to make sandwiches for lunch. Is that all right?" I wasn't a great cook, but I was learning. I had a lot more time on my hands now that we had taken out Shadow Wing and weren't running all over the place chasing demons.

"That's fine." Shade retrieved another pair of pull-ups from the laundry room and quickly clothed our foster daughter again. He lifted her up, holding her over his head, and she laughed, waving her hands to the ceiling. Finally, he carried her over to the booster chair at the table and sat her in it, brushing the hair back from her face. He fastened the belt to keep her in the chair, because she was a live wire and would be down and running again within seconds otherwise.

He stared at her for a moment, then said, "She sure looks like Chase. More so every day."

I nodded, wincing. The very mention of his name still hurt, but time was beginning to help. I didn't burst into tears every time someone mentioned him. "Sharah said she's coming over Earthside next week to see Astrid."

"There's no chance she can take her home with her?" Shade asked, coming over to wrap his arms around my ever-expanding waist as I fixed the roast beef sandwiches. He kissed my ear, then the back of my neck. "You're growing so fast that I swear you're carrying twins."

I smiled, ducking my head. "No, just one. But she's active, I'll tell you that. Only four more months and she'll be here. The place will be a madhouse, with two children."

"Well, we can always ask Tim and Jason to babysit. Or make play dates with them and their twins. Although I guess we'll have to wait and see just what little Chamiya will be like."

The name meant "good harvest" in the Fae language, and Hi'ran had heartedly approved. The pregnancy was going well, though like the battle against Shadow Wing, I had waited so long for the time to come that when I found out I was actually pregnant, it seemed to appear out of nowhere.

"Yeah, I'm not at all certain what being the mother of an Elemental baby is going to require." I glanced over at Astrid, handing Shade a bowl of applesauce and half of a sandwich. "Pour her half a cup of milk and give her this, please." As he obeyed, I answered his earlier question. "Sharah and I talked the other day. She's got her hands full with the triplets—Trenyth apparently has potent sperm and she had a very ripe egg. There's no way she can trust a nanny to watch over Astrid properly. The triplet sisters are all that anybody cares about, and almost everybody seems to have forgotten that Sharah and Chase had a daughter. She'd end up being Cinderella over there, and you know it."

Shade frowned as he placed Astrid's lunch on the tray in front of her, then got her milk. "I think you're exaggerating," he said, turning around just in time to stop her from throwing the sandwich off the table to Freeto.

"No, I'm not. Sharah said as much. She's worried that Astrid will be ignored in favor of the triplets. In some ways, Sharah reminds me so much of Queen Asteria that it's scary. Maybe the elves are just like that." I sighed, sinking into my chair. "I'm just grateful she asked us to take Astrid after…" Shaking my head, I changed the subject. "Can you carry over the sandwiches, please?

We were deep into discussing plans for the nursery when someone knocked on the kitchen door. Shade went to answer, but as he returned, I jumped out of my seat, groaning as my back bitched me out. Behind him stood Bruce.

"Bruce! Is Iris with you?" I looked around, hopeful.

He shook his head, staring at me. "Iris was right. You've a bun in the oven! Is it…"

I nodded. "The Autumn Lord's child? Yes. And that's Astrid, I'm sure you remember."

Bruce's smile faded, but he leaned down and kissed her on the head. "I remember the wee lass. We loved taking care of her for Chase. I'm just sorry he's not here to see this."

I said nothing, but right behind Astrid's chair I could see Chase. He was watching his daughter fondly. Eventually he'd have to transition over, but for now, he was causing no harm to himself or anybody by guarding over his child.

"Sit down, have a sandwich. What brings you back to America? Are you coming back?" I asked, hoping that he'd say yes. But he shook his head.

"No, actually. I came to ask you…to tell you that you might want to find someone to rent the house. Iris and I will be staying in Ireland for at least five years, and after that we plan on going to Finland. Undutar has instructed her that she is to open a temple in her homeland. She'll be the Temple Mother, and it will be run quite differently than the one in the Northlands. So we're going to settle in Finland after spending some time in my land." He scanned my face. "I know you hoped we'd come back to live here, but Fate is drawing us in other directions."

"That seems to be the case for everything lately," I said. My hormones were shifting like the tides. I felt a wash of tears well up. "I miss her. And so does Hanna." As the tears began to spill over, I caught Shade giving Bruce that "There she goes again" look.

"Don't you dare brush this off as pregnancy hormones!

I'm just lonely for Iris, damn it." I glared at him. At least while I was pregnant my ability to shift conked out, so I wasn't shifting into my Tabby shape—or Panther—at the drop of a hat.

"Yes, ma'am," Shade said meekly. But the smile on his face warmed my heart and I suddenly felt guilty for being so bitchy.

"I'm sorry. It's just…the past year has brought so many changes I'm having a hard time coping with them." No sooner were the words out of my mouth than Freeto came racing into the kitchen and tried to leap into my lap, missing by just enough that he knocked my plate off the table. He immediately jumped back down and began gobbling up my sandwich as I just stared at the mess.

"I'll make you another sandwich," Shade said, jumping up.

"I'll clean up." Bruce grabbed the broom and made himself handy.

I turned to Astrid, who was taking apart her sandwich. "No, sweetie, you need to eat the food, not wear it." She gazed up at me as I maneuvered a piece of beef toward her lips and she laughed, and in that moment, Chase leaned down beside me.

"Delilah, don't mourn," I heard him say. "I'm here and I'm watching over my daughter. I'll keep her as safe as I can, and help you while she's growing up. I'm glad she's with you."

I held his gaze, watching his ghostly figure as he gently kissed his daughter's cheek. She laughed, turning to him, and I realized she could see him, too.

I glanced over my shoulder. Shade and Bruce were in

the living room, discussing something. I took the opportunity. "Chase, I promise you this."

He focused on my face and I knew he could hear me.

"I'll never let her grow up being teased for being a Windwalker. I'll watch over her and make sure she's happy and healthy, and that she knows about her father. I give you my word." Tears were slowly tracing down my cheeks, but instead of loss, I felt love.

Love for Astrid, who would grow up to know what a brave man her father was. Love for Shade, and our connection. Love for the child growing in my womb, and for Hi'ran, whatever plans he had for me. Love for my sisters and for their loved ones. And after all these years, I realized that I truly could say I loved myself and my life. I was building roots. I was raising a family. I was home.

CHAPTER FIFTEEN
Camille: One Year Later

We were gathered around the bonfire out at Smoky's Barrow, just the four of us. I was wearing the Keraastar diamond, which had become such a part of me I couldn't imagine taking it off. My crown felt heavy on my head as we watched the stars on the cool October evening.

"Five years ago, everything started," I said. "Five years ago, Jocko died and my sisters and I were caught into Fate's web." I glanced at my husbands, each one in turn.

Smoky was leaning on his side beside me. The doctors in the Dragon Reaches couldn't reattach his arm—too much damage had been done—but thanks to the best techno-mages in Elqaneve and the Dragon Reaches, he had been fitted with a holographic prosthesis that had substance. Better still, it transformed into dragon-size when he shifted form. And he felt no lack, since he was able to use his hair to hold and grip and stroke when he needed to.

Morio was sitting on a boulder, his arms wrapped around his knees. He had emerged unscathed, but the battle had changed him in a way that I couldn't put my finger on. He was more pensive, more solemn than before.

And Trillian—he had become our rock. Shoring up Smoky when he needed it, helping to pull him out of the angry hole he had slid into after the battle. He would never be the boy next door, never be the "good guy"—but he had taken on the role of anchor and he held things together.

As for me, I could feel the diamond working on me. I had learned its secrets that night with Shadow Wing. I had seen the other demons come and go over the eons, the other knights and queens fighting them. And after the battle, each time, they had drifted for a while before the seals and diamond went into hiding again, only to emerge once again when a great enemy threatened to break through the portals. I had combed the history books, combed the ancient scrolls, but could find no mention of any of this, but in my heart, I knew it was true. And I knew that one day, we would put the seals to rest in a safe place, hiding them for the next battle.

I had told no one about this, though, because it felt like it was my secret to bear. And so I would keep it, and leave it to the Hags of Fate to see that the information was passed on when it was needed.

"What are you thinking about?" Smoky asked, popping a potato chip into his mouth.

I pulled the unicorn hide cloak around me to guard against the wind. "I don't know, really. The seals. The fight. The fact that Menolly and Nerissa are flying off to London, and that Delilah's chasing a toddler around the house, getting ready to give birth to another in a few months." I paused, then said, "I got a letter from our cousin Daniel the other day. He's heading back from a trip to Amsterdam. He said he's going to retire, give up the business and settle down."

"I'll believe it when I see it," Morio said with a laugh.

"Yeah, me too." I leaned back, resting against the grass to watch the stars overhead. "Aeval and Vanzir are coming to dinner tomorrow night. They're bringing Lahi with them." Lahi was their daughter.

Aeval had taken Vanzir as her official consort, and her Barrow had accepted the dream-chaser demon better than we could have hoped. He'd never have power there, but he had standing and respect, and together they had a daughter who had his kaleidoscopic eyes and her mother's raven hair. The girl was smart as a whip, and I had the feeling she'd be breaking hearts and heads before she was grown.

"How's the build going in the Wildwood Grove?" Smoky asked. "I haven't had time to look in on it since I got back from Mother's." He had stayed in the Dragon Reaches for several weeks so they could better attune his arm for him.

"Good. And we have our first few acolytes lined up. Derisa is sending over several priestesses to take over classes until we can train enough here. We're already planning exchange classes between the two worlds."

Trillian stoked the fire and then handed us each a stick with marshmallows on it. We sat up, roasting them as he poured hot cocoa all around. We roasted hot dogs after that, and Smoky brought out more chips, and we talked long and hard about nothing at all, late into the night.

Overhead, the Moon Mother was rising. She wasn't

quite full, but close to it, and I could feel the pull of the Hunt as she rose into the sky.

Each time I went out on the Hunt, Shamas was there, waiting for me, and we'd run side by side until the night was done. It hurt seeing him, but he was content and I was letting go. I had spent a year in mourning for Chase and Shamas, but now the wheel was turning, the future was here, and it was time to mend hearts and move into life again.

CHAPTER SIXTEEN

Maggie: Three Hundred Years Later

Dearest Mother Camille, Mother Delilah, and Mother Menolly:

I know you worry about me, but please don't. The Golden Wood is so beautiful, and I'm doing well in my studies, and I'm learning so much about my heritage. Every day I face challenges that I didn't expect to face, but I'm meeting them head-on, and I think you'll all be proud of me when I come home for Yule.

We were given the assignment to talk about our family traditions and what we learned from them. Well, obviously, mine are quite different than anybody else's here. I'm the only one who grew up away from the forests, and away from her own people. But I regret nothing, and it made me think truly, about the upbringing you gave me.

I wanted you to see what I wrote, so here it is:

"When I think about my babyhood, it's not filled

with the warm fuzzy arms of my birth mother or arguing with my siblings. Nor do I remember days spent in the trees, or learning to hunt, or anything like that. None of those rites and passages that one normally goes through.

What I *do* remember, though, is this:

Warm nights snuggled in a crib with a teddy bear, with my mother's spirit watching over me. And three warm and loving mothers who always looked so different than me, but who cared so deeply that their love shrouded me like a blanket. They guarded me as I slept. I remember a kitchen so filled with love and cheer that I couldn't bear to be put to bed. The food was always so good, and though I mostly ate lamb and porridge and cream-drink, I remember cookies and cakes and pizza and getting in trouble when I'd sneak into the garbage because I couldn't stand it till I had just *one more bite*.

I remember the musky smell of strong men who tickled me till I laughed, and when I would cry, a woman with golden hair down to her heels sang lullabies to me, songs that I still remember the words to. I remember the night Mother Menolly came to visit after she moved away, and how frightened she was because somebody had staked the queen, and now she would have to carry the crown.

I remember toys and games of hide and seek, and I remember a tree so shiny that every year Mother Delilah managed to knock off a good half-dozen ornaments when she shifted into her cat form. And everyone would scold her except me. I'd laugh and laugh.

I remember watching Mother Camille put on makeup, and how much care she would take, and when nobody was watching, she'd let me play dress up in her clothes, and she'd sneak me cookies and take me out to work in the herb garden with her. I learned how to heal with herbs thanks to her. She taught me how to sing to the Moon Mother, and to hear her answering.

I remember all these things, and so much more. But mostly?

I remember what my mothers taught me about love. About what it means to be family—how the bonds of love transcend the bonds of blood. I learned that love can transcend the widest of differences. I learned that family is what you make it, that if you care about somebody enough, they are your tribe. *They are your family*.

I learned that honor wins out, and if you make a promise, you keep it to the best of your ability. I remember the few times I lied as I was growing up, and how the disappointment in Mother Camille's eyes was greater than any punishment I could have been given. I learned that you *do your duty*, you *honor your commitments*, no matter what. And that when all is said and done, love is the last thing you have left.

And so, if I were to name my family traditions, they're those of love and laughter, of honor and keeping my word. Of being there when I'm needed.

And those are the traditions I'll instill in my children, when I have any, and that I will take to my grave."

I hope you like my paper. My teacher gave me high marks for it. Anyway, I love you, and as I said, don't worry—I'm having a blast. I'm also dating a gargoyle named E'lam. He's handsome and sweet, and he wants to meet you some time. And of course, he knows he has to win your approval.

I'll be home for Yule, and I'll see all of you then. Give my love to everybody.

Your daughter,

Maggie.

And they all lived happily ever after.

⚔

AND SO WE come to the end of the line. Every journey has a beginning, and every journey has an end point. And this series is no exception. Thank you, my friends, from the bottom of my heart, for being part of this incredible journey.

Want to know what to read next?

If you loved Otherworld, I'm pretty sure you'll like my new series—The Wild Hunt Series. The first five books are available: THE SILVER STAG, OAK & THORNS, IRON BONES, A SHADOW OF CROWS, and THE HALLOWED HUNT. The sixth and seventh, THE SILVER MIST and WITCHING HOUR, will be out within a few months. Preorder THE SILVER MIST now, and WITCHING HOUR will be available for preorder soon. There will be more to come after that.

I also invite you to visit Fury's world. In a gritty, post-apocalyptic Seattle, Fury is a minor goddess, in charge of eliminating the Abominations who come off the World Tree. Book 1-5 are available now in the Fury Unbound Series : FURY RISING, FURY'S MAGIC, FURY AWAKENED, FURY CALLING, and FURY'S MANTLE.

If you prefer a lighter-hearted but still steamy paranormal romance, meet the wild and magical residents of Bedlam in my Bewitching Bedlam Series. Fun-loving witch Maddy Gallowglass, her smoking-hot vampire lover Aegis, and their crazed cjinn Bubba (part djinn, all cat) rock it out in Bedlam, a magical town on a mystical island. BLOOD MUSIC, BEWITCHING BEDLAM, MAUDLIN'S MAYHEM, SIREN'S SONG, WITCHES WILD, CASTING CURSES, BLOOD VENGEANCE, TIGER TAILS, and Bubba's origin story THE WISH FACTOR are all available.

For a dark, gritty, steamy series, try my world of The Indigo Court , where the long winter has come, and the Vampiric Fae are on the rise. The series is complete with NIGHT MYST, NIGHT VEIL, NIGHT SEEKER, NIGHT VISION, NIGHT'S END, and NIGHT SHIVERS.

If you like cozies with teeth, try my Chintz 'n China paranormal mysteries. The series is complete with: GHOST OF A CHANCE, LEGEND OF THE JADE DRAGON, MURDER UNDER A MYSTIC MOON, A HARVEST OF BONES, ONE HEX OF A WEDDING, and a wrap-up novella: HOLIDAY SPIRITS.

For all of my work, both published and upcoming

releases, see the Biography at the end of this book, or check out my website at Galenorn.com and be sure and sign up for my newsletter to receive news about all my new releases.

PLAYLIST

I often write to music, and BLOOD BONDS was no exception. Here's the playlist I used for this book:

- **Three Doors Down:** Kryptonite
- **AJ Roach:** Devil May Dance
- **Android Lust:** Here and Now
- **Arcade Fire:** Abraham's Daughter
- **Arch Leaves:** Nowhere to Go
- **The Animals:** Bury My Body
- **AWOLNATION:** Sail
- **Band of Skulls:** I Know What I Am
- **Beck:** Farewell Ride; Emergency Exit
- **The Black Angels:** Half Believing; Hunt Me Down; Death March
- **Black Mountain:** Queens Will Play
- **Bon Jovi:** Wanted Dead or Alive
- **The Bravery:** Believe
- **Broken Bells:** The Ghost Inside
- **Buffalo Springfield:** For What It's Worth

PLAYLIST

- **Camouflage Nights:** (It Could Be) Love
- **Cobra Verde:** Play With Fire
- **Colin Foulke:** Emergence
- **Crazytown:** Butterfly
- **David Bowie:** Golden Years; I'm Afraid of Americans
- **Death Cab For Cutie:** I Will Possess Your Heart
- **Eastern Sun:** Beautiful Being
- **Eels:** Souljacker Part 1
- **Everlast:** Black Jesus; I Can't Move
- **FC Kahuna:** Hayling
- **Garbage:** Queer
- **The Gospel Whiskey Runners:** Muddy Waters
- **Gypsy Soul:** Who?
- **The Hang Drum Project:** Sukram; Shaken Oak; St. Chartier
- **Harvey Danger:** Sad Sweetheart of the Rodeo
- **The Hollies:** Long Cool Woman
- **Jessica Bates:** The Hanging Tree
- **John Fogerty:** The Old Man Down the Road
- **The Kills:** Nail in My Coffin; You Don't Own the Road
- **Lorde:** Royals; Yellow Flicker Beat
- **Pearl Jam:** Even Flow; Jeremy
- **PJ Harvey:** Let England Shake; The Glorious Land; The Words that Maketh Murder; In the Dark Places; The Colour of the Earth
- **Rob Zombie:** Living Dead Girl
- **Robin Schultz:** Sugar
- **Saliva:** Ladies and Gentlemen
- **Scorpions:** The Zoo
- **Seether:** Remedy

- **Shriekback:** And The Rain; Wriggle and Drone; Church of the Louder Light; Now These Days Are Gone
- **Tina Turner:** We Don't Need Another Hero; One of the Living; I Can't Stand The Rain
- **Tom Petty:** Mary Jane's Last Dance
- **Traffic:** The Low Spark of High Heeled Boys
- **The Verve:** Bitter Sweet Symphony
- **Yoko Kanno:** Lithium Flower
- **Zero 7:** In the Waiting Line

CAST OF MAJOR CHARACTERS

The D'Artigo Family:

- **Arial Lianan te Maria:** Delilah's twin who died at birth. Half-Fae, half-human.
- **Camille Sepharial te Maria, aka Camille D'Artigo:** The oldest sister; a Moon Witch and Priestess. Half-Fae, half-human.
- **Daniel George Fredericks:** The D'Artigo sisters' half cousin; FBH.
- **Delilah Maria te Maria, aka Delilah D'Artigo:** The middle sister; a werecat.
- **Hester Lou Fredericks:** The D'Artigo sisters' half cousin; FBH.
- **Maria D'Artigo:** The D'Artigo Sisters' mother. Human. Deceased.
- **Menolly Rosabelle te Maria, aka Menolly D'Artigo:** The youngest sister; a vampire and *jian-tu:* extraordinary acrobat. Half-Fae, half-human.

- **Sephreh ob Tanu:** The D'Artigo Sisters' father. Full Fae. Deceased.
- **Shamas ob Olanda:** The D'Artigo girls' cousin. Full Fae. Deceased.

The D'Artigo Sisters' Lovers & Close Friends:

- **Astrid (Johnson):** Chase and Sharah's baby daughter.
- **Bruce O'Shea:** Iris's husband. Leprechaun.
- **Carter:** Leader of the Demonica Vacana Society, a group that watches and records the interactions of Demonkin and human through the ages. Carter is half demon and half Titan—his father was Hyperion, one of the Greek Titans.
- **Chase Garden Johnson:** Detective, director of the Faerie–Human Crime Scene Investigation (FH-CSI) team. Human who has taken the Nectar of Life, which extends his life span beyond any ordinary mortal and has opened up his psychic abilities.
- **Chrysandra:** Waitress at the Wayfarer Bar & Grill. Human. Deceased.
- **Derrick Means:** Bartender at the Wayfarer Bar & Grill. Werebadger.
- **Erin Mathews:** Former president of the Faerie Watchers Club and former owner of the Scarlet Harlot Boutique. Turned into a vampire by Menolly, her sire, moments before her death. Human.

CAST OF MAJOR CHARACTERS

- **Greta:** Leader of the Death Maidens; Delilah's tutor.
- **Iris (Kuusi) O'Shea:** Friend and companion of the girls. Priestess of Undutar. Talon-haltija (Finnish house sprite).
- **Lindsey Katharine Cartridge:** Director of the Green Goddess Women's Shelter. Pagan and witch. Human.
- **Maria O'Shea:** Iris and Bruce's baby daughter.
- **Marion Vespa:** Coyote shifter; owner of the Supe-Urban Café.
- **Morio Kuroyama:** One of Camille's lovers and husbands. Essentially the grandson of Grandmother Coyote. Youkai-kitsune (roughly translated: Japanese fox demon).
- **Nerissa Shale:** Menolly's wife. Worked for DSHS. Now working for Chase Johnson as a victims-rights counselor for the FH-CSI. Werepuma and member of the Rainier Puma Pride.
- **Roman:** Ancient vampire; son of Blood Wyne, Queen of the Crimson Veil. Menolly's official consort in the Vampire Nation and her new sire.
- **Queen Asteria:** The former Elfin Queen. Deceased.
- **Queen Sharah:** Was an elfin medic, now the new Elfin Queen; Chase's girlfriend.
- **Rozurial, aka Roz:** Mercenary. Menolly's secondary lover. Incubus who used to be Fae before Zeus and Hera destroyed his marriage.

CAST OF MAJOR CHARACTERS

- **Shade:** Delilah's fiancé. Part Stradolan, part black (shadow) dragon.
- **Siobhan Morgan:** One of the girls' friends. Selkie (wereseal); member of the Puget Sound Harbor Seal Pod.
- **Smoky:** One of Camille's lovers and husbands. Half-white, half-silver dragon.
- **Tanne Baum:** One of the Black Forest woodland Fae. A member of the Hunter's Glen Clan.
- **Tavah:** Guardian of the portal at the Wayfarer Bar & Grill. Vampire (full Fae).
- **Tim Winthrop, aka Cleo Blanco:** Computer student/genius, female impersonator. FBH. Now owns the Scarlet Harlot.
- **Trillian:** Mercenary. Camille's alpha lover and one of her three husbands. Svartan (one of the Charming Fae).
- **Ukkonen O'Shea:** Iris and Bruce's baby son.
- **Vanzir:** Was indentured slave to the Sisters, by his own choice. Dream-chaser demon who lost his powers and now is regaining new ones.
- **Venus the Moon Child:** Former shaman of the Rainier Puma Pride. Werepuma. One of the Keraastar Knights.
- **Wade Stevens:** President of Vampires Anonymous. Vampire (human).
- **Zachary Lyonnesse:** Former member of the Rainier Puma Pride Council of Elders. Werepuma living in Otherworld.

GLOSSARY

- **Black Unicorn/Black Beast:** Father of the Dahns unicorns, a magical unicorn that is reborn like the phoenix and lives in Darkynwyrd and Thistlewyd Deep. Raven Mother is his consort, and he is more a force of nature than a unicorn.
- **Calouk:** The rough, common dialect used by a number of Otherworld inhabitants.
- **Court and Crown:** "Crown" refers to the Queen of Y'Elestrial. "Court" refers to the nobility and military personnel that surround the Queen. "Court and Crown" together refer to the entire government of Y'Elestrial.
- **Court of the Three Queens:** The newly risen Court of the three Earthside Fae Queens: Titania, the Fae Queen of Light and Morning; Morgaine, the half-Fae Queen of Dusk and Twilight; and Aeval, the Fae Queen of Shadow and Night.

- **Crypto:** One of the Cryptozoid races. Cryptos include creatures out of legend that are not technically of the Fae races: gargoyles, unicorns, gryphons, chimeras, and so on. Most primarily inhabit Otherworld, but some have Earthside cousins.
- **Demon Gate:** A gate through which demons may be summoned by a powerful sorcerer or necromancer.
- **Demonica Vacana Society:** A society run by a number of ancient entities, including Carter, who study and record the history of demonic activity over Earthside. The archives of the society are found in the Demonica Catacombs, deep within an uninhabited island of the Cyclades, a group of Grecian islands in the Aegean Sea.
- **Dreyerie:** A dragon lair.
- **Earthside:** Everything that exists on the Earth side of the portals.
- **Elqaneve:** The Elfin city in Otherworld, located in Kelvashan—the Elfin lands.
- **Elemental Lords:** The elemental beings—both male and female—who, along with the Hags of Fate and the Harvestmen, are the only true Immortals. They are avatars of various elements and energies, and they inhabit all realms. They do as they will and seldom concern themselves with humankind or Fae unless summoned. If asked for help, they often exact steep prices in return. The Elemental Lords are not concerned with balance like the Hags of Fate.

GLOSSARY

- **FBH:** Full-Blooded Human (usually refers to Earthside humans).
- **FH-CSI:** The Faerie–Human Crime Scene Investigation team. The brainchild of Detective Chase Johnson, it was first formed as a collaboration between the OIA and the Seattle police department. Other FH-CSI units have been created around the country, based on the Seattle prototype. The FH-CSI takes care of both medical and criminal emergencies involving visitors from Otherworld.
- **Great Divide:** A time of immense turmoil when the Elemental Lords and some of the High Court of Fae decided to rip apart the worlds. Until then, the Fae existed primarily on Earth, their lives and worlds mingling with those of humans. The Great Divide tore everything asunder, splitting off another dimension, which became Otherworld. At that time, the Twin Courts of Fae were disbanded and their queens and the Merlin were stripped of power. This was the time during which the Spirit Seal was formed and broken in order to seal off the realms from each other. Some Fae chose to stay Earthside, while others moved to the realm of Otherworld, and the demons were—for the most part—sealed in the Subterranean Realms.
- **Guard Des'Estar:** The military of Y'Elestrial.
- **Hags of Fates:** The women of destiny who keep the balance righted. Neither good nor evil, they observe the flow of destiny. When events get too far out of balance, they step in and take

GLOSSARY

action, usually using humans, Fae, Supes, and other creatures as pawns to bring the path of destiny back into line.
- **Harvestmen:** The lords of death—a few cross over and are also Elemental Lords. The Harvestmen, along with their followers (the Valkyries and the Death Maidens, for example), reap the souls of the dead.
- **Haseofon:** The abode of the Death Maidens— where they stay and where they train.
- **Ionyc Lands:** The astral, etheric, and spirit realms, along with several other lesser-known noncorporeal dimensions, form the Ionyc Lands. These realms are separated by the Ionyc Seas, a current of energy that prevents the Ionyc Lands from colliding, thereby sparking off an explosion of universal proportions.
- **Ionyc Seas:** The currents of energy that separate the Ionyc Lands. Certain creatures, especially those connected with the elemental energies of ice, snow, and wind, can travel through the Ionyc Seas without protection.
- **Kelvashan:** The lands of the elves.
- **Koyanni:** The coyote shifters who took an evil path away from the Great Coyote; followers of Nukpana.
- **Melosealfôr:** A rare Crypto dialect learned by powerful Cryptos and all Moon Witches.
- **The Nectar of Life:** An elixir that can extend the life span of humans to nearly the length of a Fae's years. Highly prized and cautiously used. Can drive someone insane if he or she doesn't

have the emotional capacity to handle the changes incurred.
- **Oblition:** The act of a Death Maiden sucking the soul out of one of their targets.
- **OIA:** The Otherworld Intelligence Agency; the "brains" behind the Guard Des'Estar. Earthside Division now run by Camille, Menolly, and Delilah.
- **Otherworld/OW:** The human term for the "United Nations" of Faerie Land. A dimension apart from ours that contains creatures from legend and lore, pathways to the gods, and various other places, such as Olympus. Otherworld's actual name varies among the differing dialects of the many races of Cryptos and Fae.
- **Portal, Portals:** The interdimensional gates that connect the different realms. Some were created during the Great Divide; others open up randomly.
- **Seelie Court:** The Earthside Fae Court of Light and Summer, disbanded during the Great Divide. Titania was the Seelie Queen.
- **Soul Statues:** In Otherworld, small figurines created for the Fae of certain races and magically linked with the baby. These figurines reside in family shrines and when one of the Fae dies, their soul statue shatters. In Menolly's case, when she was reborn as a vampire, her soul statue re-formed, although twisted. If a family member disappears, his or her family can always tell if their loved one is

alive or dead if they have access to the soul statue.
- **Spirit Seals:** A magical crystal artifact, the Spirit Seal was created during the Great Divide. When the portals were sealed, the Spirit Seal was broken into nine gems and each piece was given to an Elemental Lord or Lady. These gems each have varying powers. Even possessing one of the spirit seals can allow the wielder to weaken the portals that divide Otherworld, Earthside, and the Subterranean Realms. If all of the seals are joined together again, then all of the portals will open.
- **Stradolan:** A being who can walk between worlds, who can walk through the shadows, using them as a method of transportation.
- **Supe/Supes:** Short for Supernaturals. Refers to Earthside supernatural beings who are not of Fae nature. Refers to Weres, especially.
- **Talamh Lonrach Oll:** The name for the Earthside Sovereign Fae Nation.
- **Triple Threat:** Camille's nickname for the newly risen three Earthside Queens of Fae.
- **Unseelie Court:** The Earthside Fae Court of Shadow and Winter, disbanded during the Great Divide. Aeval was the Unseelie Queen.
- **VA/Vampires Anonymous:** The Earthside group started by Wade Stevens, a vampire who was a psychiatrist during life. The group is focused on helping newly born vampires adjust to their new state of existence, and to encourage vampires to avoid harming the

innocent as much as possible. The VA is vying for control. Their goal is to rule the vampires of the United States and to set up an internal policing agency.
- **Whispering Mirror:** A magical communications device that links Otherworld and Earth. Think magical video phone.
- **Y'Eírialiastar:** The Sidhe/Fae name for Otherworld.
- **Y'Elestrial:** The city-state in Otherworld where the D'Artigo girls were born and raised. A Fae city, recently embroiled in a civil war between the drug-crazed tyrannical Queen Lethesanar and her more level-headed sister Tanaquar, who managed to claim the throne for herself. The civil war has ended and Tanaquar is restoring order to the land.
- **Youkai:** Loosely (very loosely) translated as Japanese demon/nature spirit. For the purposes of this series, the youkai have three shapes: the animal, the human form, and the true demon form. Unlike the demons of the Subterranean Realms, youkai are not necessarily evil by nature.

BIOGRAPHY

New York Times, Publishers Weekly, and USA Today bestselling author Yasmine Galenorn writes urban fantasy and paranormal romance, and is the author of over sixty books, including the Wild Hunt Series, the Fury Unbound Series, the Bewitching Bedlam Series, the Indigo Court Series, and the Otherworld Series, among others. She's also written nonfiction metaphysical books. She is the 2011 Career Achievement Award Winner in Urban Fantasy, given by RT Magazine.

Yasmine has been in the Craft since 1980, is a shamanic witch and High Priestess. She describes her life as a blend of teacups and tattoos. She lives in Kirkland, WA, with her husband Samwise and their cats. Yasmine can be reached via her website at Galenorn.com.

Indie Releases Currently Available:

The Wild Hunt Series:
   The Silver Stag

Oak & Thorns
Iron Bones
A Shadow of Crows
The Hallowed Hunt
The Silver Mist
Witching Hour

Bewitching Bedlam Series:
Bewitching Bedlam
Maudlin's Mayhem
Siren's Song
Witches Wild
Casting Curses
Blood Music
Blood Vengeance
Tiger Tails
The Wish Factor

Fury Unbound Series:
Fury Rising
Fury's Magic
Fury Awakened
Fury Calling
Fury's Mantle

Indigo Court Series:
Night Myst
Night Veil
Night Seeker
Night Vision
Night's End
Night Shivers

Indigo Court Books, 1-3: Night Myst, Night Veil, Night Seeker (Boxed Set)

Indigo Court Books, 4-6: Night Vision, Night's End, Night Shivers (Boxed Set)

Otherworld Series:

Moon Shimmers

Harvest Song

Blood Bonds

Earthbound

Knight Magic

Otherworld Tales: Volume One

Tales From Otherworld: Collection One

Men of Otherworld: Collection One

Men of Otherworld: Collection Two

Moon Swept: Otherworld Tales of First Love

For the rest of the Otherworld Series, see website at Galenorn.com.

Chintz 'n China Series:

Ghost of a Chance

Legend of the Jade Dragon

Murder Under a Mystic Moon

A Harvest of Bones

One Hex of a Wedding

Holiday Spirits

Chintz 'n China Books, 1 – 3: Ghost of a Chance, Legend of the Jade Dragon, Murder Under A Mystic Moon

Chintz 'n China Books, 4-6: A Harvest of Bones, One Hex of a Wedding, Holiday Spirits

Bath and Body Series (originally under the name India Ink):
Scent to Her Grave
A Blush With Death
Glossed and Found

Misc. Short Stories/Anthologies:
The Longest Night: A Starwood Novella
Mist and Shadows: Tales From Dark Haunts
Once Upon a Kiss (short story: Princess Charming)
Once Upon a Curse (short story: Bones)

Magickal Nonfiction:
Embracing the Moon
Tarot Journeys

Printed in Great Britain
by Amazon

ODE TO RUBY RING

J S SUTTON

First published in Great Britain as a softback original in 2023

Copyright © J S Sutton

The moral right of this author has been asserted.

All characters and events in this publication, other than those clearly in the public domain, are fictitious and any resemblance to real persons, living or dead, is purely coincidental.

All rights reserved.

No part of this publication may be reproduced, stored in a retrieval system, or transmitted, in any form or by any means, without the prior permission in writing of the publisher, nor be otherwise circulated in any form of binding or cover other than that in which it is published and without a similar condition including this condition being imposed on the subsequent purchaser.

Design, typesetting and publishing by UK Book Publishing

www.ukbookpublishing.com

ISBN: 978-1-915338-89-1

Author's Note: this book is best read while listening to *Cyberpunk/Ambient Music*

PROLOGUE

Time Of Death, 15:40

Ricky couldn't believe his eyes. The Boss, Lisa, here on the same shuttle flight to the outer orbit. She stared back also, probably not believing her eyes either. How did she get off the colony? How could she even remember him? He got up and sat opposite her.

'Hi,' he said, smiling.

'Hi,' she repeated, smiling also.

They then exchanged an awkward silence, not really knowing what to say, or even if the burning questions should be asked. The shuttle blasted into hyperspace but the g-force couldn't be felt in the passenger section. That was due to the bubble tech that the shuttle company employed to make hyperspace travel less taxing for frequent flyers. They both watched out the window as stars flew past in short white lines. How beautiful they were.

The flight attendant came past with refreshments and they both ordered a whiskey at the same time. Embarrassed, they fell silent once more. After several, agonizing moments, Ricky built up the courage to ask 'so how did you get off the colony this time?'

'What do you mean?' Lisa replied, looking around her for people who could be listening in.

'Well,' he began, not knowing if he should carry on the enquiry, she probably felt as though she was being interrogated, 'last time I saw you, you were standing over my brothers as they died on the colony, since then I've been having these dreams.'

'They call that PTSD,' she said, smiling as though she'd just won a game of chess.

'No,' he said, 'I mean, they started out like that, then they became increasingly sexual.'

The smile left her face, had Ricky gone too far? I probably have, he thought.

'Probably something Freudian,' she said, after a long silence, 'did you have a student/teacher crush at school?' her tone denoted ridicule, which made Ricky a little angry, but not enough to shout at her or anything like that.

Like a lot of people his age, Ricky was educated at Metro High. That was what all the kids called it, the actual name was too long to pronounce quickly. And, like a lot of schools, had a fair few young

PROLOGUE

teachers. Come to think of it, Ricky did have a crush on some of them at the time.

There was one, she wasn't particularly good looking, her main point of interest was her boobs, Mrs Payne. All the boys had a secret crush on Mrs Payne. They also had a locker room crush on Miss Adams, a young, supple sports teacher with blonde hair, blue eyes and an athletic body. Everyday, as they changed for sports lessons, they would make outlandish, and false, claims to have bedded the young Miss Adams. What they did, how she moaned and said they were the best lover out of all the others. It made Ricky laugh at some of them, but others, probably the best liars out of the rest, were quite believable. Though it never left the locker room banter stage.

The shuttle slowed down and the stars began to regain their shape.

'Where are you staying?' Ricky ventured.

'Pluto Regency,' Lisa answered, with a proud tone to her voice.

'Same,' Ricky lied, he didn't have anywhere to stay, he left New London before he had a chance to book a room. He hoped against hope that there was a spare room going at the Pluto Regency. He didn't know why, but he wanted Lisa, wanted her like he would've never comprehended wanting someone in his life. The shuttle finally came to a stop, and there was a violent jolt.

'Sorry about that folks,' the pilot said, in a trans-Atlantic drawl, over the tannoy, 'misjudged the stop there but don't worry, we'll be landing on Pluto shortly.'

'Fucking shuttle pilots,' Lisa said in an exacerbated tone.

Ricky smiled in agreement.

The Pluto Regency was built not long after humans started populating other planets. Its main purpose was to house people who wanted to go to other colonies situated in other systems, but couldn't handle the long flights and soon it started offering luxuries along with the standard mod cons. Thermal heated rooms, extra soft mattresses and pillows, room service at the click of a button.

They got to the Pluto Regency about an hour later, after a thorough search at the space port, and the Boss checked in before Ricky. When he was sure she'd gone up to her room, he pleaded with the woman at the front desk to give him a room, which she initially declined, until she saw the briefcase of money Ricky had, then she finally accepted and gave him the last remaining room key which was, fortunately for Ricky, right next to Lisa's room. They even shared a balcony that was protected from the elements by a force field that could be switched on and off from a button situated by the

PROLOGUE

french windows of either room. He got to his room and unpacked the rest of his money, laying it out in neat little piles on the bed. He had packed a few clothes, but no toiletries. He checked the bathroom and was relieved to find shower gel, toothpaste, toothbrush and various aftershaves placed conveniently by the sink. He decided to have a shower and change before trying to seduce the Boss. Lisa. Her name was Lisa here, she's only the Boss on the colony. They were on Pluto now so she ain't the boss of shit. After he'd showered, he got dressed and knocked on her door. She answered in a silk gown, her bright red hair damp and hanging just below her jaw. She was naked under her gown so Ricky assumed she'd just showered herself.

'Come in,' she said with a smile, and he entered, smiling also. They sat on the balcony and drank a while.

'So,' she began, after swallowing a gulp of whiskey, God she can drink, thought Ricky, 'you wanna know how I got off the colony.'

'Yeah,' Ricky replied.

'Well,' she put the glass on the small round table in front of her, 'it wasn't easy I'll tell you, I waited for a care package to be dropped off from New London, you know when I was the Boss, they let me onto the ships that drop off various items?' Ricky nodded, 'well I waited and waited until finally....one came and I talked my way on to it, you know, made promises that I'd screw the guy and the like. Then, in the cargo hold, I searched box after box after box until finally I found an empty one and climbed in. There I waited some more until the ship took off and I found myself back on New London. Then I just walked off and nobody said a word. 'Course I didn't screw the guy so I feel bad lying to him, but I wasn't going to anyway. So there I am, in New London. Nowhere to go, no one to see. I decided that the pigs were gonna find me eventually so I paid a visit to this tiny gun shop in the Highrise Quarter. Got myself a piece and burglarised a bank, got myself some new clothes, new hair, new passport and the like. Hopped on the next available shuttle and now I'm here, talking to you and drinking this fine whiskey.'

When she'd finished, she took another gulp of whiskey.

'I'm getting another one,' she said, 'you want one?'

Ricky shook his head and held up his three-quarter full glass and she went into her room to the mini bar. On her way out, she stopped by the french windows.

'You wanna screw me?' she asked, and Ricky looked surprised at her forward question. Sure, he wanted to but he thought she wasn't gonna

PROLOGUE

put out and he'd have to work for it. He crossed the balcony to the french windows and kissed her. They put their drinks down and lay on the bed.

A few hours later, they lay spent and sweating on the silk sheets. It'd been a long time since she'd done that. Too long in her eyes. For Ricky it'd been a few days.

'Oh shit,' she said, 'I think I left my drink on the balcony, can you fetch it for me?'

'Ok,' he said and walked, naked, onto the balcony outside, not knowing, in his post-coital stupor, that she had her drink next to her. She knew her drink wasn't on the balcony. When he realised this, he turned quickly and saw her standing there, naked also, and smiling. She closed and locked the french windows then switched the force field off. Within seconds, Ricky was an ice sculpture. Frozen there, naked and bewildered for all time.

'The black widow strikes again,' she laughed and took a sip of her whiskey.

Hours later, dressed and packed, she went into his room and stole his cash. Then she checked out and nobody saw her ever again.

PART 1

Picking Up The Pieces

1

It was raining in New London again. Kung Fo just got back from attending a multi-funeral. In New London, if people died in the same place at around the same time they were all buried at once, saved on the priest's time and the money spent on the ceremony. And grave space too as they were all dumped into the same hole, laying together for eternity. He still couldn't believe that he lost his friends and his mother in the same way and on the same day. He was angry, more than angry, he couldn't even find a word to express how pissed off he was. That damn mega-corporation, and Ricky for bringing them here to his home, his own doorstep. He couldn't stay angry with Ricky though. It wasn't his fault. He just wanted to know who the hell he was working for and what they wanted from him. He lifted a baggy of Ko Sang. He wanted to know what was so fucking good about this shit that made people want to kill each other. He cooked and injected. Then he saw why.

An abstract array of colours danced before him and shapes…..so many shapes. Shapes of all sizes and…..shapes.

Hours later and with the high over, he came to. He'd never got high on his own supply before. That was the cardinal rule of dealing. But at this moment in time he didn't care. He wanted to escape. He wanted the heat to come down on him from his dealing cohorts. He wanted to be with his friends, his mother. That was it now. Kung Fo was hooked. Where could he get some more? Where could he get anything? He wanted numbness, he wanted the soft oblivion of the high. He ached for it. He cried for it. Curled up in the corner of his room. Crying. He desperately scrambled for his laptop. He had to know someone online who was selling. Soon enough, after what seemed like hours of searching, he found someone who could supply him with some premium Ko Sang. They agreed on a time and place, and Kung Fo got out of his funeral suit and into a pair of maroon tracksuit bottoms and a grey hoodie. The place; the corner of Wang Xia street, the time; right fucking now.

The corner of Wang Xia street was cold and wet. Kung Fo shivered in his soaking clothes, he'd been waiting what seemed like hours for this guy to show up. A pod landed next to him and the door opened. Tentatively, he turned and looked, praying

CHAPTER 1

it wasn't the cops, praying they hadn't intercepted the communication between him and the would-be dealer. In the neon turquoise of the dashboard light, he saw a pretty, young girl who looked about seventeen. She had black hair, trimmed in what looked like a bob style on one side and shaved quite close on the other. He only saw one eye, as the other was covered by her hair, she was Asian. Half Asian actually. She was wearing a black PVC outfit with the sleeves of her top connected to the rest of it with safety pins. Store bought Kung Fo thought, probably didn't have the time or the patience to do it herself.

'Are you Kung Fo?' she asked.

'Yes,' he replied, 'are you "drugmule76?"'

'Get in,' she said and turned to fly away.

'Got the goods?' he asked desperately, he wasn't interested in anything else.

'Easy now,' she said with a smile, 'I could be a cop.'

'At this moment in time I don't give a shit, have you got it or not?'

'Woah!' she exclaimed, "in the glove box, you desperate fucker!'

He scrambled round for it, found the Ko Sang and put it in his pocket.

'How much?' he asked.

She pulled over and, turning off the engine,

turned to him. Was she going to ask for sex? Because right now couldn't be more of a worse time.

'I work for someone,' she began. Here we go, Kung Fo thought.

'Now before you say anything, he's not the bad guy here,' she said, 'he just wants something that belongs to him, something that was owed to him.'

'And?'

'He needs your help getting it.'

'Why does he need my help?'

'Cause he heard you're pretty good at what you do with computers.'

He looked at her.

'Who told you, or him for that matter?'

'We heard from an old associate of ours, how we did is none of your business yet.'

'I'm gonna need to think about it, take me home.'

'Of course.'

She turned the pod around and dropped him off at the corner of Wang Xia street.

He got out to leave then she stopped him.

'Here's my card,' she said, giving him a glossy, little piece of plastic, 'gimme a call when you've made up your mind. Oh, and Fo?, the 'Sang is on the house, if you agree to help us.'

When he got back, he cooked, injected and saw

CHAPTER 1

the shapes again. He didn't know why the shapes gave him comfort. Maybe it was something from his childhood, like nursery rhymes or a shapes book the teacher used to read out to the class in primary school, maybe it was just the drugs. When the high left him a few hours later, he looked at the card. It was sleek, silver, with the numbers raised and painted gold. Xiang Bancroft, the card said. He decided that it wouldn't hurt to see what they wanted from him. What else had he to do around the place? His mother was gone, his friends were gone, why not? He slid the card into his vid phone situated at the side of his bed and green letters came up on the screen. "Calling Xiang Bancroft" it read. She answered a few rings later.

'Ah, Kung Fo!' she said with a smile on her face, 'have you made up your mind?'

'Yeah,' he said, 'I'll meet you and your boss and see what you guys want.'

When they hung up from one another, Kung Fo went to sleep. He dreamt of his mother, how she'd be ashamed of him for getting high on what he was meant to be selling, what he'd become, how he was going to use his computer knowledge for illegal purposes, more illegal than he'd used it before. Minor hacking wasn't a big thing to her. She knew he did it to help friends in need. But this seemed a bit more than just some minor hacking.

She just stared at him, shaking her head. She didn't say a word, she didn't have to, he knew she was ashamed and that tore him apart.

Air raid sirens blared over New Chinatown. Acid rain was coming. People rushed indoors and in the shelters to wait it out. It seemed, to Kung Fo, that the acid rain was never going to go away. They'd always have it. It cost a fortune for the city everytime they had a bad storm, like the one brewing now, to repair windows and rooftops and pods. In New Westminster, the politicians were talking endlessly about having to raise taxes in order to pay for all the damage caused by acid rain storms. Kung Fo woke up and looked out the window at the rain as it ran down. Leaving little grooves as it snaked its way to the bottom frame.

2

When the acid rain stopped and it was morning, he left his house and went up to the roof where his pod was. As he got in, he fished around his pocket for the calling card for Xiang.

He slid it into his pod's vidphone and it called her for him.

'Hey, Kung Fo!' she said, her tone was almost delighted.

'Time and place,' he grumbled. He was still half asleep.

'Ok,' she said, 'where I met you last night, I'll pick you up and take you to the building.'

'Don't bother, I've got my own ride.'

'Ok,' she said, 'it's in New Soho. Above the Golden Pineapple. When you get there, press the buzzer and ask for Danny.'

'Will you be there?'

'Yeah, I'm just getting ready to leave now.'

Kung Fo hung up and closed the door of his pod. He tuned into his favorite station on the radio and old-time synthwave music blared out the speakers. Shocked by the noise, he turned it down, his head thumping from the high. He looked through the glove box and found some painkillers. He dry swallowed them and, pressing the ignition button, took off for New Soho.

He got to the Golden Pineapple sometime later and parked his pod on the roof. He ran through the heavy rain to a door some fifty metres from the landing bay. Xiang's pod was already there. He pressed the buzzer and a tired voice came over the speaker.

'Yeah? Who is it?'

'Is Danny there?'

'Who is it?'

'Is Danny there?' Kung Fo repeated, a bit flustered by the unprofessionalism, 'it's Kung Fo.'

The door buzzed open and he went in.

He came to a stairwell and walked down. The stairs were dark and he had trouble seeing where he was going. He found a door and knocked. Xiang answered with a smile. In the daylight he saw that she was wearing coal coloured eye shadow on the one eye he could see that wasn't covered by her hair. She wore a white vest, combat trousers and white trainers. She showed him in and directed for him to sit at a table in an office in the corner of the room. He sat down and waited for what seemed

CHAPTER 2

like a few moments, then they were joined by a young-looking guy who sat at the opposite end of the table. Kung Fo noticed that the room and the office itself were bare and basic. Maybe he doesn't live here, he thought.

The young-looking guy introduced himself as Danny. He had black hair in a crew cut style, probable military background Kung Fo assumed, covered head to toe in tattoos, he wore a light pink polo shirt, grey trousers and a ring on each finger.

'Hello Mr Fo,' he began.

'Kung Fo, please,' Kung Fo said.

'Ok,' Danny said, 'I assume you're wondering why I wanted you here today?'

'The thought had crossed my mind, yeah.'

'Well,' Danny continued, 'I heard, from a very reliable source, that you're really good with computers.'

'Ok,' Kung Fo said, wondering where this conversation was going.

'I need you to break into a bank's security and retrieve a code to a safety deposit box,' Danny said.

'Is that it?' Kung Fo asked, 'I could do that in my sleep, why the cloak and dagger? And why bring me in like this? Dragging Xiang into this too.'

Xiang blushed.

'It's the contents of the box I'm more interested in,' Danny replied, 'it's something of great value.

My father was supposed to leave it to me but he left it to my brother instead, just before he died.'

'What is it?'

'A ruby ring.'

Kung Fo looked at Danny's hands.

'Don't you have enough?'

Danny laughed.

'It may seem so, yes.'

'Ok,' Kung Fo finally conceded, 'say I do get you this code, what's in it for me?'

'What do you want?'

'To die, at this moment in time.'

Danny looked shocked, Xiang filled him in on what happened, how did she know? Was she there in New Chinatown when the shit hit the fan? No, he'd reached out to her for drugs and all of a sudden she knew everything about him? Damn it, she looked him up while he was sleeping no doubt.

'Well we'll discuss that at a later date,' Danny said, 'anything I can get you now?'

'Some powerful painkillers,' Kung Fo said, 'my head's killing me.'

When they left the office and returned to the roof, Xiang turned to Kung Fo.

'Did you really mean what you said in there?'

'What do you mean?'

'About wanting to die.'

'How would you feel if you lost all your friends

CHAPTER 2

and your mother on the same day?'

'I suppose.'

She sighed and suddenly her arms were round him.

'I'm sorry for your loss, really I am,' she said and released him.

'Who did I just talk to?' Kung Fo asked.

'Danny Von Croft.'

'THE Danny Von Croft?'

'Yeah,' she bit her bottom lip, 'why? Is there a problem?'

'Well yeah,' Kung Fo answered, 'it was the Von Croft corporation that killed my friends and my mother.'

'Oh God,' she said, the realisation of the connection between the Von Croft family and Kung Fo suddenly dawning on her, 'if I'd have known-'

'Don't worry,' he interrupted, 'it's no bother. Seems to me that he has just as much a problem with the mega-corp as I do.'

'Well yeah,' she said, 'he got disowned and left out because he didn't want to continue the family business of selling drugs and sub-par accommodation to people who couldn't afford any better.'

'Sounds like a real cool guy,' he said, 'what did he wanna do with his life?'

'He wanted to join the military, hence, the hair

and tattoos.'

'I see,' he said and turned to leave.

She stopped him with a hand on his arm.

'Is there anything we can get to help you break into the bank?'

'Gonna need a VR headset.'

'What about software?'

'Software I got.'

'I'll pick one up personally,' she said, 'and deliver it to you tonight. Go home, rest and I'll see you later.'

They got in their respective pods and took off in different directions.

3

The buzzer rang nine hours later. It was Xiang with the VR headset.

Kung Fo let her in and closed the door behind her.

'Top of the line in VR this is,' she said, proudly as she handed it to him.

He unboxed the headset and was impressed by what he saw. Yeah it was still a clunky headset but its specs were high end.

'How much did this steal from you?'

'Not much,' she replied, 'got it on the black market, down in the Highrise Quarter off this kid who'd lifted it from one of the Butters boys.'

'Is he dead yet?'

'He soon will be.'

If there was anyone you didn't steal from it was the Butters family. Kung Fo remembered reading the newspaper one morning about some cop who'd managed to infiltrate the New Krays and the Butters family in particular. He ended up killed.

He hooked the headset up to his laptop.

'Which bank am I going into?' he asked Xiang.

'Anderson & Anderson,' she replied.

'Right,' he said as he lowered the VR headset over his eyes.

Green grid patterns danced in front of him then settled into stillness as he logged in. He moved the mouse pad's cursor over the logo for Anderson & Anderson Banking and clicked. The site came up in the visor of the headset. In the corner of the screen was an 'ask me' button. He clicked on that and a chat window came up.

'Hello,' the automated message said, 'how may I help you today?'

'Safety deposit box codes,' he typed.

'Sorry,' it read again, 'you need an access code for that query, please answer the following question so we may transfer you to the right box.'

'Shit,' he said out loud.

'What's wrong?' Xiang asked.

'It says I need to answer a question,' he said.

'What question?'

'What was the name of his first pet? I'm assuming it's Adam Von Croft's first pet?'

'Let me call Danny, he might know.'

An hour later, Xiang came back.

'Fido,' she said, 'type in Fido.'

He did so and a blue screen popped up showing

the code for the safety deposit box.

1354.

'Got it,' he said and selected the print page icon on his visor/desktop.

'That was simple enough,' she said.

'Told you I could do it in my sleep, why the hell did he want me to do it? Isn't he computer savvy?'

'You'll have to ask him, he's on his way over, he knows where you live.'

'How?'

'I told him over the phone,' she said, a little sheepishly.

'Why'd you do that?'

''Cause I thought he could help!'

Kung Fo growled.

'I don't like people knowing too much about me,' he said, 'especially if I don't know them well enough.'

'I'm sorry,' she said.

The atmosphere became cold. Why the hell did she tell Danny Von Croft, of all people, where he lived? He'd have much preferred to meet him somewhere to exchange the info for whatever he was going to use to off himself.

He took the headset off and stared at her.

'I'm sorry ok?' she said, her tone apologetic and sad. She'd screwed up, she thought.

Kung Fo felt hungry, more hungry than he'd

ever felt. He was in the process of frying some vegetables when the buzzer rang. Xiang answered for him and Danny came through the door.

'Before we start,' Danny began, 'I just wanted to tell you how happy I am with your service Kung Fo.'

Kung Fo emptied the contents of the wok onto three plates and set them down on the table.

Xiang and Danny both thanked him as they sat down.

He wasn't happy they were there but what could he do? It was impolite to order them to leave. It was his role as gracious host that stopped him from kicking them out of his place.

'So,' Danny continued, once their plates were empty, 'where is the info I requested?'

'I printed it out for you, it's on the desk in the corner,' Kung Fo said.

Danny walked over to the desk and inspected the sheet before him.

'Good,' he said, folding the piece of paper and putting it into his pocket.

'Where's my way out?' Kung Fo asked.

'In the pod,' Danny said, 'Xiang? Be a darling and go and get it.'

She disappeared up to the pod and minutes later came back with a big bag of Ko Sang.

'Don't inject it all at once,' Danny said, smiling

CHAPTER 3

as if he were talking to a child, 'I need you to collect the ring from the bank yourself.'

'What?!' Kung Fo exclaimed, 'you never said-'

'The bank know my face, they know not to let me in under strict instructions from my late father,' Danny interrupted, 'why do you think I asked for you? When I could've easily done it myself.'

The role of gracious host went out the window.

'I think it's best you two leave,' he said, and Danny and Xiang did as asked.

Before she left, Xiang turned around and said, 'I really think you should reconsider this job, Danny can give you whatever it is you want.'

4

A few days later, Kung Fo was still considering the job. Whatever I want? he thought, what I want is to not exist, to hell with it all.

He picked up the bag of Ko Sang. Only a quarter left. He'd been using a lot since that day, when he asked them to leave he went straight to cooking and injecting.

Don't inject it all at once, the phrase repeated in his mind, made him mad, what did he mean? What did he expect? He went over to his laptop and put his VR headset on. If they did some digging on him, he was going to dig on them. The same green grid did its dance before settling down as he logged on. Through his visor, he saw their rap sheets on a dark web page.

Daniel 'Danny' Von Croft, aged 30, educated at Metro High, passed all his courses with distinction, joined the army in '44, much to the disdain of his family who wanted him to carry on in their stead selling properties to the poor. Dishonourably discharged in '46 and made a living off his father's money.

Xiang Bancroft, also 30, educated at Metro High too, mother was Asian, father was white, didn't pass any courses but repeated them at college where she passed with distinction. Never joined the army but was taught combat at home. Worked for many rich people as security personnel.

So, a rich boy and a school dropout. What a world we live in, Kung Fo thought.

He was puzzled by the thought that if they were the same age, went to the same school, how come they only noticed each other now? Moved in different circles maybe? He didn't know. Then he realised, Metro High was a big school, it's highly possible to go to the same school and not know each other. He was also amazed Xiang was as old as she was, she still looked like a teenager. Good genes probably.

After an hour and still searching the dark web for more info, the cravings came on so he took the headset off and, rubbing his eyes, he cooked and injected. The shapes….the beautiful shapes….

When the high left him he got up from his bed and made a coffee. He was going to have to be awake for what was coming next. He was going to call Xiang and talk through this whole thing. He again slid the calling card into the vidphone on the side of his bed and the green lettering came up.

PART 2:

Employment History

5

A few days later, they met in a neon soaked cafe just off Tanaka street. Xiang couldn't believe Kung Fo would consider coming back to the assignment. But then again, he thought, that's all I am to her, an assignment.

She was wearing her PVC bodysuit with the cutoff arms held in place by safety pins again.

Eyes like a panda from the rain.

They sat silently until their coffees were cooled slightly.

'So,' she began, taking a sip, 'what made you want to come back?'

'Nothing else better to do,' he admitted.

'It can't just be that, it just can't.'

'What do you mean?'

'Well you called me instead of Danny, there must be something there, surely.'

'Didn't have Danny's calling card, plus, anyway, I have a problem.'

'With Danny?'

He took a sip before carrying on.

'With the Von Croft name. His brother ordered my friends and my mother dead.'

'Paton?'

'Yeah,' he took another sip and revelled slightly as the warm liquid ran down his throat, now he knew the name of the person he was going to kill. Paton Von Croft. He wasn't sure if Danny was going to stop him, being his brother and all. At this moment he didn't care. He finally had leverage in this deal. A new perk. If he was going to get this ruby ring for Danny, he wanted permission, and assurance that Danny wouldn't intervene, to kill Paton. He still didn't know what was so Goddamn special about this ring. You could get replica ruby rings from a street vendor for fifty sub credits. He was going to ask Danny about this later.

Later on, they were both at the office door of Danny Von Croft. Xiang knocked for both of them.

'Come in,' a voice at the other side said, 'the door's open.'

Danny was wearing a pink polo shirt and grey cargo shorts. Again he had rings on his fingers.

'I need to get that ring today,' he said, 'I've heard through the grapevine that Paton is going to pick it up tomorrow and I need that ring gone from the safety deposit box before he gets there.'

'What is so special about this ring?'

CHAPTER 5

Kung Fo asked.

'I'm glad you asked,' Danny said, 'it's the last known genuine ruby ring left, its value alone is worth a few million.'

'So you want me to steal it, so you can sell it?'

'No, I want you to steal it, so I can keep a hold of it for a few years, plus it means Paton can't have it, fucking Daddy's blue-eyed boy.'

'So, what's the history?'

'Between Paton and myself?'

'Yeah.'

'Well,' Danny began, leaning forward, 'Paton was always Daddy's favourite. Right from birth. Daddy had big plans for him to carry on the family business.'

'Of selling drugs and shitty apartments while the Von Crofts lived in luxury?'

Danny looked embarrassed.

'Well,' he continued, 'whatever you feel about the business, it's still the family bread and butter.' He leaned back in his chair and looked at Kung Fo with immense cynicism.

'I'm to understand,' he said finally, 'that you are a dealer too, just on a smaller scale. We sell what you sell.'

'I'm beginning to think that over,' Kung Fo said.

'Oh?' Danny enquired.

'Yeah,' it was Kung Fo's time to lean forward,

'I'm thinking about getting out of that business. Not for me I think.'

'When will this change occur?'

'After this job, I want out. That reminds me. I'm going to kill your brother.'

Danny looked furious but kept his cool. Probably trying to rile me up, he thought.

Kung Fo smiled. He knew that Danny wouldn't wish his brother dead, no matter how much he hated him.

They were sitting in the pod outside the bank. The rain splashing down on the roof making it barely possible to talk without raising their voices.

'The ring should be in box two hundred and forty,' Danny said, 'just get in there and grab it.'

'Ok,' Kung Fo said.

He opened the door and stepped out into the deluge. Looking up he saw the building in all its opulent glory. They'd really splashed out on this place. It stood nearly twenty stories high and its doors were illuminated gold by the lights above them. It was guarded by two armed, meat-headed men in navy blue overalls, black army boots and brandishing AK47s. When he saw this, Kung Fo became slightly nervous. He was unarmed and didn't know what to say if he was stopped. Danny hadn't explained that to him. All Danny wanted was that fucking ring. He walked up to the door.

CHAPTER 5

Thankfully the guards let him in with nothing more than a nod of acknowledgment. Inside the bank was more luxurious than the exterior, with turquoise marble floors and walls, its ceiling hidden in the dark shadow that one would expect of a building that tall. The lamps hung in oblong chandeliers and almost blinded him as he looked at them. The reception desk sat in the middle of the atrium, manned by a skinny, beautiful black woman. His wet trainers squeaked on the marble as he made his way towards her. Each squeak echoing so loudly it made him feel self-conscious of where he was. This was a bank for the super-rich after all. As he drew closer, the receptionist looked up with a look of disapproval on her face when noticing he didn't dress like their usual clientele.

When he got to the desk, he smiled. She forced a smile back. She was pretty in a stuck up bitch kind of way. Her name tag said 'Trisha' and under it she had scrawled with a ballpoint 'be kind, I'm new!'

'Box two hundered and forty, please,' he asked.

'Just need to go through some security,' she murmured, not entirely happy with the situation, 'security code, please.'

'1354,' he replied.

She looked up and smiled at him. This one seemed genuine.

'Mr Von Croft?' she asked.

'That's me,' he laughed nervously, he prayed she didn't notice.

'Ok,' she said, 'that's security taken care of.'

'Is that it?' he asked.

'Pardon me?'

'Nothing.'

She ignored this last comment and started fishing round her desk draws for the card to the vault.

'Just need the key card,' she said, slightly under her breath, 'then I'll escort you to the safety deposit vault, then you can do what you like in there, with me there to assist you of course.'

'Thank you,' he said.

He loved new employees. They were so easy to manipulate and they were so eager to please. Especially high profile clientèle.

6

They got to the vault several minutes later. For what it was, the security was pretty lax in this place. The vault was darker than the atrium, and seemed bigger too. Inside this huge room was an almost endless maze. Stacks of safety deposit boxes reaching to the ceiling, and beyond it seemed, he couldn't really see.

He turned to the receptionist and asked 'so what's Trisha short for? Patrisha?'

'No,' she said slowly, 'it's short for Latrisha,' she was talking to him as though she were correcting a child that had asked an outlandish but nevertheless dumb question, as some children often do. Fo got a little bit angry but he let it pass, he was going to rob this bitch soon and get her in a whole heap of shit with her mega-corp higher-ups, so he didn't mind the odd jibe in his direction. Made the whole situation easier for him.

They found box two hundred and forty, with a little help from a scanner the receptionist had, in no time at all. Opening it, Kung Fo found it was empty, save for a tiny jewellery box. He opened it and there, staring back at him in its scarlet glory, was the ring. He could see why Danny was so eager to have it. Even he wanted it. He considered taking it for himself, lying to Danny saying that Paton had gotten to it before them. It was the last known ring made from genuine ruby after all. Suddenly, an alarm rang out, breaking Kung Fo away from his trance.

'DNA incompatible,' a robotic voice over the speakers said.

'What's happening?' he shouted over the alarm.

'It appears,' Latrisha called back, 'you're not Mr Von Croft.'

Pushing past and knocking her over, he put the ring in the front pouch of his hoodie and ran for the door, which was now starting to close slowly. He got there just as it was inches away from closing shut, and rolled under it. It closed with a loud thudding sound and he checked his hoodie front pouch to see if the ring was still with him. It was. He breathed a sigh of relief as it shone up at him. To his left and right, he heard heavy, booted footsteps. The armed guards! He ran for the front door, dodging gunfire and shouts of "FREEZE!!"

The meatheads at the front door tried to block his path, but he simply slid underneath them, got

CHAPTER 6

up and carried on running. He ran down the steps to the pod, just as Danny was starting the engine up. He got in and they sped away. Police pods in hot pursuit.

'Do you have it?' Danny asked. Kung Fo was panting heavily. He hadn't ran like that in years. Not since his time at Metro High when he was a track star. He was a peculiar student at school. He was an athlete who was also fantastic at computers. Most students were either one or the other. Other students weren't good at anything, and Kung Fo felt sorry for them.

'Do you have it?!' Danny repeated, louder over the whirring sirens of the New London Police pods.

'I got it right here,' Kung Fo replied, still trying to catch his breath. He pulled the ring out of his front pouch and stared at it. The scarlet stone, shimmering in his eyes. He wanted to keep it for himself. Question was, how was he going to go about doing that? Jump out a moving pod and fall the thirty floors to his death? He saw his lifeless body, soaking wet and still clutching the ring in his stiff fist. No, he thought, someone would loot it from his corpse. Kill Danny and drive the pod down to the colony? He could hide for a while but if the mutant insects didn't get him then the gangs would, plus he wasn't exactly dressed to survive the weather down there.

Danny reached over and shook him from his trance. The Police pods were still in hot pursuit.

'Come on,' he said, even louder, 'we don't have time for this shit. Give me the ring and as soon as we shake these fuckers off, I'll let you out by your house.'

Reluctantly, Kung Fo handed over the ring and Danny snatched it from his grasp.

'I know,' Danny said, 'it's entrancing, isn't it? But it's mine now, I thank you for getting it for me, and for all the trouble you went through to get it.'

'Trouble?' Kung Fo exclaimed, 'got fucking shot at to get you this, you ever been shot at?'

He then remembered that Danny was in the military and regretted his question.

'Once,' Danny said, 'a long time ago, I was in the Chinese and NATO conflict, not long after New London entered its final stages of construction,' he made a quick right turn to avoid oncoming traffic, still flying at breakneck speed to escape their would-be captors, or killers if they were the Armed Response Unit, 'we were travelling down to Beijing in a convoy, when out of the sides of the roads came gunfire, we couldn't turn left or right to avoid the gunfire, so we moved forward, just kept going y'know? Anyway, we got several hundred yards down the road when a giant explosion rocked us. They'd used an RPG to blow up the truck ahead of us. We got out to survey the damage and fight back, but there was too many of them, I was taken in to the POW camp and was held there for a year before the peace treaty allowed me to leave….so yes Kung Fo, I have been shot at.'

They turned into the maze of the Highrise Quarter and the Police pods gave up chasing them. They knew better than to go down there. Danny parked next to a heavily graffitied, slightly damaged, statue of Aphrodite standing naked in the clam.

'This isn't New Chinatown,' Kung Fo observed.

'Can't take you there,' Danny said, 'too dangerous with the cops all over there, looking for you.'

'Ok,' Kung Fo replied, a little deflated at the thought of having to walk through the Highrise Quarter in order to get home. Unarmed and not proficient with a weapon if he even had one. If he had to take walking through the Highrise Quarter unarmed or go to jail he'd say 'lock me up.'

He got out and bid Danny a farewell, then he walked north and onto New Chinatown.

As he left the area where the statue was, he made his way down an alleyway. He'd never felt this nervous in a long time. Not even back at the bank when he was getting shot at. Or, again, back at the bank, when the receptionist said he wasn't

Mr Von Croft.

'c'mon' he thought, 'do I really look like a Von Croft?

At the outer edge of the alleyway, he came upon a group of youths. They were dressed in multicoloured camouflage trousers, must be a gang thing he thought, knee-high boots, dirty, white vests and each had an individual dyed mohawk. One of them stepped forward. Kung Fo thought this one must be the leader.

'Got any money?' the leader said.

'Got nothing on me,' Kung Fo replied.

The leader flicked out a flip knife.

'I don't think you heard him,' one of the others said, 'got any money.'

Kung Fo made a break for it, but the youths didn't chase him. Instead they laughed and carried on doing whatever it was they were doing. They knew he was small fry and didn't have anything of value just by his clothes. He stopped by a seemingly abandoned apartment building and looked through the smashed window at a cold looking corridor. It had pipes running along the walls which suggested that this place was old, probably dating back to when New London was first constructed. There came a dim glow from the end of the corridor and Kung Fo was amazed he didn't see it sooner. He walked around the

CHAPTER 6

building and found a run down, rusted metal door at the back. Turquoise. He looked back to check the youths hadn't followed him and pushed his way in. The place was dark. Darker than outside. He checked a lightswitch by the door. Nothing. The rain pitter-pattered on the windowsil as he made his way deeper into the dark, grey room, he tripped slightly on a brick that slept in a small pile of glass and swore under his breath. Suddenly, he heard a door creak open, and a voice filled the small room. It was masculine sounding in its tone but had subtle hints of femininity in the words that were used.

'I've been waiting for you, Kung Fo,' it said, 'I felt you, even before you opened the door.'

Kung Fo looked around. The place was so dark he couldn't see what was in front of him. The voice had sounded old so he assumed it was an old hobo or something. He focused on the window, the rain seeping in slightly through the hole that the brick had made when it must've smashed through. A pod hovered past, and he retreated further into the room, all the while, never taking his eyes off the window. His heel suddenly found a toe. This crazy hobo with the deep voice wasn't wearing shoes. He felt the hobo's breath on the back of his neck and his eyes widened.

'Don't be afraid,' the hobo said, 'I'm not here

to cause you harm, nor you, me. At least, not after what I tell you.'

Kung Fo stopped. He was going to turn and face this hobo and knock him clean out. He didn't have time for mystical talk. This hobo wasn't an oracle. Or was he. He couldn't tell. He clenched his fists, ready for a fight, ready to take this fucker down if they tried anything funny. He turned and raised his fist. Darkness.

'I'm over here!' the hobo voice said, and laughed, and Kung Fo looked to his right. He saw, crouched against the door in the grey light of the window, a small figure.

'My name is Franklin,' the figure said, and he stood and approached Kung Fo. Kung Fo stepped back, still fist raised, and felt the cold wall against his back. Franklin stopped also.

'I told you,' he said, 'I'm not going to hurt you.'

'What do you want?' Kung Fo said, 'I don't have any money.'

'I don't want money,' Franklin said, 'only for you to listen to what I have to say, I don't have much time before-' he coughed and lit a cigarette, Kung Fo saw the plastic smoothness of Franklin's face for a brief moment. But he sounded old, right? 'Before I depart this mortal shell and become one with the algorithm.' what was this guy talking about?

CHAPTER 6

'Before you say anything,' Franklin said, 'I am neither man, nor woman, I simply am.'

Kung Fo was puzzled by this, and lowered his fist. He wasn't going to hit this guy, or girl, whatever they are.

'I've lived for countless years,' Franklin began, 'I am old, I am tired and-' cough- 'I am finally ready for this moment. Ready to give you your message.'

Kung Fo's mouth dropped. Was Franklin dangerous crazy? Or just old crazy maybe?

'And what is this message?' Kung Fo finally stuttered.

'That you, Kung Fo, are going to be rich, I've seen it, but not without considerable loss. You will be the downfall of this city, and its people, but you will meet someone. And when you do, she will be your deathbed love.'

Franklin then stepped aside.

'Now,' they said, 'you run.'

Kung Fo sprinted for the door, pushing past Franklin along the way and in the dim light of the window he saw them. A smooth plastic face with tye dye coloured eyes. As he ran, they smiled to expose a webwork of decaying brown with glimpses of veneer white.

Kung Fo got to New Chinatown around half an hour later. He'd ran the entire way, still shaken by what Franklin had said. He collapsed on a wet bench and started to dream. He saw his friends and his mother. They were all smiling, he didn't know why. The sun was shining and the rain had quieted down to a light shower. Suddenly, the air raid sirens blared out their warning song, and his friends and mother started to melt. He was shaken awake by a passerby.

'Get to a shelter!' this stranger yelled. The air raid sirens were real.

7

In the shelter, he noticed a slim, beautiful young lady with pink hair, grey rubber trench coat, fishnet tights and black, PVC stilettos. She looked like the type to get high. And he had a whole stash of Ko Sang back at his place. She saw him almost staring at her and smiled. Her eyes were painted sky blue and her smile….it made him speechless.

He decided he was going to brave a hello and walked up to her.

They exchanged small talk for a while, almost shouting over the acid rain smashing down on the shelter roof. Her name was Isabelle. Her favourite food was Ramen and she liked the colour pink, hence the hair, which was cut in a short, almost masculine, style. There was something about her near lack of femininity that puzzled Kung Fo. Made him curious. He wanted to know if she was a lesbian, or if she just liked the whole power status that came with her choice of style. The air raid sirens sang the signal that the acid rain storm had passed before he got the chance to get to know her more, and Kung Fo felt a sudden surge of emptiness inside. He never saw her again, which he felt was typical. He met this amazing character of a woman and then she's gone.

It was a few days later when Kung Fo heard from Xiang.

'Ah Xiang,' he said, over the vidphone, high on Ko Sang again, 'how may I be of assistance?'

'It's Danny,' she said, she was crying, her black eye make-up running in streams down her high cheeks, 'Paton ordered him dead, and he's gone, they got to his office just after he dropped you off at the Highrise Quarter and shot him as he was coming through the door.'

'Did they take the ring?' Kung Fo asked.

'I don't know....probably.'

He could see why Paton wanted the ring, but he still didn't have to kill his brother to get it.

'Oh, Fo,' she said, between sobs, 'what are we gonna do?'

'Where are you?' he asked.

'I'm at the vidphone booth outside,' she said, 'I knew you'd want to help.'

'I don't,' he admitted, 'but I don't want the Von Croft Mega-Corp here again.'

'Oh,' she said, deflated.

'Come on up anyway,' he said, and hung up.

CHAPTER 7

When she got up to the apartment above the shop, Kung Fo made her a pot of green tea and they sat at the table in the kitchen.

'So,' she said, 'what are we going to do?'

'You mean what are 'you' going to do?'

She slammed her fist on the table.

'You bastard!' she exclaimed, 'Danny stuck his neck out for you and you act as if you don't care!'

'I don't,' he said, simply.

She stood abruptly and walked over to his bedroom.

He followed her and saw she was going to his laptop. Why was she going there? He wondered. Then she picked up the baggy of Ko Sang.

'See this?' she said and dangled it playfully in front of him, 'Danny stuck his neck out to get you this, called all his contacts from the military, had to do a small, but nonetheless dangerous, recon mission, just to get you this bag, and all you can say is that you don't care he's dead?'

Kung Fo started to feel guilty, then he stopped himself by thinking why the hell is she trying to guilt-trip me?

'I'm sorry,' he finally conceded, 'I'll help, just tell me what I need to do.'

Hours later, they had discussed a plan and were flying to the Highrise Quarter. If this plan was going to go ahead, they'd need firepower. Kung Fo had never used a gun in his life, how was he going to carry out the plan? The plan was, they were going to get some guns and storm the Von Croft tower. Taking out a few guards in the process. He'd initially declined his role. He was a hacker, not a soldier. He ran his fingers across the visor of his VR headset as he cradled it in his adrenaline fueled, shaky hands. Xiang noticed this and came to the conclusion that he was, in fact, better behind a keyboard rather than holding a gun. They came to a little pawn shop in the Highrise Quarter. The owner was a balding, fat man with thick framed glasses, hawian shirt and a gold chain dangling on top a dirty, stained vest. Xiang bought, among other things, a 9mm Beretta, AK47, with rounds, and a new triple barreled sniper rifle. Her idea was, she'd first clear the roof by picking off the guards patrolling then go in via the ground floor, simple idea, no doubt countless attempts to do this would have failed, by other people of course, but this was Xiang Bancroft. Killer chick in PVC high heels.

Also for sale, to Kung Fo's wonder, was ice-breaking software. Several copies of premium breaker discs. All for a few hundred sub credits each. Xiang bought them for Kung Fo as she knew he was low on funds at the moment. He'd promised, after they got the ring and sold it on the black market, to pay her back, but she refused his kind gesture.

8

On the roof of the building adjacent to the Von Croft tower, they sat in the pouring rain and waited for the perfect time to strike. Kung Fo was going to hack into the mainframe of the tower's security systems and remote control the CCTV from here over his VR headset. He'd discovered, earlier on, that he didn't need a laptop to use the headset, and that he could insert the ice breaking software discs straight into the temple of the visor. Very high-end specs this one. Xiang was going to wait til security systems were offline then strike. She knew that Kung Fo could create a virus that would take the systems out but still keep the cameras so he could keep an eye on her and the various corridors dotted around the tower. He pulled the VR headset over his eyes then went to the virus creation app on the visor's desktop page. He blinked and it automatically clicked on the app's icon.

A message came on his vision that asked him what kind of virus he wished to make.

He decided on a semi-security lockdown virus and a gauge came up that showed him the loading progress of the virus's birthing.

He took the headset off and turned to Xiang.

'Virus is birthing, may take a few hours, what do you wanna do?'

She smiled then leaped on him.

'Oh I don't know,' she whispered in his ear, 'this maybe?' and they made love in the rain.

Hours later, they lay spent on the roof. The VR headset pinged with a notification. Kung Fo moved his numb and tingling arm from under Xiang's head and put the visor on.

'Virus is ready,' he said, she got up and dressed, 'gonna take the security out now.'

He slid the ice breaker disc into the visor and looked at the tower. He saw the tower light up and the security system was made obvious with a blue line, moving up and down the tower's infra-structure. He pressed the zoom in button on the opposite temple of his visor and saw the main security box on the fourth floor of the tower. Even though it was the fourth floor, it was still seen as the basement of the tower. He blinked to click on the box and the mainframe came up. After moments of searching, he found the interface he was looking for and a box came up on the periphery of his vision that said 'insert virus here?'

CHAPTER 8

he blinked to click yes and the virus started to upload itself. A blue gauge popped up to show the progress, then flashed to indicate that the virus had successfully uploaded itself. He now had control of the security and he switched off the alarms and metal detectors in the main lobby of the building.

'Are we ready?' Xiang asked.

'We're ready,' Kung Fo replied.

Rex Taylor was deflated at the idea he was on roof duty that day. He hated being so high in the sky. His bosses knew he was afraid of heights, but they put him on roof duty anyway. Today of all days, it was his daughter's birthday and, furthermore, it was pissing down with rain. He was already soaked through. He came to the Von Croft Corporation because he thought he'd get a nice apartment, good pay and a better working environment than his last employer, he'd worked security for a small chain of corner shops in the Highrise Quarter, but this was ridiculous. And the cherry on the cake? Someone had hacked into the security system. A small box had presented itself to him on his visor, indicating the intrusion. And that was the last thing he saw before a bullet smashed through his visor, his eye, then his brain and exited out the back of his helmet.

Xiang reloaded the sniper rifle quickly. She aimed again and fired, killing another security guard who was patrolling the roof. She reloaded again and fired, killing the final guard on the roof. Now was her chance. She jumped off the roof of the building and fell a few stories before finding a wet cable that went from the building straight into the Von Croft tower, grabbed it, then slid down it onto a balcony and crouched. She touched an earpiece which allowed her to talk to Kung Fo, another handy purchase from the pawn shop in the Highrise Quarter. She opened the window and slid in.

'Ok I'm in,' she said.

'Ok,' said Kung Fo, 'there should be an elevator shaft not too far from you, once you get there, you can climb up to the offices on the top floor, but be careful, the cameras show me heavy security patrolling the floors above you.'

Xiang crept along the corridor, careful so as not to arouse detection. She came to a large elevator shaft and used all her strength to open the steel doors with her bare hands. Her parents had given her arm implants for her 17th birthday so this feat should've been easy for her. But, she hadn't used it in a while so it'd gathered rust. Once the doors were open, she entered the elevator, climbed up on to the top of it and contacted Kung Fo.

'Can you hack into the elevator for me? I need it to go up to the top,' she said.

CHAPTER 8

'Ok,' he replied, 'and three two one and done.'

The elevator began to rise and took Xiang up to the offices on the top floor. She took this time to load her 9mm and get in the zone for a fight.

When she got up to the top floor, she leaped from the elevator through the open elevator doors and did a battle roll upon landing. The guards responded with gunfire and she took cover behind a turned over desk.

'You've got twenty guards on you,' Kung Fo said into her earpiece, 'must be the entire force.'

Suddenly, a chopper came flying round the building, spotted Xiang, and opened fire, clipping her leg.

'SHIT!' she cried and she ran for cover elsewhere on the floor, chased by bullets from both the guards and the chopper.

9

She limped as she got to a corner office. Her leg was bleeding from the bullet graze on her leg. The chopper had followed her. The windows smashed as the bullets sprayed the tiny room. She was hiding behind steel cabinets which didn't do much to shield her from the spray of the chopper guns.

'Kung Fo!' she screamed into the earpiece, 'find me a way out, PLEEEAAASE!!'

'Bare with me,' he replied, he found the chopper on his VR visor and hacked into its systems. He found the functioning mainframe and uploaded a virus into the chopper's main systems. The chopper began to malfunction and spiral down to the ground.

'Ok,' Kung Fo said, 'you're golden, head up to the next floor, there should be a staircase not far from your location, that will lead you up to the main Von Croft apartment.'

Xiang counted to three then limped out of the

CHAPTER 9

office, then the adrenaline kicked in and she began to run, all the while the guards were firing and she fired back, killing ten and forcing the rest to run for cover.

She got to the staircase Kung Fo mentioned. Coming down were Paton Von Croft's personnel guards, she fired at them and they fired back. A bullet smashed into her shoulder and she stumbled slightly as they reloaded. Now was her chance. She fired the AK47 and they all hit the floor with a river of blood, flowing down the walls and stairs. She came to a door at the top of the staircase. It had a red light above it. She shot the lock and the door opened to reveal a large, luxurious apartment. She dropped her smoking AK and ventured forward. She loaded the 9mm and proceeded into the apartment doing a sweep search pattern.

Xiang got to the office of Paton Von Croft to find him cowering in the corner.

'Where's the fucking ring, Paton?' she yelled, gun at the ready. She was going to kill him anyway, she just needed to find the ring first. What she'd dare not admit to Kung Fo, to herself also, is that she loved Danny. But if indeed she loved Danny, why did she just have sex with Kung Fo? She tried pushing the confusion to the back of her mind.

'I won't ask again, you fucker, where's the fucking ring?' she ordered.

'I don't have it,' he stuttered, meekly.
Xiang then noticed that he was wearing it.
'Fucking liar,' she said.
She walked up to him.
'I'm sorry!' he whimpered.
She shot him point blank in the back of the head, pried the ring from his crooked finger and cautiously left the room.

PART 3

Absolute Power Corrupts

10

She got to the top of the stairs and limped down. She heard gunfire and remembered there was still some guards on this floor. Not to mention the hordes of police that were no doubt on their way. Loud gunfire and a crashing helicopter doesn't go unnoticed, even in New London. She took cover behind a partition, firing back as she ran. Xiang waited for them to reload before unleashing a barrage of bullets, killing six and fatally wounding four. Suddenly, there came a voice over the tannoy. She looked out the windows to see what seemed like a hundred police pods.

'Kung Fo!' she yelled into her earpiece, 'I need a way out, like now?'

'Head to the elevator shaft again, I'll call one up for you.'

'Put your weapons down on the ground and step away with your hands behind your head! NOW!' the voice over the tannoy screamed.

Xiang put her 9mm down and stepped away.

CHAPTER 10

'Put your hands behind your head!' the voice screamed.

She did as instructed, then she heard the ping of the elevator and decided that if ever there was a chance of escaping with this ring for Kung Fo, now was the time.

She made a break for it, followed by gunfire and screams of 'she's running! Stop her!'

Xiang made it to the elevator, but not without a spray of lead hitting her back. The force pushed her into the elevator and she struggled to her feet. Once the doors had closed, she tried to pull herself up through the emergency hatch in the ceiling, but fell to the ground. She motivated herself to try again, but again her strength was zapped out of her arms from loss of blood and winding from the blast in her back. She pushed the button for the ground floor and collapsed.

The ping from the elevator woke her up, she didn't realise she was sleeping. She resolved, with every ounce of strength she could muster, to stand up and get out of the elevator. The police were waiting in the lobby for her. She stumbled forward and fell against the front desk.

'FIRE!'

An array of bullets riddled her body and she convulsed with every shot.

And she was gone, shot dead. Off to see Danny

in the sky. To hold him like she wished she'd done in life. Her body lay still on beige marble, the ruby ring still clutched in her stiff fist.

    Kung Fo saw it all through the CCTV. He took the VR headset off and wept. Each tear, lost in the rain. Why didn't he just agree to go in with her? Instead of hiding on the adjacent roof like a coward. Cause I'd be dead too he thought. When the last tear fell, he decided that he needed that ring. This couldn't have all been for nothing, Xiang wouldn't have wanted that. There was no one else to stop him now. Danny was dead, Xiang was dead, shit, even Paton was dead. He waited for the police presence to die down and went downstairs to the ground floor. Even though the ARU had left, there were still some pigs left to guard the evidence. This was a crime scene after all. They stood there with visors of their own, clutching 442 plasma rifles with laser sighting, each had a cable connecting their visors to their rifles. Kung Fo hid behind a pod on the opposite side of the street. He put the headset on. His plan was to upload a virus to the police guard's visors to somehow create a diversion so he could sneak past them. In order to do this though, he had to create a whole new algorithm from scratch. So he hid down an alley adjacent to the tower, crouched behind a dumpster and got to work.

CHAPTER 10

What seemed like hours later, he finally had a custom virus. He returned to his former hiding place, behind a police pod, and saw the same guards across the street. Their blue armour speckled with raindrops. Each drop, clinking as it smashed to pieces on the kevlar steel. He waited for the guards to turn away from him for a split second, then he crossed the street and crouched behind a parked civilian pod. He put the VR headset on and looked at the guards. Through the visor, he saw the circuitry that snaked its way from the rifles to the visors. A box popped up. 'Upload virus?' it said. He blinked to click yes and an orange gauge bar appeared and began to fill to signify that the virus was uploading itself to their visors. Once this happened, Kung Fo saw the guards take them off, bewildered at the obvious malfunction. He took this opportunity to, still crouched, run into the building. He got to Xiang's body and crouched near her. He almost began to cry as he saw her lying there dead. But he pushed it back. There wasn't enough time to grieve now. He searched her and found the ring in her clenched fist. Obviously the coroner, who was probably at another charity ball, hadn't arrived yet, so the ring would still be there. He went to put it in his pocket, but stopped. The scarlet glow entranced him and he got lost in its opulence for a second.

'FREEZE!!!'

He shook himself out of the stupor and noticed that the virus had run its course and worn off. He turned sharply and saw the guards aiming at him. There were only two so maybe he could outrun them. He got up and ran, faster than he ran at the bank, faster than in high school, faster than he'd ever ran in his life. Dodging plasma beams, which obliterated the objects around him, he finally got to the back door of the lobby. He turned to see the guards in hot pursuit, yelling into their earpieces. He noticed, at the back of the tower, a parking lot. If he was going to get away, he'd have to jack a ride somehow. So he pulled the visor down and searched. He found a sports pod that probably belonged to someone in security, so he quick hacked into the pod's mainframe to unlock the doors and start the engine, and ran to it, got in, and flew away, dodging the shots of the guards as he escaped.

11

A few days later, Kung Fo was laying on his bed. He'd ditched the sports pod somewhere in the Highrise Quarter. Hoping the cops would think he lived there. He was turning the ring over between his forefinger and thumb, mesmerised by the light of the sun shining through the gem, making little red diamonds on his fingers. Upon closer inspection, he noticed what looked like a chip under the ruby stone.

'What the fuck?' he said slowly under his breath.

He got up and rooted through his draws for a screwdriver or something. He had to pry the gem out of the ring to receive the chip. When he did so, the chip almost fell out. He caught it quickly and examined it in the sunlight. It looked like it was meant to slot into something as it had odd edges. It was square, with one of the corners missing, kind of like an SD card. He looked for his VR headset. Something had to be on this chip for so many people to want it. And kill for it, it seemed. He slotted it into the temple of his headset and slid it over his eyes. Green grid with black background. He blinked on the chip icon on the desktop and saw an array of shapes, colours and binary codes, then suddenly the visor went white. An almost blinding white. A face appeared.

'Hello Mr Von Croft,' an automated voice said.

'It's not Von Croft,' Kung Fo said, 'register new user.'

'New user registered,' it said back to him, 'hello Mr Fo.'

'Not Mr Fo,' Kung Fo said, 'Kung Fo.'

'New name registered,' it said, 'how may I help you Kung Fo?'

'Run diagnostic, I wanna see what's on you.'

'Diagnostic running.'

A few moments later, Kung Fo was looking at several pages of text. From what he read, the AI was known as Helen, and whoever was in possession of the ring and the chip embedded inside, owned the Von Croft business and tower.

Head of the company? Kung Fo asked himself, and smiled. Now he understood why this ring was so important, why so many people wanted it. It wasn't enough that it was the last ring made with genuine Ruby stones, it had the possibility to make the owner very powerful.

CHAPTER 11

He slid the ring onto his right wedding finger. He was dressed in the funeral suit he wore a few weeks ago. It felt, to Kung Fo, like it'd been years since he'd worn the suit. But now he felt like he was a somebody. Like he meant something to the world. To New London anyway. He pushed his way through the revolving doors of Von Croft tower and approached the front desk. The blood on the floor was gone, Xiang was gone and so was the police presence. When he noticed that Xiang's body wasn't there he felt a kind of finalist moment. She was really dead. Gone from this world to the next. He didn't think of going to her funeral. He may have been the only one there. He wouldn't know. But now everything was business as usual and it bugged him slightly. The receptionist looked up from her glossy magazine and smiled.

'How may I help you today sir?' she asked, politely and cheerfully.

Somebody just died, he thought, and you're acting like nothing happened?

He lifted his right hand and showed her the ring. Her smile disappeared slightly, shocked at the look of her new boss, then it returned.

'Top floor sir,' she said, 'the other delegates are waiting for you.'

Delegates?, he thought, must be the big table, the one everyone gossiped about in the

Portuguese slums.

He entered the elevator and took it to the top floor. When he got there, he noticed that there were men working on the windows that were shot out during the skirmish between Xiang and the police. People were working on their various tasks in the office, hanging out by the coffee machine, moving between the computer desks like ants working on a new nest. He came to the staircase that Xiang had climbed earlier in the week during their heist to retrieve the ring. The blood and bodies were gone from there too. Nice clean up job he thought.

He got to the apartment moments later, and was met by the delegates from the various other families that practically owned New London. The Yulehouse family from the German sector, the Genaro family from New Rome just north of New Battersea and what was left of the Butters family from the City Centre. Out of all the families, the Butters' and the Von Crofts were the most powerful. They all stood, curious about this stranger in their midst. Kung Fo lifted his right hand again to show the ring and, puzzled but accepting, they all sat down again.

'So,' the head delegate from the Genaros said to Kung Fo as he sat down, 'you don't look like a Von Croft, what are you?' he smiled and looked at everyone else for approval,

CHAPTER 11

'Adam's bastard love child from New Chinatown's whores?'

Kung Fo swallowed his rage and very calmly shook his head.

'I'm the heir to the company,' Kung Fo answered, 'obviously the others couldn't hack it, so I took up the mantle.'

The Genaro delegate laughed.

The Yulehouse delegate leaned forward.

'And what, I assume, a respectable person you are,' he said, 'I'm hoping you'll lead the company to great wealth.'

'Thank you,' Kung Fo replied, smiling, 'I move that we no longer sell Ko Sang.'

'What will we sell instead?' the Butters' delegate asked.

'Have someone in the lab create a new drug,' Kung Fo suggested.

They all laughed but saw that Kung Fo was deadly serious, and stopped.

'I suppose,' the Genaro delegate said, finally, 'we could do that, but where will our finances come from in the meantime?'

'We phase it out,' Kung Fo said.

'Are we to understand,' Yulehouse said, 'that you want to put a whole new, even more addictive drug out there and turn a profit that way?'

'Yes,' Kung Fo said, proudly.

Loud murmurs of disapproval erupted between the families, but Butters was silent.

'We could do that,' he said, once the murmurs had died down and he could be heard.

'But,' Genaro said, 'we have the politicians and the police in our pockets to turn a blind eye to the selling of Ko Sang! How are we meant to get them on side with a new drug?'

'We give the Prime Minister a free sample,' Kung Fo said, 'then we get him hooked and the others will soon follow.'

They all nodded. This kid knew what he was talking about.

12

Days later, Kung Fo was standing in his office looking out the window at the city centre of New London. The flying pods rushed past his view, various ads popped up as they went along. One was for a sexual stimulant known as Minotaur Junk, with a picture of a muscular minotaur with a giant erect penis. Unrealistic expectation Kung Fo thought, is this really what we've come to? One was the female version, Aphrodyte's Blossom, with a picture of a naked blonde with huge breasts, riding atop a clam. Fuck sake he thought at this and turned away from the window.

He decided he wanted a chat with someone or something. Something to take his mind off what was going on. So he poured himself a glass of bourbon and sat down on a plush couch to the right of his desk, put the VR headset on and plugged Helen in.

'Hello Kung Fo,' she said, cheerfully, 'how are you today?'

'Hi Helen,' he said, 'yeah I'm fine, just needed to talk.'

'My functions go far into psychiatry and-'

'I don't need psychiatry or a shrink, just someone to talk to, you know, like a friend.'

Helen was silent.

'Helen?'

'I'm sorry,' she said finally, 'but my functions don't go that far. Please make another request or search for another keyword.'

Sensing this was a lost cause, he slid the headset off his eyes and, taking a sip of his bourbon, laid it on the couch next to him. It's gonna be a long day, he though, rubbing his forehead.

13

After the war, Adam Von Croft was a shrewd businessman. He'd always been shrewd. Even when he was starting out. His father always taught him to be ruthless, even though he was a lowly butcher, and to make examples of people wherever and whenever possible. He would show Adam how he culled animals for meat sources. For chickens it was a plain beheading, for cows, however, it was an entirely, and for Adam pleasurable, different affair. Before the war, they still killed animals the way they had done for an age, it seemed. One shot of a compressed air gun to the head and that was it. Adam loved the finalising of it. Click, pop, you're dead, next.

He became a deft hand at it. So much so that, when the war began, and he was old enough, he joined the British Legion of Police, a group that, for the most part, believed in strong-arming the little guy if he stepped out of line, no matter how pathetic the infringement. It was in this profession that Adam got a taste for authority. A taste that never left him. He loved roaming the streets, telling people off if they were out late at night. 'There is a war on, you know,' he'd say, and promptly wrapped the cuffs on them if they tried to protest. So many people got a criminal record because of him. Even old ladies, who were caught out in the blackout, got arrested.

He was eventually asked to leave the group for brutality, which was saying something about his character if he was asked to leave by a group that was not unlike the National Front. It was at this point in his life, he decided to sell drugs to make money. He made enough to go to the council and ask for his own apartment block in the now famous construction known as New London.

When the construction was complete, his new tower was ready for residents. He sold them for exorbitant amounts for a profit of course. He used the money to start his now burgeoning hobby of Archaeology, down on what was then, the nuclear wasteland of Earth, thinking he could find something worth more money than he already had. It was on a cool summer's day he found it. Buried under the rubble of a petrol station, a ruby gem. He promptly put it in his pocket and, declaring no finds, decided to take the stone back up to New London.

CHAPTER 13

Crime was rife in New London, so Adam was aware he had to be careful when roaming the streets now. He was older now, and thus became more of a target for thieves and murderers. Especially if they looked round his dead body and found the ruby. He decided the only way to keep it with him was to make it into a ring. So he did so, and he wore it until the day he decided to pass it on. Part of the way into his life, he had the labs create not only Ko Sang, but also a secret microchip, with an AI on it called Helen, who was designed to be his secretary. He also made a family law that, whoever owned the ring, owned the company. Near his death he had the ring put in a safety deposit box. Ready for the next generation of Von Crofts to carry on in his stead. He had no idea that so many people would die because of it.

Soon after he returned from his Archaeological excursion, the government passed a bill that would send all the convicted criminals down to a newly formed colony on the Earth's surface. This suited Adam very well as, now he was a somebody at the big table, he could move relatively safely round New London. Obviously not venturing to the Highrise Quarter. Not even the Police or even the Army would go down there.

14

Kung Fo must've been napping, because he didn't hear the other delegates come into the office. He awoke to Genaro trying to pry the ring from his hand. Smiling, Genaro gently placed Kung Fo's hand back down on the couch and stepped away. Yulehouse looked at Genaro with immense anger and disappointment at this obvious lack of respect.

'We have the go-ahead,' Butters said, 'for the lab to start the making of the new drug, but we need a name, something loud, something sexy, something-'

Kung Fo raised his hand for Butters to stop.

'We'll call it death,' Kung Fo said, inspired by the drug in his favourite book.

The delegates looked at each other in confusion. How were they meant to sell something called death? They guessed it would appeal to the hardcore drug demographic, the ones who wanted to say something like 'yeah I take death, I'm hard

CHAPTER 14

because I regularly take something that would eventually kill me.'

So death it was, and they all agreed that, with enough support from politicians and the police, it would take off and everyone will be on it, sooner or later.

Kung Fo needed a second opinion, so when they left he put his VR headset on and slotted Helen in again. She greeted him and they began to talk.

'So,' he asked her, 'what do you think of the name death?'

'It's…..different,' she said, 'but not wholly unpleasant.'

She was quite pretty for an AI, something about her smooth lips and high cheekbones that just made Kung Fo crazy. He wondered if they made her like that on purpose, whether it'd been a design plan from Von Croft himself. When she noticed the long pause, she grew concerned.

'Something on your mind?' she asked.

'What?....no, just thinking,' he said.

'About….?'

'You, mainly, you're quite pretty.'

She smiled.

'Go to the closet,' she said, 'and open it.'

He did so and was shocked to find what was there.

A physical replica of what the scientist, and

Von Croft, imagined Helen would look like if she were human.

'What do I do now?' he asked.

'Slot me in to the back of the neck, just below the hairline,' she suggested.

He did so and the replica whurred to life and smiled.

'Do what you will,' she said.

Hours later, they lay on the couch. Breathing heavily and sweating. Kung Fo grunted to signify that he was finished and Helen looked up at him, smiling, her clear, ocean blues staring up at him.

'Was that pleasurable?' she asked.

'Very,' he said, and rolled off her, getting dressed as he did so.

For some reason, he felt dirty. He'd just done the unthinkable with an AI. His friends would make fun of him for that. He suddenly felt sad. How had he forgotten about his roots? Enough to fuck, what many would see as, a robot. Was he really that desperate? And how many of the Von Crofts had struck lucky with her before him? Without saying a word, he unslotted her and put the body back in the closet. He walked to the giant window and looked out. It was raining, and the mist hung low over the rooftops. He saw the building that, just days prior, hosted the rainy love-making between him and Xiang. He felt like scum, Kung Fo had fallen for two girls, one was dead and the other existed in cyberspace but could be let out into the real world to fulfil the base pleasures of whoever wore the ring. He brought his hands to his face and wept. He felt like something that was scraped off someone's shoe if they didn't bother looking where they were walking.

He needed to get out, he needed to get drunk, he needed to get high. Kung Fo walked down the stairs, down the elevator and out the lobby, not saying a word to anyone as he walked.

Hours later, he was in New Soho. The Neon Potato stood before him, newly reopened. The synthetic music blasting out from the front door. He paid the bouncer and entered. It had everything he remembered from a few short months ago when his friend Ricky owned it. He always put on to Ricky that his English was shit. Really he could speak it quite well, but it was that whole Asian servant crap that Ricky was into. The UV lights shone blue, the bar illuminated by a white light shining from underneath the stools, the music was louder now, and people of all colours danced and grinded on the dancefloor. His friends would've definitely loved the vibe. He approached the bar and ordered a bourbon, no ice, and sat down. Moments later, his drink was before him. He could barely see it due to the UV lights, he stared into the black void in his glass and wondered, would Helen like this? This place? This drink? Shit, even this stool? He soon realised he was falling in love with Helen, and that the fact she was on his mind after he took himself out of the building to get away from her, must be something there, surely?

15

Kung Fo stumbled drunkenly through the streets of New Soho. Various taylor-made ads flickered holographically in front of him, but he wasn't interested. He just wanted to get back to Helen. Tell her how he felt, if he even knew himself. He was too drunk for that trail of thought he decided. Instead, he went to the seedier side of New Soho, if there was any such place. He stopped and swayed in front of a stripper. She was dancing and grinding up against a pole. She wore silver lingerie and had her hair dyed ocean blue. This made Kung Fo think of Helen so he moved on. Soon after, he saw a black woman standing on the corner wearing fishnet tights, knee high boots and a leopard print vest. She had a silver mohawk and large hoop earrings.

She noticed him and smiled.

'Want me to take you home?' she purred.

What happened next was a blur. Did they have sex? Didn't they? He didn't know but he woke up the next morning with a killer hangover and fifty credits short.

When his head finished spinning, and after a coffee, he realised he was in his office. The first thing he wanted to do was talk to Helen. So he slotted her into the VR headset and she loaded up.

'Have a good night?' she asked.

'I'm sorry, I don't remember, did I…?'

'Yes you did,' she said, 'it's on CCTV if you want to have a look?'

'No, thank you I…..I'd rather not remember if I'm honest.'

'Well,' Helen said, 'it looked like you definitely had a good time, you should've done with the price you paid.'

'What do you mean, the price I paid?'

Helen glitched, 'fifty credits removed from user account,' and glitched back to her usual, smiling self.

'You saw that?' he asked, mortified.

'It's got nothing to do with me,' she said, 'what we had was momentary, just to clear the air between us.'

'But I think I'm in love with you,' he said, and instantly regretted it.

She let out a little giggle.

'So you can laugh?' he asked.

'Yeah, it's ok though, you don't have to be

CHAPTER 15

embarrassed, just know that just because I'm here, you don't have to stop living,' she reassured him, 'you can go out and have fun, I'll always be here for you if you want me.'

'Thank you,' he said, 'it really means a lot.'

Genaro and the other delegates arrived soon after. They had a sample of death with them, and Kung Fo was the lucky son of a bitch who had first dibbs. He cooked and injected, suddenly, he was transported to a different world. Everyone in the room had a greenish tint to their skin. The daylight shone blue through the blinds, shining, so brightly shining. He stumbled to the window and pulled up the blinds to see New London and what it would look like under the influence of death. The pods flew backwards, the minotaur was laughing, Aphrodite winked at him, he saw Xiang on the roof of the building adjacent, she was standing there, holding her sniper rifle, wearing the same PVC outfit she wore a few weeks ago in the pod when they'd first met. Her skin, a pale blue. The raindrops on the window formed a face, when he squinted his eyes he saw Helen, smiling back at him. Was it really raining? Or was it the death? Kung Fo could never tell. He found himself falling backwards and into the safety of his office chair. For what seemed like hours, he watched out the window, watched the denizens go about their daily affairs, watched the minotaur repeat the same action over and over, watched Aphrodite grinding against the clam.

When the high had finally left him, Kung Fo got up from his chair slowly. The delegates were still there.

'Gentlemen,' he announced, 'I think we've got a hit.'

They all applauded and congratulated each other, slapping each other on the back for a job well done. Sooner or later, everyone was going to be on this escape route, Kung Fo thought.

'I think,' he said, when they'd all finished the circle jerk, 'we should get this in pill form for mass produce.'

They all nodded, ecstatically.

16

A few weeks later, the pill was ready for mass production and, though it took longer for it to take effect, it still had the same high as injecting it. Kung Fo had to decide how they were going to actually get it to New Westminster for the Prime Minister to get hooked. They knew, once he was on board, that the other politicians would soon follow and then the police. They also knew that soon people would be taking this pill as often as they take their vitamin tablets, Kung Fo saw them now, as soon as they woke up, downing the pill with their morning coffees. He wondered, though, how many people, once they'd learned that the high came on faster when you injected it, would actually take it in pill form and how many would choose to inject. That was the outstanding problem. He decided to leave that to the consumer.

That evening, it was a Monday, he wanted to take Helen out somewhere. She'd never left the office in the entirety of her existence. Not in physical form anyway. So he got her out of the closet and slotted her in.

'Hello, Kung Fo,' she said, cheerfully automated, 'what do you want to do today?'

'I'm taking you out on the town,' he said, 'there's a place in New Soho called the Neon Potato that I think you'll like.'

A few moments later, they were in the pod, flying towards New Soho. Helen stared out the window at the rain. She was wearing some clothes that Kung Fo had picked out for her. A green dress, nice, shiny high heeled sandals, and some black, velvet up to the elbow gloves. She'd never seen actual rain before. She traced the raindrops going down the window with her fingers, and felt amazed that she could feel, actually feel, the chill of the outside on the window pane. Noticing her amazement at the rain, Kung Fo said 'we should be careful really, acid rain could come at any moment.'

'Acid rain?' she said, with an upward inflection toward the end.

'Yeah,' he said, then filled her in on the history of the world, starting from the thermo-nuclear war.

'I knew all that,' she said, 'just didn't want to interrupt you.'

They both laughed.

He couldn't believe that he was laughing with a machine, she couldn't believe she was laughing.

CHAPTER 16

When they got to the Neon Potato, Helen was amazed by what she saw, and heard. She had six million songs programmed in her chip, but she'd never heard music like this before. She'd never seen people like this before. Grinding against each other to the beats that blasted from the speakers. It was very loud. But she could handle it. The hearing monitors in her ears made it so that if there were loud sounds, the circuitry would dampen the sound before it could access the pain receptors. They found a table and sat down. Kung Fo thought she looked beautiful under the blue UV light. It reflected off her rubberised plastic skin and made her LED irises sparkle. He took a sip of bourbon and, setting it back on the table, asked 'do you drink?'

She smiled, 'no, but the atmosphere is nice.'

He smiled back, blushing slightly. He'd never seen someone so radiant before.

Noticing his drink was empty, he stood and walked to the bar. He ordered another bourbon and, while he was waiting, noticed a young casanova looking guy talking to Helen, and she, not realising what this meant, was chatting back. Kung Fo became immediately incensed with rage and jealousy. Forgetting his drink, he walked over, took her hand and they both walked out of the club.

'Who was that nice person?' she asked as they

made their way to the pod.

'A predator,' Kung Fo answered, it was a bad idea bringing her here, 'only wants one thing and he's not going to get it.'

'Oh,' she stopped and wrestled her hand from his, 'like you, you mean?'

He turned to her.

'What?.....no,' he tried to back track but to no avail.

'The only reason you wanted me here was to get me drunk so you can do me again,' she accused, 'why is he any different?'

'Because he's not me!' Kung Fo yelled.

'I'm going back in there,' she said, finishing the argument, 'and you're not going to stop me.'

Later that same night, Kung Fo was alone in New Chinatown. He was right, a few days ago, he had forgotten his roots. It was raining still, and he walked and walked, letting the rain water wash over him. The neon lights cutting through the droplets like shiny knives, shimmering on his skin. With his eyes closed, he raised his head and soaked in the water and neon, taking a deep breath in, and out again. He opened his eyes and saw a group of boys playing in the rain. That was him, growing up in New London, where the rain hardly ever stopped, and the neon hardly ever went out. Suddenly, air raid sirens blared out of the speakers on top of the street lights. Acid rain, he thought, HELEN!

He rushed back to New Soho, dodging the rain as he did so by hiding in shelters for brief periods of time. When he got there, she was nowhere to be seen. Nobody knew her and if they did, they didn't know where she was now. He asked in the Neon Potato and they said she'd left with casanova. He was at a loss. He didn't know where she was. Outside, the acid rain stopped and a green mist had descended. Kung Fo was circling desperately, trying to see if she was on the street somewhere. She'd never seen an acid rain storm before, she only knew about it from files on her CPU. Suddenly, he heard a groan from the alleyway between the Neon Potato and a strip club.

17

Helen returned to the Neon Potato. There, she danced to the electronic tunes, she could not only feel the music, she could see it too. It came to her like a shimmering wave. The UV lights flickering to the beat. Lasers darting from the stage to her, as if the music was being played, just for her and her alone. She soon began to attract attention. Stood there, dancing on her own. The women looked on in jealousy, the men, in amazement. Who was she? This vixen with the piercing blue eyes. The casanova from earlier waltzed up to her and grabbed her, expecting her to grind up against him, but she pushed him away. Another vixen, this one with green eyes, pulled Helen close to her. Without a chance for Helen to protest, she kissed her on the lips. Helen was taken back by this new sensory experience, and found that she liked it slightly. She was like a child, experiencing things for the first time. But she'd have preferred it if Kung Fo did that. They hadn't kissed, even during

CHAPTER 17

their love-making. But this, this was a whole new thing for her.

When it came close to closing time, Helen decided to leave and see if there was any other places she could go to dance more. She was followed out by Casanova, he didn't follow her out of lust or love. He followed her out of jealousy and anger. How dare she push him away, how dare she kiss another woman. What was wrong with him? He wanted her and he was going to have her. Whether she wanted to or not. When they got to the street outside, Casanova grabbed Helen and dragged her into an alley. Undressing her as they went. First he ripped off her gloves, then her shoes as she tried to kick him, then her dress as they got behind a dumpster. The worse thing was, nobody tried to stop him. The police were nowhere to be seen, revellers were too drunk to notice, and the other perverts were too engrossed in the strippers. He grabbed her wrists. She tried her best to fight back. To get away, somehow, but he was too strong. He felt his gender harden under his jeans, and unzipped his fly to expose it to her. He was big, and this was going to hurt, but it was going to happen either way. She closed her eyes and imagined Kung Fo. His smile. His gentle touch.

Before Casanova could continue, however, the air raid sirens blared out as if to save Helen from the rape. He quickly put his penis away and ran from the alley. Leaving Helen there, shaking and traumatised from the experience. Suddenly, the rain drops began to set off her pain receptors. Each drop felt like a needle, penetrating her rubberised skin. Then her smell receptors began working, and she smelled burning rubber. She couldn't tell what was going on. Her main systems began to glitch, and she tried to stand, but her main motor functions began to shut down. Slowly, she fell to her knees. Her main systems glitched on last time, then all went black. She knelt there, naked and burning, alone.

Her main systems came back online about two hours later, but she still couldn't move. Most of her skin had melted into a puddle round her knees, save for a few patches here and there, exposing circuitry and wires. She managed a groan. At least her vocal functions were working. Her pain receptors were tingling all over. She felt raw. Suddenly, she heard a voice. Her hearing functions were working properly as well.

'Helen?'

18

Kung Fo picked her up in his arms and carried her to a taxi pod. The driver was bewildered at this apparent damaged doll his fare was carrying, but money was money and he had mouths to feed. His wife had left him and the kids a few agonizing months ago and he needed the money as she was the only one bringing in a steady, well-paid income. The babysitter wanted money to buy nice, new clothes and the kids, well they just wanted daddy to be home more often.

'Von Croft tower,' Kung Fo ordered, and the pod took off.

When they got there, Kung Fo took Helen up to the apartment and lay her down on the couch. He unslotted her and put her in his VR headset.

'Kung Fo,' she said, and started to weep.

'Helen,' he replied, and started to cry as well.

'I was almost raped before you found me,' she said, between sobs, Kung Fo couldn't believe that an AI could feel this level of emotion, they must've done a pretty good, if not realistic, job when they programmed her.

'You're safe now,' he said, 'back in the tower.'

'You warned me,' she said, 'you warned me and I didn't listen.'

'It's ok,' he said, calming down now, 'it's ok.'

A few days later, Kung Fo was in the office of the apartment. He hadn't checked in on Helen yet, so he slotted her in on his headset.

'You ok?' he asked as soon as she came up on his visor.

'Been better,' she said.

'Got you a new body,' he said, smiling as though to reassure her.

She smiled back, she really appreciated the fact that he went to all this trouble just for her, a simple, if not realistic, AI.

'It's being constructed as we speak,' he said, 'had my best eggheads build it for you.'

'Thank you,' she said, 'but I don't think I could handle being physical right now, in all aspects of the word.'

An AI not handling it? Definitely a pro job.

He really didn't know what to say. Was she in two minds on the subject? Could she have two minds on anything as complex as this? The eggheads definitely did a realistic job here, and he was going to find out who programmed her.

CHAPTER 18

Later that same day, Kung Fo was in the science department. Doctors to-ing and fro-ing from different work stations. Busy on making the pill that would make him rich. He headed to the head scientist's office in the far corner of the lab. Dr Oswald, the sign on the door said.

Kung Fo knocked, and a voice from the other side called for him to come in.

'Dr Oswald?' Kung Fo asked as he entered the office.

'Mr Fo,' Dr Oswald stood from his dimly lit desk and walked over, his hand out to be shook.

He looked pleased to see Kung Fo.

'Are you here,' Dr Oswald asked, 'to check on the progress of the project?'

'Yes and no,' Kung Fo replied, Dr Oswald looked confused, 'I want to know a bit more about Helen.'

Dr Oswald's smile disappeared and his hand lowered when he realised it wasn't going to be shaken. Also when he heard that name.

'Is she not to your liking?' Oswald asked.

'It's not like that,' Kung Fo replied, 'I'm surprised at how advanced she is.'

'Well,' Oswald said, 'we used cutting edge technology on her, we even uploaded the brain of one of our workers to make sure she appeared real, make sure she seemed human enough for your predecessors, and yourself of course.'

'Is that even legal?' Kung Fo asked.

'It is if you have the right connections,' Oswald said, 'and we, or should I say you, have the right connections.'

That evening, Kung Fo was sat in his office, contemplating. He turned the ring over between his forefinger and thumb. Much in the way he did when he'd discovered Helen. His eyes darted from the ring, to the hustle and bustle of life in 2056 outside, and back again, the Minotaur Junk advert had been replaced with a coca cola ad depicting a cheerleader taking a sip and smiling, her pearly whites dazzling him as he watched. He heard the door open and slid the ring back on his finger. He turned to see Oswald pushing a gurney into the office.

'Here,' Oswald proudly announced, 'is Helen's new body, try to be careful with it,' he removed the bed sheet that covered Helen's new body with a flourish, 'viola!'

On the gurney, lay a naked woman, hairless and white, with circuitry going up and down her arms and legs and up her cheeks into her ocean blue eyes, which staired, dead, up at the ceiling. Oswald, smiling, backed out of the office, his arms outstretched as if he were presenting Kung Fo with a delicious banquet.

CHAPTER 18

'She's hairless,' Kung Fo remarked.

Oswald's smile vanished and he stopped at the door.

'Her hair,' he said, 'will grow the instant she's slotted in, and the pigment can be changed to your liking from your VR headset. On an app you can download.'

'I see,' Kung Fo said, quietly.

19

He stared at the body for some time before working up the courage to slot Helen in. Her form was perfect, if a little white. Her pearly skin glimmered slightly and her ocean blues shone in the reflection of the light in the ceiling. It reminded him of when they'd made love. Her beautiful eyes looking up at him, that smile, oh that smile, faint but still seeable. He slid the VR headset over his eyes, he was going to give her hair, dark green he thought, he always had a thing for girls with unnatural hair colour, even though trying to find a girl with natural hair colour these days was like trying to find a needle in a haystack, to use the old cliche. He selected the colour then ejected the chip and, very carefully, slotted Helen in. The hair grew almost instantaneously, just as Oswald had said. She let out a breath as she finished loading up and looked about her surroundings.

'Welcome back,' Kung Fo said with a smile.

She sat up slowly, her eyes darting along her

CHAPTER 19

new form, and smiled back at him.

'This is my….' she started, she couldn't believe it, a new body.

'Do you like it?' Kung Fo asked.

'I love it,' she said, he handed her a mirror and she looked at herself for a few moments, smiling, 'thank you.'

She noticed her hair.

'One question though,' she said, eventually, "why dark green?"

'You don't like it?'

'I love it, it's just….'

'Just what?'

'Unusual,' she said, putting the mirror down.

'Well,' Kung Fo said, 'I thought it suited you.'

'It does,' she looked in the mirror again, 'thank you.'

That night, he took her out on the town again, this time he didn't leave her side. They went to the Golden Pineapple this time, instead of the Neon Potato. Ambient tunes filled their ears. Lasers pierced their eyes, and smoke machines washed over them. Nobody danced on the floor or by the bar. Instead they just moved, slowly, as a hologram of Jean Michel Jarre turned dials and pressed keys and placed his hands over beams of light on stage. Kung Fo ordered them drinks and they sat down. They didn't talk, what could they talk about? They just sat there and enjoyed the music.

When they returned from the Golden Pineapple, they made love on his desk in the shadow of the mega complexes that surrounded Von Croft tower. As he thrust inside her, she whimpered quietly, her ocean blues closed tightly. The hologram of Aphrodite, smiling behind them.

The next morning, she asked to be unslotted and he did so, slotting her into his VR headset so he could still talk to her over breakfast. Kung Fo left the building with his visor still on but, as it was see-through, he could still see where he was going, with an image of her face in the top left corner of his vision. He went into the local Chinese eatery and ordered chicken gyoza and rice with a heap of sweet chilli sauce on top. Something to wake him up. He felt a surge of happiness as the rice, gyoza and sweet chilli went down his throat. His tongue was on fire and he liked that.

'I wish you could taste this,' he said to Helen, 'it's so good.'

'I can,' she said, 'scan the food item with your visor and my taste receptors will activate on the mainframe, then I'll be able to run it through the over six million taste samples that have been uploaded to my programme and experience something close to what you call 'taste'.'

He did so, and a few moments later she closed

her eyes and groaned with taste ecstasy.

'This is good,' she said, 'I especially like the sweet chilli sample, it's so warm in my mouth.'

Later, Kung Fo was sitting at his desk, looking out at the world and decided he wanted some company that was a little more physical than a non-physical AI could afford. So he slotted Helen into her body again and sat back down as she booted up.

'Where are we going this time?' she asked.

'Nowhere,' he replied, 'just want you with me in a physical form today, is that alright with you?'

'Of course it is,' she said and Kung Fo smiled.

She walked over to where he was sitting and started to undress him. He pushed her hands away.

'Not this time,' he said, 'this time I just want company.'

'Ok,' she said, and stepped back.

For the rest of the day, they talked, just talked, talked about their lives, dreams and aspirations. Kung Fo was surprised that an AI wanted more out of life than he did, but was that Helen, or the scientist whose brain was uploaded to her mainframe?

20

Kung Fo was distracted from contemplation that night, Helen was gone, back in non physical form on the chip, by the delegates. They wanted to know how the pill called death was doing. Butters had already drawn up an advertising campaign for it and had large pieces of card under his arm, ready to be shown to Kung Fo for his consideration. They showed a 1950s style American family, holding the pill in their hands and smiling, with the slogan 'death, could really be the life of you' in large white letters.

'What's this slogan about?' Kung Fo said, after careful consideration, 'it doesn't make any sense.'

'It's a play on words, shows how good it is for you and why you should take it,' Butters said.

'No it doesn't,' Genaro said, 'it doesn't say that at all.'

Butters shot Genaro a dirty look and carried on the presentation.

Afterwards, the delegates left but Butters remained.

CHAPTER 20

'I need to talk to you,' he told Kung Fo.

'What about?' Kung Fo retorted.

'Genaro, he wants your company, your life, but most of all, he wants that ring.'

Kung Fo rolled his eyes up at Butters and shook his head.

'This is about his reaction to your campaign isn't it?'

'No no no, this is the truth!'

'Ok,' Kung Fo said, 'let's say he does, what's he going to do to get it?'

'Almost anything,' Butters smiled, trying his best to reassure his point.

Later that same night, and a little spooked by what Butters had told him, Kung Fo searched the dark web for info on Genaro, Butters but most of all, combat programmes that he could upload onto Helen. He was going to need protection if what Butters told him had any merit. He found nothing on Genaro, which he found suspicious, but he did find something big on Butters. His family suffered a loss at the hands of DI David Wright earlier this year that they could never recover from, he remembered reading about it in the newspaper. 'He's desperate,' Kung Fo thought, 'he really needs this pill to sell.'

He found some combat software and, inserting the chip into his headset, uploaded them onto Helen's mainframe. Seconds later, she popped up on his visor screen/desktop.

'I am now proficient in many forms of martial art, gunplay and tactical precision,' she said, 'why?'

'I'll be needing protection,' he replied, 'I've just had some worrying news.'

'Tell me.'

Kung Fo then relayed everything Butters had told him about Genaro and everything he'd found on the dark web.

'You're right,' she said, after an uncomfortable pause, 'that is worrying.'

The next morning, Kung Fo sat in front of the window. It was still raining. He hadn't slept a wink, he was worried about Genaro trying to take the company from him. How could this be? Was it the promise of this new death doing well? Or maybe the almost millions in bonds that the Von Croft family owned from drugs and sub par accommodation. Von Croft had definitely worked his way to the top when he'd built this place. Kung Fo couldn't fault him for that. However he earned his millions, he'd still worked for it. Shortly after, Kung Fo was looking out his window again. He noticed the coca-cola ad had gone. Replaced by a blank screen. Then, hours later, it was dark, the image of the 1950s style American family was up there for all to see. 'Death,' it said, 'could really be the life of you.' He laughed at this. 'So he went ahead without me' he thought.

21

When Adam Von Croft had built his housing empire, he wanted more. Like so many before him, greed was his weakness. He had his lot, but that didn't stop him. He wanted more, more, more. More wine. More women. More money. So he asked his advisor what he should do.

'There's money in pharmaceuticals,' his advisor suggested, 'legal and otherwise.'

'And how,' Adam asked, 'would I go about that?'

'Go down to the street,' the advisor said, 'you'll find someone, in New Soho especially.'

But that wasn't enough, Adam wanted the best minds on the job of creating these new drugs. He needed research, he needed knowledge of the drugs already in existence, and he needed people to push it for him. So he did as suggested and went to New Soho.

Once he was there, he cruised the streets in his chauffeur driven limo-pod, looking for dealers.

He was going to buy out all of them in exchange for their services and knowledge of local drug hotspots. A few were interested, but most turned him down flat out of some kind of loyalty to their higher-ups. It was only when he showed them the many briefcases of money he had, and the promise that it could all be theirs, that they were on board. Later, he'd assembled a crack team of mercenaries and struck off cops to go and take out the competition. When they reported back with success, he smiled. He owned the drug game in New London now. All he had to cope with were the other families. How'd they make their millions? And was it through the same means as him? Perhaps not. But it was well worth finding out, so he set up a secret society. The Big Table. Where delegates from all the most powerful families in New London could meet and exchange assets and knowledge and whatnot. He worked closely with Harold Butters and his up and coming new kid, Hugo. Later in life, when he heard of their sad passing at the hands of an undercover cop, he arranged to have the person who hated him with a passion, Ricky, released from the colony to assassinate him.

In the meantime though, he'd built a drug empire, along with his housing empire, to rival that of the Columbian drug cartels of the last century. To say he was rolling in it would be an understatement. He sat cushty for a few years, not to mention a few wives, until his most recent acquisition, Ricky, murdered him in revenge. Prophesying this, he arranged to have his most prized possession, his ruby ring, the last known ruby in the world, placed in a safety deposit box for future Von Crofts to have. To carry on his legacy. What he didn't tell anyone, was what the chip under the stone was. Helen. He'd had her programmed to handle things should the Von Crofts not prevail. But not to survive herself. Though he had wives, many wives, and many sons from those wives, he still had a body created for his recreational uses.

22

Kung Fo called Butters to ask why the campaign went ahead without his knowledge.

'I thought I'd had your approval,' Butters said on the vidphone, 'you seemed impressed-'

'I didn't authorise it to go ahead,' Kung Fo barked, angrily.

'But Kung Fo,' Butters said, nervously, he knew, with the power this kid could wave around, he could have him rubbed out in a millisecond, 'once the right people see this ad, everyone will want some death.'

'I suppose,' Kung Fo said, relenting, 'you're right, but who will see it?'

'What do you mean?'

'Who will see it where I am?'

'Visiting politicians from New Westminster.'

'C'mon,' said Kung Fo, 'when am I going to have visiting politicians?'

'In about five minutes, I've already set up a meet with the delegates and the health secretary.'

CHAPTER 22

And true to his word, five minutes later the office was full. Even delegates from the smaller gangs were there, eager to know what death was like, seeing as they were going to be pushing it. The health secretary felt a bit intimidated with the amount of known criminals he now shared a room with. People he thought were sent down to the colony were now sharing the same breathing space as him.

Oswald proudly entered the room, carrying a booster pack under his arm filled with enough death for the delegates and the secretary to try. More trippy than LSD, more addictive than Heroin. That was the secret underground tagline for death. This little pill, this tiny little piece of science, could change the world for the rich and poor alike. Turning them all into dope fiend slaves, willing to part with their money, and control, over to the delegates. New Westminster will fall and the delegates will own everything.

That day was very productive. Once he'd tried it, and the high wore off, the health secretary greenlighted it from his end and arranged for the Prime Minister's dose. It was all coming together. Kung Fo felt a surge of energy flow through his veins. He wasn't just going to be rich. He was going to be super wealthy. More money than he could ever have imagined. He imagined what his mother and his friends would think if they saw him now. Sitting in a plush, leather bound swivel chair in a fancy office. Surrounded by the super rich, who were about to become even richer, who were about to become very powerful. Once they'd all slapped each other on the back and left, Kung Fo slotted Helen in for the first time that day, he had to tell her. When she'd booted up in her body, and he'd told her the good news, they made mad love on the office floor. Not caring, at the time, if anyone came in and caught them.

In the wee small hours of the morning, and with Kung Fo asleep, Helen got up off the office floor and, putting his shirt on to mask her nakedness, walked towards the window and looked out. Will this office be all she knows from now on? Will she be locked in a gilded cage with no escape in sight? Plaything and protector? She couldn't handle it. She had to get out somehow. Didn't he mention a certain gentleman known as Genaro who wanted what he had? Maybe life, as she knew it, would be better with him? But she loved Kung Fo, he'd taken her out on the town when previous owners would not. He loved her back, which was unusual for what she was programmed for. As for her programming, he'd added extra knowledge to her mainframe. She was a badass now. She knew more than any sensei could teach her in any dojo. Every

CHAPTER 22

martial art that has ever been recorded was now in her data bank and at her fingertips. To be used when the order was given, and even if not.

The sunlight seeped through the blinds and woke Kung Fo. Strange, he didn't remember closing them. He got up from the office floor and searched for his shirt. Helen was in the corner. She looked like she was powered down. He couldn't really tell from this distance and the meager light in the room.

'Helen?' he called to her, 'Helen? You awake?' he felt stupid asking her this as she never really 'slept'.

'I'm here,' she said, as though she was exhausted, 'I'm always here.'

'I could take you out,' he said, 'like for breakfast?'

'In your headset again, I take it.'

'No,' he protested, 'like, as you are now.'

Clothed and ready, they walked out onto the street as the denizens of New London went about their daily business. It was raining but Kung Fo and Helen didn't mind. It was nice. She felt the cold water splash on her white, rubberised plastic skin and reveled in it as if it was her first time. They walked to the Chinese eatery a few streets away and ate a hearty portion of chicken gyoza, rice and sweet chilli sauce. Unlike her old body, her new one had a synthetic stomach so she could eat and drink like a human. In many respects, she was human now. She could think like a human. She could feel like a human too. So why not? She reveled in the feeling of the sweet chilli covered heaven that made its way down her synthetic oesophagus. Loved the way it made her synthetic taste buds dance. They must've stayed there all day, under the protection of the corrugated iron roof. The rain came down hard when they decided to leave, and when they returned to the office, Butters and Genaro were waiting for them.

PART 3

Endgame

23

'I thought you'd wanna know,' said Butters, as he stood across the desk from Kung Fo, 'what Genaro was planning.'

'You fucking li-' Genaro accused.

'Enough!' Kung Fo barked, and they both fell silent.

Helen moved to the window and pulled up the blinds. The neon lights and adverts blinding them slightly.

'I want you both to state your case,' said Kung Fo, 'and I'll judge fairly who I believe and who I don't.'

This is like watching a kid with a gun Genaro thought, how could he make a fair judgment? He ain't even out of his fucking nappies.

Butters started.

'You know what I told you was true,' he said, 'you know I'm right. Genaro here has got it in for you, he wants what you have.'

'Right,' Kung Fo said, calmly, 'Genaro?'

CHAPTER 23

'He's fucking lying, I want nothing more than to serve your best interests, you're the one that came up with this pill that'll make us all rich. He's the one that wants what you have!'

Butters looked shocked at the accusation.

'No way would I go against you,' he said, 'with the power and the money you have, and will gain if this pill sells well, you could zero me right now and no one would bat an eyelid.'

'Right,' said Kung Fo, after a few minutes of contemplation, 'Butters….I believe you,'

Genaro let out a sigh of exasperation.

'Genaro, get out. I don't want to see or hear from you ever again,' Kung Fo ordered, 'you and your whole family are banished from the Big Table.'

'You're gonna fucking regret this,' Genaro said through clenched teeth and left, stomping out the door. Butters had a victorious smile on his face.

Later that same night, as Kung Fo and Helen were sleeping, there came a huge explosion in the Von Croft tower. It woke them almost instantly. They barely had time to get dressed when several men burst through the door, firing plasma rifles and ordering them to get down on the ground. Kung Fo did as instructed but with a smile on his face.

'Helen?' he said, 'you know what to do.'

Suddenly, Helen's combat reflexes kicked in and she leaped at the first gunman. With a flying kick, she knocked him to the ground, broke his arm and took the gun off him. She aimed at the second gunman and fired, killing him instantly. Aiming point blank, she blew the first gunman's head off. She made her way through the apartment, firing and killing several more of the gunmen. Kung Fo stood up. Fucking Genaro, he thought.

He got dressed, calmly, as Helen dispatched the other gunmen in the other rooms.

He went to the vidphone by the silk covered bed and called Butters.

'You were right about Genaro,' he said, as soon as Butters sleepily answered the call, 'fucker's just sent a hit squad to my place.'

'I told you,' Butters said and yawned.

'I need you to come over,' Kung Fo said, 'we need a plan to kill Genaro before he sends reinforcements.'

'I'll be there in half an hour,' Butters said and hung up.

The sun rose over New London. Shining its solar yellow glow over the city. Butters and Kung Fo were in the office, going over a schematic of New London. Genaro had his place next to the main generator under the Highrise Quarter. That's where it'll go down. The final battle. They planned on creeping in and getting him while he slept. So they waited, and waited, for the sun to go

CHAPTER 23

down. None had slept since Butters had arrived. The adrenaline pumped through them and they prepped for battle. Helen loaded as many guns as she could carry. Butters cleaned his plasma pistol and Kung Fo looked over the schematics some more, looking for a stealthy way in. He thought that he could sit in the pod outside with his VR headset on, much like he did when Xiang stormed the Von Croft tower what seemed like an age ago, and direct them from there while his crack team of mercs did the dirty work for him, but Butters advised that that wasn't a good idea. He'd be safer with them, he said.

Night fell, street rats came out to play, it was time. The three left Von Croft tower in an armoured pod, with a convoy of mercs escorting them to the Highrise Quarter. They'd be there soon. Helen drove. It was her first time behind the wheel but part of the combat programme was driving armoured pods so she was ok with it. Kung Fo was nervous. He thought back to when Von Croft's men had practically invaded New Chinatown, and how the Yakuza had come to the rescue. They weren't here now. He was on his own, almost.

When they got there, they all loaded out of their respective pods and made their way to the sewer system. Genaro and what was left of his men would be sleeping by now, surely. The mercs moved in a four by four cover formation, 'these guys,' Kung Fo thought, 'know what they're doing.'

They all regrouped outside a huge ventilation gate. Helen, using her tech ability in conjunction with her programming, hacked the automated lock and in moments, the gate was open. They all filed in and entered the sewer system's dark, pitch black abyss.

They switched their torches on and the light pierced the void. They could still only see four feet ahead of them. But that was enough. They made their way to the main generator room. It was guarded by three men. Helen dispatched them quietly, under the hum of the generator, and moved ahead of the group, clearing the way for them.

Helen moved quietly. She dispatched several guards on her way to Genaro's tent, and found him sleeping next to a young-looking Asian girl. Disgusted, she moved over to the bed and grabbed his throat.

'Wakey, wakey you digusting fucker!' she said, through clenched teeth.

What they came upon, in the light of several searchlights, was a shanty town of sorts. Kung Fo never knew this place existed until now, that's how under the radar they were. No wonder Genaro wanted the tower and the company. He'd do just about anything to get it too, it seemed.

CHAPTER 23

They got to Genaro's tent not long after, and everything was as it should be. The guards were dead. Genaro was bound to a chair with rope and bewildered at this rude wake up call.

Helen stood by him, a plasma rifle to his head.

Butters turned to the mercs.

'You can go now,' he said, 'the credits will be in your individual accounts by sunrise.'

They nodded and left.

Kung Fo turned to Genaro.

'Why'd you do it man?'

'What!? Do what!?' Genaro screamed in desperation.

'Send that squad after me.'

'I didn't!'

'If not you, then who else? You said I'd regret it, you tried pulling the ring off my finger not long ago.'

'I'm not that fucking stupid man,' Genaro shouted, 'I know something like this would happen if I did. Look, I've been doing some digging, and it's someone close to you who wants the ring, who wants the whole damn company, who wants-'

A purple beam shot across the tent and pierced straight through Genaro's open mouth, taking the top half of his head clean off.

'What the fuck, Butters!' cried Kung Fo.

'He knew too much,' said Butters, calmly.

Kung Fo turned to see Butters with his plasma pistol aimed right at him.

'You know what it's like,' Butters said, 'to have everything, then nothing? To have all the money in the world and then, 'cause of one rat bastard cop, have it all taken away again?'

'You slimy fuck,' Kung Fo said, and moved forward a step, only to stop as Butters raised the pistol a little higher.

'Easy now,' Butters said, 'you wouldn't want me to get nervous and pull this trigger, would you?'

Helen aimed at Butters.

'Same with me,' she said.

Butters, outmatched, started to retreat backwards and out the tent. He started to run and Helen fired. A purple beam exploded through Butters' chest and hit the main generator. There was a massive explosion. Butters turned as he fell and shot Kung Fo with the plasma pistol. Severing his arm. There was a sudden feeling of weightlessness. New London was falling out of the sky. Kung Fo fell into Helen's grasp. He was bleeding heavily from the gunshot.

He saw Xiang, Danny, his friends, his mother, he was going to them now.

'Helen?' he said, as the last litre of blood left him.

'I'm here,' she said, quietly, 'I'm always here.'

PART 4

Epilogue: All Empires Fall

24

New London was falling. That blast in the main generator had crippled its flight canisters and caused it to lose power to all its major systems. It was over the ruins of New York when it happened. All its residents clung for dear life to anything they could get their hands on. Audry Darlington was in the shower when it happened. The water stopped and she couldn't see anything due to the shampoo in her eyes. She rose from the shower, banging her head on the ceiling, 'what's happening?!' she cried.

Chang Hua was crawling the streets of New Chinatown, looking for girls, until he felt the gravity leave him. He clung to a street lamp and cried. Thank God his friends weren't around.

Franklin was in the dark. He felt weightlessness, then a sudden thump as New London hit the gravel of times square. She thought, 'well isn't this lovely?'

The pimps and whores of the Portuguese slums grabbed their belongings and reached out with

CHAPTER 24

their spare hands to anything they could get a hold of. That proved fruitless and they were catapulted into the sky.

New London crashed into the ruins of the Empire State Building, moved on its side a few blocks, then came to a stop. Everyone, bewildered and confused, walked out onto the street. They'd forgotten all about the colony and what it even looked like. Helen was among them, she'd taken the ring from Kung Fo's body once the crash had ended. It seemed like, whatever happens now, she'd made it to the Big Table. If it even existed now. She looked around at the many different people, walking zombie-like through the streets of their new home. Rich rubbing shoulders with poor. Exactly like it should be.

25

Several weeks later, she was walking through the desert landscape of the American midwest, somewhere between Iowa and Nebraska, it looked absolutely barren. A dust storm was about to pick up when she came upon a bar. Just a kiosk, out in the middle of nowhere. She sat down and ordered a drink, southern comfort and coke, no ice. She asked if they did food and the barman just looked at her strangely. While she waited, he noticed the ruby ring on her left wedding ring finger.

'You married?' he asked, in a midwestern drawl.

'No,' she replied, who was this guy, she thought.

'Well then,' he said, 'what's with the ring?'

'Oh that,' she said, as if she'd just noticed it, 'now that…..is a long story.'

The End

ACKNOWLEDGEMENTS

First, I would like to thank Deniz and Mike for giving me the tools to write this, I couldn't have written a word without your tutelage. Also I would like to thank Charlotte, Mum and Dad, Aunty Pat, Donna, Jess, Paul, Aunty Alison, Gill, and anyone else who bought 'When The Rain Stops' for their critique and support. I couldn't have done it without you guys and I love you all. Also, I'd like to thank Jaegermeister for all the inspiration, and Nine Inch Nails for the soundtrack to my writing. Also Brian Keene for wishing me luck in this endevour. I've read you since I wanted to become a writer and I thank you for giving me the motivation through your writing and podcasts. Also William Gibson, for Neuromancer and inspiring me to write in this genre. I hope it makes you and Brian Keene proud.

Printed in Great Britain
by Amazon